SHADOWS, MAPS,
and other
ANCIENT MAGIC

SHADOWS, MAPS, AND OTHER ANCIENT MAGIC
(DOWSER 4)
Copyright © 2015 Meghan Ciana Doidge
Published by Old Man in the CrossWalk
Productions 2015
Salt Spring Island, BC, Canada
www.oldmaninthecrosswalk.com

All rights reserved under International and Pan-American Copyright Conventions. No part of this book may be produced in any form or by any electronic or mechanical means, including information storage and retrieval systems, without permission in writing from the author, except by reviewer, who may quote brief passages in a review.

This is a work of fiction. All names, characters, places, objects, and incidents herein are the products of the author's imagination or are used fictitiously. Any resemblance to actual things, events, locales, or persons living or dead is entirely coincidental.

Library and Archives Canada
Doidge, Meghan Ciana, 1973 —
Shadows, Maps, and Other Ancient Magic/Meghan Ciana Doidge — PAPERBACK

Cover design by Elizabeth Mackey

ISBN 978-1-927850-24-4

Dowser Series · Book 1

SHADOWS, MAPS, and other ANCIENT MAGIC

Meghan Ciana Doidge

Published by Old Man in the CrossWalk Productions
Vancouver, BC, Canada

www.oldmaninthecrosswalk.com
www.madebymeghan.ca

For Michael
The yin to my yang.
Or maybe it's the other way around?

Author's Note:

Shadows, Maps, and Other Ancient Magic is the fourth book in the Dowser series. The Oracle series is also set in the same universe as the Dowser series.

While it's not necessary to read both series, the ideal reading order is as follows:

- Cupcakes, Trinkets, and Other Deadly Magic (Dowser 1)
- Trinkets, Treasures, and Other Bloody Magic (Dowser 2)
- Treasures, Demons, and Other Black Magic (Dowser 3)
- I See Me (Oracle 1)*
- Shadows, Maps, and Other Ancient Magic (Dowser 4)
- Maps, Artifacts, and Other Arcane Magic (Dowser 5)
- I See You (Oracle 2)

Other books in both the Oracle and Dowser series to follow.

*I See Me (Oracle 1) contains spoilers for Dowser 1, 2, and 3.

I had new cupcakes to bake, a new treasure to hunt, and a new dragon in town — literally. Who wouldn't be ecstatic filling their days with chocolate, trinket collecting, and martial arts training?

Yeah … me.

Because no matter how much chocolate I ate, I couldn't fill the dark pit in my soul. A darkness born from blood alchemy. A darkness that reeked of the black magic I now knew I was capable of creating.

Maybe it was time to walk away.

But what if there were important things left to do? What if I was the only one who could do what needed to be done?

I wasn't sure I could handle the responsibility, but as long as I had my chocolate stash and a good friend to back me up, I was willing to give it a try.

Chapter One

The blade was inches from my neck before I felt it. Thankfully, I had my blond curls clipped back today. Otherwise, I would have gotten an unwanted and unneeded haircut. I flung myself sideways, rolling over my shoulder and coming up on one knee to block the reverse strike with my jade knife.

The over-the-head blow glanced off my knife and was knocked to the side, but the force of it reverberated down my arm in a wash of pain. I slid back on the white stone floor even as I rolled forward onto the balls of my feet to step into my attacker. This close, his sword was all but useless.

Unfortunately, he was faster than me, or I would have managed to gut him.

Instead, he grabbed the wrist of my knife hand and twisted my arm up over my head, then around my back. This forced me to pivot away or have my shoulder dislocated. He pinned my knife hand, the wrist still painfully twisted between my shoulder blades. I had to rise up on my toes to lessen the pain of the hold.

"Branson!" I screeched, completely forgetting the formality with which I was to address the sword master of the dragons. "I was meditating."

He brought his blade up to my neck. I managed to get my left hand around his wrist, but had to practically lay my head back against his shoulder to avoid having my throat slit.

"I don't think you are capable of such, warrior's daughter." Branson's voice was deep, his tone brusque. He was wearing traditional black training leathers, with a laced vest that left his well-muscled arms bare.

I twisted his wrist to try to get the blade away from my neck. His forearms were adorned with tattoos of water dragons, which I'd mistaken for snakes when I first met him.

I gained an inch.

The sword master hadn't spoken directly to me for over a week after that display of ignorance. Drake — the fourteen-year-old apprentice to Chi Wen the far seer and adoptive son of Suanmi, the fire breather — had delighted in relaying Branson's drills during my period of punishment.

"Are your fingernails green?" Branson asked now, completely bemused.

"Jade is the new black, baby," I said. "You should see my toes."

Then I kicked him in the head.

Well, first I twisted my own head quickly to the right, dropped underneath the blade at my neck, and spun away to face him again. Unfortunately, he was still holding on to my wrists, so my arms were now crossed in front of me. I threw all my weight backward. This off-balanced the sword master enough that he stumbled forward, letting me snap a kick between our crossed arms directly underneath his jaw. I had always loved having long legs.

Oh, yeah. Befuddlement of ancient beings was my new secret weapon.

Branson grunted, lost his hold on my wrists, and staggered back. My entire right leg went so numb that it wouldn't actually take my full weight.

I'd been sitting cross-legged and eyes closed in the center of the dragon nexus when Branson attacked me. The circular room was supported by gilded columns, between which nine ornately carved doors were situated. Two archways stood across from each other, leading deeper into the nexus — to the residences of the guardian dragons, as well as the library and the training rooms.

Still listing to the left, I raised my knife before me as I faced off with the sword master.

I was wearing my standard uniform of printed T-shirt and jeans. And though my brand-new teal-with-white-piping Liz Fluevogs offset my black-and-white 'UM — Element of Confusion' top in an utterly cute way, I really needed to see about getting the shoes fitted with metal plates and toes. All the better to kick indestructible people in the head.

It was my day off from training and the bakery, so I really hadn't expected to be attacked. But I was never without my jade knife, not since I'd found the large stone along the Fraser River outside Lillooet and hand carved it myself. I hadn't even known I was an alchemist at the time, and therefore capable of creating magical objects. I'd just seen the stone and known it should be a knife — a knife imbued with so much of my magic now that no one could disarm me, not without knocking me out. Nor could anyone touch the knife without my permission without being burned by it.

Branson shook his dark head as if clearing it.

I smirked. I'd never managed to rattle him before.

He slowly raised his golden double-edged sword to answer my poised knife. His blade was a slimmer, longer version of the bejeweled broadsword that my father Yazi, the warrior of the guardians, wielded. Its pommel and hilt were utilitarian, though.

Branson had been in training for the mantle of the warrior before he'd been gravely wounded as a fledgling. No, dragons weren't completely indestructible. Just don't mention that to any of them. Occasionally, the sword master's old wound showed up as a limp. Despite that, and the fact that he was at least a hundred years older than my three hundred and fifty year old father, I'd never knocked him off his feet.

"I'm not here for a lesson, sword master," I said, struggling to remain polite — and to hide the fact that I still couldn't feel my right leg. My wrist also felt severely sprained from being twisted harshly behind my back. "I await the treasure keeper."

Branson grinned, but it did little to lighten his perpetually stern face. He had that same hint of Asian ancestry to his features that Drake did. I didn't think he and the fledgling guardian were related, but I was far from an expert on dragon genealogy.

"Life is a lesson," Branson said.

Ah, damn. Dragons only got all preachy right before they kicked my ass. Granted, I usually deserved an ass kicking — I attracted trouble almost as easily as I attracted or found magic. Except that dragon-inflicted bruises usually took a couple of days to heal, and I had a birthday party to go to tonight.

I narrowed my eyes at my trainer, causing all the overly golden hues of the room to blur together behind him. Dragons adored surrounding themselves with gold and jewels and art, and it was a little much sometimes. The heart of the dragon nexus was all gaudy Greek temple mixed with oriental motifs, though each door was carved in artwork that represented the specific territories of each guardian. The room was also saturated with guardian magic, hence me not tasting Branson's magic as he approached.

The narrower my eyes got — I was working on my intimidation factor — the wider Branson's grin grew. Indigo eyes, blond curls now falling out of my hair clip, and sun-kissed skin didn't much help in that department. I was fairly certain it was my ample assets that made me less than imposing, though, since I was the spitting image of my father and he scared the crap out of everyone even while laughing. Actually, it was the absolute power that rolled off him when he laughed that was terrifying.

I'd narrowed my eyes too far. Now my eyelashes were making my vision fuzzy.

I sighed, opened my eyes, and gave my knife hand a roll. The overly stretched tendons and ligaments crunched, but then snapped back into their proper place.

That was better.

I smiled, extended my left hand forward to balance my right, and stepped sideways to circle Branson.

If he wanted a tussle, I was up for it. Bruises or no bruises.

The sword master lost his grin as he stepped opposite to me. He watched my every move, my every twitch, with deadly intent. I was never going to get the upper hand when he was focused like this.

I thought about flashing him to throw him off — and not just because I kept wondering how his sword-callused hands would feel sliding up my inner thighs. A totally inappropriate thought, yes. But then, I hadn't had sex in way over a year. I hadn't been kissed in ten months. Even my constant chocolate high couldn't keep my serotonin levels up perpetually.

I decided against the flashing because I knew Branson would be utterly aghast — and might even refuse to be in the same room with me ever again. Plus, I wasn't wearing my prettiest bra at the moment. It had been far too long since I'd had any reason to wear anything other than a serviceable sports bra.

Attempting to not massively broadcast my intent, I abruptly lunged forward, thrusting my knife for Branson's heart.

Then, completely blindsided, I got shoulder checked by a small mountain.

This knocked me flying off my feet and cracked my head against one of the nine pillars that encircled the heart of the dragon nexus.

Remember the only way to reliably disarm me these days?

Yeah, knock me out.

So that happened.

Waking up after getting your neck broken was never fun. I knew because this was my second time. The first time, I'd been visiting a morgue with a vampire and was flung head first into a cement wall by a zombie. A zombie who'd been the corpse of someone I'd really, really hoped to thoroughly date. A zombie piloted by my dead sister, Sienna. I still mourned for what might have been, had Hudson survived my sister's bloodlust. Yeah, silly me. Who agrees to go to a morgue with a vampire, right?

This time, by the taste of honey-roasted almonds that lingered in my mouth, I'd been attacked by Drake. Yeah, the fourteen-year-old fledgling guardian had just — utterly playfully — tried to kill me.

Despite the fact that my brain felt completely shattered in my skull, I attempted to open my eyes.

Qiuniu, the most breathtakingly beautiful man I'd ever had the absolute privilege to lay eyes on, was leaning over me.

"Gran will be pleased," I muttered. My voice was cracking. Pearl Godfrey, aka the chair of the witches' Convocation, aka my grandmother, had decided that the healer was the perfect pairing for her granddaughter. Yes, one of the nine guardian dragons of the world. Despite the fact that his dark caramel skin, high cheekbones, and deep brown eyes were completely gorgeous, his guardian status was terrifying enough to keep my hormones way in check.

"Your neck is still vulnerable, warrior's daughter," Qiuniu said. "I would recommend you protect it better." My throat had been nastily gouged out by the five-inch claws of a demon, ten months ago on the beaches of a resort town on the west coast of Vancouver Island. A demon from the horde raised by my now-dead sister. Yeah, there was definitely a pattern to the last year of my life.

"I didn't expect to get attacked in the dragon nexus … twice," I muttered.

Qiuniu rewarded my grumpiness with a blinding smile. "Shall I heal you, alchemist? Though you are not moments from death as I was led to believe."

The healer glanced over his shoulder, turning his body just enough that with a slight and painful twist of my head I could see Drake behind him, shuffling anxiously from foot to foot. Even from my supine vantage point, I could tell that the fourteen-year-old had grown at least two inches since I'd last seen him. He also needed a haircut. His dark bangs were brushing his impossibly full lashes. I was surprised Branson hadn't taken clippers to him yet. The trainer had often muttered about my hair being an impediment to my achieving my "perfected warrior form."

"I'm sorry, warrior's daughter," Drake called out apologetically. His voice was far too loud against the serenity of the nexus. Well, the typical serenity. You know, when I wasn't getting attacked and almost killed. "I'd forgotten how delicate you are."

"She is only half-dragon, fledgling," Branson admonished. He was standing, sword sheathed and hands crossed behind his back, to one side of Drake.

I might adore being treated like I was precious, but I wasn't interested in being insulted or underestimated by immortal creatures.

I sat up.

Qiuniu shifted back on his haunches to allow me space. "I would be pleased to heal you, Jade Godfrey."

His utterance of my given name flooded through me like the tingly warmth that came from sipping great champagne. You know, like panty remover.

I gritted my teeth against the feeling and cranked my neck right, then left. Qiuniu actually flinched from the cracking sound. Blood rushed into my skull with a painful pulse, pounding right at the top of my spine. Good. The pain would keep me from getting all cozy with the guardian. I wasn't at all interested in mixing up magic and emotions anymore. And by emotions I meant sex, of course.

"I'm good," I said. This came out gruffer than I intended, but Qiuniu, who was the second-youngest guardian next to Haoxin, didn't take offense as easily as some of the older guardians.

He smiled, sweetly disappointed. The guardian's healing was administered via a searingly hot kiss. At least it was when he'd healed me in the past. I momentarily wished my stubbornness away ... it was a great kiss, and I didn't want to be bruised all evening ...

Then, with a wash of golden magic that literally took my breath away, the portal behind me opened. The portal that led to the territory of Australia.

Qiuniu stood in a smooth movement, so swift I could barely track it. And I was sitting inches from him.

Drake froze, with the foot he'd been about to transfer his weight onto jutted out to one side.

Chocolate — an intense, spicy blend of smoky smoothness without a hint of bitterness — flooded my taste buds as the warrior of the guardians stepped into the nexus behind me.

"Hey, Dad," I said weakly, cranking my aching neck around to lay eyes on my father as the portal snapped shut behind him. Though I knew him to be over three hundred and fifty years old, Yazi appeared to be no older than thirty-five. His tanned skin and sun-bleached blond hair screamed 'surfer dude.' His grim scowl and the golden sword he carried casually by his side screamed 'pissed-off demigod.' The fact that his hard-shelled, samurai-inspired armor was splattered with blood and ash didn't ease the intimidation factor.

"Jade," he said. My name came out as a growled threat to everyone arrayed in front of me.

Branson and Drake instantly dropped to one knee with their eyes downcast. Qiuniu twitched, as if he'd stopped himself from doing the same.

A different kind of pleasure flooded through me, and I tucked my chin to hide the smirk that was now spread across my face. What a freaking brat I was. All pleased that my father had rushed to the apparent scene of my death ... for the second time. I'd never had a dad growing up. Yazi and I had only met just over a year ago. I told myself I was allowed to be pleased that he cared for me.

"Healer," Yazi said.

"Warrior," Qiuniu answered.

"Thank you for attending my daughter."

Qiuniu inclined his head. "My pleasure."

Err, wrong thing to say. Yazi narrowed his eyes further. By the look of his armor, he'd been off saving the world from some terrible something that I wanted to know nothing about.

I scrambled to my feet, not at all worried about looking dignified or powerful now. "It was an accident," I said. My words were breathy and rushed. My throat was still healing. I threaded the fingers of my left hand through the wedding rings I'd soldered like charms to the gold necklace I wore twined three times around my neck. The wedding rings contained glimmers of residual magic, which I'd mortared into the necklace with my own magic. As with my knife, I'd created the necklace before I knew I was an alchemist. I wore it constantly. As best as I could tell, given that I couldn't actually see or taste my own magic, it seemed to collect more of my residual power daily. In the past, I'd used it to shield myself from harmful spells, but in tense situations — like this one — it was more of a comfort blanket.

Yazi frowned, then loosened the fingers of his sword hand. His gold broadsword simply winked out of existence. The intense taste of the warrior's magic lessened enough that I could pick out strains of the other magic swirling to surround me now. Qiuniu always somehow carried music with him wherever he went. I never knew the tune, but I could hear hints of it. The pounding at the base of my skull eased a bit.

Yazi stepped toward me and placed his fingers underneath my chin. I'd never seen him not smile for such an extended period of time before. He applied pressure to my chin and I obligingly lifted it.

"You attend, healer, but you don't heal?" he asked without looking away from me.

"The alchemist refused me, warrior."

A slow, wide grin spread across my father's face, transforming him from a forbidding warrior into a good-natured buddy type. "Did you now?"

I grinned back at him. "It was just a scratch."

He threw back his head and laughed. The nexus shook. Or maybe it was just that all the magic in the air bloomed at this sound. That was my dad. He could lop the heads off three demons in a single blow and make magic dance with a chortle at the same time. He would be terrifying if I didn't love him so much.

I glanced, still grinning, at Qiuniu. He looked less than pleased. Not that his fine features could ever really look sour, but it was the twist of his lips that betrayed his displeasure.

I stifled my grin. "I apologize, healer. I would never wish to waste your time."

He nodded. "Happily, I was in the nexus when Drake came to me. Not to worry, warrior's daughter."

"Speaking of hasty fledglings," Yazi said.

I opened my mouth to intervene, to protest Drake's innocence. My father shook his head at me. I snapped my mouth shut.

"You're still working off your last escapade, Drake," the warrior continued.

"Luckily Suanmi doesn't put much value on my life, so this shouldn't add to the fledgling's probation," I said. I really wasn't great at keeping my mouth shut when a friend was on the chopping block. The fire breather, Suanmi, loathed me. Actually, she loathed the happenstance of my birth. Conceived of a witch and a dragon during a fertility ceremony of the Kalkadoon — aka a tribe of Australian Aboriginals — I was unnatural. Suanmi had declared me 'an abomination' when she'd first laid eyes on me. It didn't help that my presence in the nexus only encouraged Drake to disobey the restrictions and requirements of his guardian apprenticeship and training.

My father huffed at my interruption. Drake, who was still down on one knee, squirmed uncomfortably.

"Indeed," Qiuniu said. He laughed softly.

Suanmi's hatred was amusing, I guess. If she didn't scare the hell out of me, I might have laughed along with the healer. As it was, I'd seen her cremate a demon by merely whispering in its ear, so I endeavored to stay way off the fire breather's radar. This was a simpler task now, because after Drake had accidentally accompanied me on a scouting trip that ended in a triple demon summoning in London last year, Suanmi had demanded a separate training schedule for him. Which was fine because it opened up the mornings I needed to be at the bakery anyway. Well, my mornings ... time didn't exist the same way in the nexus. But I missed hanging out with the fledgling. He carried a lightness with him that I had a difficult time emulating these days, though my beleaguered soul was slowly healing.

Drake peered up at me. His dark brown eyes were almost hidden behind his bangs. I stepped forward to brush the hair off his forehead.

"You need a haircut," I chided with a smile.

And that was all it took for him to spring, grinning, to his feet. "I have missed you, warrior's daughter. I will be careful with your head from now on."

Qiuniu choked back a laugh. My father expelled another huff of displeasure.

"Branson," Yazi said.

The sword master rose to his feet but kept his eyes downcast.

"I entrusted my daughter to your care, my friend," Yazi continued.

"Yes, warrior," Branson said. "I have failed you."

"No," I cried. "It was a terrible test. There's so much magic here, I didn't feel Drake approach —"

"Then that is the skill you will hone next," Yazi said, as if being inundated and overwhelmed by the power of the dragons was nothing.

Branson looked at me thoughtfully. His gaze then fell to my wedding ring charm necklace. "Perhaps the necklace the alchemist wears could be —"

"I'm awaiting the treasure keeper," I blurted, interrupting what I was sure was about to become a lesson plan that would occupy months, if not years, of my time. Months that I greedily wanted to myself.

Qiuniu stifled another laugh. I was so glad I amused him. Not.

Branson inclined his head. "As you will, warrior's daughter." Then he looked to Yazi, who nodded back at him. Branson, taking this as permission to leave, spun away and strode off through the far archway.

"You hurt his feelings," Drake said. He sounded surprised.

"His ego," Yazi corrected. "Not a bad lesson for you to learn today, Drake, apprentice to Chi Wen."

Drake nodded reverently to my father, who touched my shoulder lightly but then turned to Qiuniu. "I must return," he said. "Do you have a moment, healer?"

"For you, warrior, always."

Yazi turned back to open the portal behind him.

Qiuniu, a step behind my father, brushed by me with a whisper. "Next time." His breath tickled my skin, spreading the warmth of his healing power across my cheek and down my neck. Sneaky bugger.

My father turned back to glower at the healer, but he stepped through the golden magic of the portal without another word as he did so. He wasn't big on goodbyes. I was just coming to realize that my mortality was a thorny issue for him.

With a wink back at me, Qiuniu was swallowed by the portal. The door snapped shut.

"The healer wants to bed you," Drake said. His tone suggested he was mystified by this discovery.

"Drake!"

"What? Did I use the expression incorrectly? The healer wants to take you to bed? To his bed?" the fourteen-year-old continued. "To have sex, you know."

"Stop. Talking."

"Guardians don't wed. A marriage is traditional in your culture, isn't it?"

"I'm not going to sleep with Qiuniu."

Drake nodded sagely, but doubtfully.

I narrowed my eyes at him, completely forgetting it was a useless gesture against a dragon, even if he was only fourteen. "Don't pretend you know different," I snapped.

Drake, grinning madly, scrambled back a few steps and drew his sword in a flash of gold. "Pull your knife, warrior's daughter!" he shouted. "Get back on the broken horse!"

I sighed. "That's not the expression —"

Drake whipped his head toward the door to his immediate left. The white-paneled one, decorated with hundreds of ornate gold fleurs-de-lis. As in, actual gold. The crazy grin was gone from the fledgling's face. He looked back at me with wide eyes, opened his mouth to say something, but then seemed to change his mind.

"What?" I asked.

"Got to go," he said. Then he took off through the archway that Branson had exited through. He didn't even bother to sheath his sword.

What the hell?

Portal magic bloomed behind the door that led to the territory of the guardian of Western Europe. I half-turned toward it, fear pooling in the pit of my stomach, but not knowing what to do. I hadn't seen Suanmi in over ten months, not since that terrible night in London. Not since I'd begged her for help with my sister. She'd told me to "clean up my own mess," and warned me that if I didn't do so, she'd put me out of my misery.

I didn't want to run. I also really didn't want to be eviscerated with a single breath.

The portal opened. A foot shod in a drool-worthy Louboutin pump stepped through. Yes, a nude patent leather Very Prive peep-toe pump with the Louboutin signature red sole, which cost more than a month of rent on my apartment and bakery combined.

I clutched my necklace, practically praying for its shielding protection. I didn't draw my knife, though my every instinct was screaming at me to do so.

As Suanmi the fire breather walked through the portal, I stepped my right foot behind my left ankle and bowed my head in a formal curtsy. I utterly refused to fall to my knees, not unless she forced me there. Suanmi's navy blue Chanel pencil skirt skimmed her gorgeous legs just below her knees. The Louboutin heels and pristine nylons, which she wore despite it being late summer, swathed slim calves that didn't look anything like the calves of the forty-five-year-old woman Suanmi pretended to be. Or maybe 'pretend' was the wrong word. Maybe that was just the point at which she'd decided to stop aging naturally? She was only a hundred or so years older than the treasure keeper, Pulou. If you could refer to being six hundred years old as 'only.'

I kept my eyes cast downward, my fingers twined through the rings of my necklace. The magic — the utter power of the fire breather — thundered around me, and I fought the need to give in to it, to fall to the ground and rail against its crushing force. Suanmi never bothered to dampen her magic, not the way my father, Pulou, and even Qiuniu did around me.

Suanmi didn't even pause. She stepped by me without acknowledgment, and that was fine by me.

I tried to focus on the clicking of her heels, counting her steps to the archway and beyond. Acting on the instinct to protect myself, I took all the magic raging around me and willed it into my necklace. I begged the necklace to hold it at bay, so I didn't make a fool of myself in front of the guardian of Western Europe for the third time of our brief acquaintance.

The heel clicks stopped.

I inhaled and held my breath.

Suanmi pivoted back to me. "Half-blood," she snapped. Then, softening her tone until her French-accented English was almost lyrical, she continued. "The treasure keeper requires your skills." The fire breather didn't quite pull off the word 'skills' without some deep derision attached.

I nodded but didn't look up. "Thank you, guardian. I await him."

Suanmi laughed, the sound of which tinkled over me like broken crystal. I tamped down on the impulse to brush it away from me, knowing that would look utterly crazy.

"Do you not know how to call him?" Suanmi asked, her voice deadly soft but sharp. "I suppose it is beyond you to do so."

I didn't answer. I didn't know how to answer.

She waited. And waited.

I slowly lifted my head. I locked eyes with the guardian I most feared. She lifted her chin a little.

"You're shorter than I am," I blurted without thinking.

She took a step toward me and a flush of fear ran down my spine. I spread the fingers of my right hand as wide as I could, in order to force myself to not call my knife forth.

Then Suanmi smiled. A tight, dark-edged smile. "Pulou, treasure keeper," she called out. Her commanding voice reverberated through the round room. "The alchemist attends you."

A portal to my right opened in a blinding flash of light, seeming to swallow the echo of Suanmi's words as it snapped shut again.

The fire breather turned her back to me.

"Thank you," I whispered, and instantly wished I hadn't spoken. Being polite was just too ingrained in my upbringing.

"Just do your job, half-blood." Suanmi spoke without looking at me.

"I ... I also regret ..." I was stumbling over the words I knew I should keep to myself, but that my guilt forced me to speak. "I regret not bringing Drake immediately back when he followed me through the portal into Scotland ... and then London. I would never hurt him —"

"No. You aren't powerful enough to do so." Suanmi was looking at me again with a perfectly refined sneer. Her dark hair was smoothed back from her pale, unlined brow. She was poised and collected.

I was a grubby child.

"True," I said. "It's too bad I'm useful to the treasure keeper."

"Indeed."

I lifted my chin, allowing myself a tiny bit of defiance. And with that choice, that gesture, the dragon magic settled around me to a bearable level.

Suanmi frowned as if she'd seen what I felt.

I straightened my spine further, then settled my shoulder blades down my back. No more cringing for me.

Then I smiled.

Suanmi spun away without another word.

I didn't collapse with relief, but only because I was afraid she'd come back.

I took two steps to the left — so I was once again in the very center of the room — and settled down into a cross-legged position. I pulled my all-time favorite Amedei 70 percent single-origin Madagascar chocolate bar out of my Matt & Nat satchel. The bar was mangled. Even I couldn't get hit by a small mountain and not get crushed. Thankfully, I had no problem licking the shards of goodness off the inner foil wrapper.

It was one thing to stand up to Suanmi — the fire breather, and one of the nine guardians of the world. But it was completely another thing to waste chocolate out of some silly sense of perceived dignity.

Chapter Two

I wasn't sure how much longer I waited for Pulou. Time moved oddly in the dragon nexus — if it actually moved at all, which some days it didn't. It could have been minutes, but I really hoped it wasn't days. I'd arrived — via the portal in the bakery basement — a little after eight o'clock, knowing I might have to camp out all day to have a chance of seeing the treasure keeper.

Kandy, Kett, and I had been going on collection runs for Pulou for the last six months or so. These missions couldn't really be classified as treasure hunting. They were barely even training exercises. I hadn't pulled my knife during any of these so-called assignments, not once.

Kandy, my werewolf BFF — who managed to maintain her bright green hair no matter where in the world we were — was disappointed that there had been no call for breaking and entering, spelunking, or skydiving on any of the missions yet.

Kett had faded away about three months ago. And who could blame the vampire? He was the executioner for the Conclave. He had way better things to be doing. Not that I was at all sure what those 'things' were exactly.

So, yeah. I was bored out of my mind. Which was why I was completely determined that I was about to hand over my last benign artifact.

A pen.

Yes, a sorcerer-charmed pen that wrote by voice command. It had stopped responding to its owner's requests a few months ago, and now wrote whatever and wherever it wanted to. The sorcerer from whom I'd collected it practically threw it at me in relief when Kandy and I went to pick it up. The only amusing part of the so-called mission was his harried look and the cursive ink markings all over his face and neck. Hebrew script, I imagined, since we were in Tel Aviv. Not that I'd taken the time to explore the city.

Today, Pulou would authorize a real mission — something with some importance — or I was taking matters into my own hands. No one could accuse me of being rash. I'd taken the time to heal. I'd trained. I'd explored my magic until I bored myself utterly. Hell, I was so bloody boring that I couldn't manage to be in the same room with myself for more than a few minutes without wishing someone else was around. Someone interesting. Someone with a life beyond the bakery, and plucking trinkets out of the hands of witches and sorcerers without a single protest from them.

Was a lick of resistance too much to ask for? A simple offensive spell? Or even a protection ward that I had to exert actual effort to thwart?

I'd jumped through all of Pulou's hoops since Tofino. Since Sienna's death. And because the treasure keeper had me running around with training wheels for the last six months, it meant that Blackwell could have been running all around Europe with that damn circlet of his. I'd wanted to rip it from his bony hands the first moment I laid eyes on it. No sorcerer, least of all one as evil as Blackwell, should have access to a magical object that dampened or impeded the powers of any Adept who wore it. No one would wear such a thing voluntarily. And the circlet wasn't made to be used benevolently. That, I was sure of.

I'd had the opportunity to face off against Blackwell last January when Desmond, the Lord and Alpha of the West Coast North American Pack, had asked me to come to Portland to identify the magic of a teen that was supposedly being stalked by Blackwell. Instead of blindly joining the pack hunt, I chose to do the right thing by the teen — namely, distract Desmond and the pack, then get Chi Wen involved. Last I heard, the far seer had taken Rochelle, who turned out to be a fledgling oracle, under his wing, and Blackwell was in the wind.

Now it was time to figure out my own guidelines and make my own choices. I knew good from evil. Hell, I could taste it.

Today, I would finally get Pulou's permission to go after Blackwell. I knew exactly how to word the request, to present the evidence, and outline my plan. I'd been working on the wording for over three months, once I'd figured out that there was a proper way to ask. Dragons had a lot of rules and regulations. Extreme power came with extreme guidelines, it seemed.

I would have gone without permission months ago, because Blackwell pissed me off so much, except I was kind of banned from Europe. London, specifically. And just taking the circlet from Blackwell might get me into a whole lot of trouble from the Convocation, who strictly governed the behavior of witches and considered me subject to their will, though I was only half-witch. The sorcerers' League wouldn't be too happy about the theft either, despite how I got the sense there was no love lost between them and Blackwell.

Then there was the sticky bit about the elder vampire of London being seriously pissed with me. Not because I almost got Kett — his grandson by blood — killed, but because he'd had to divide his power to save him.

However, if the theft was dragon certified, then it became a 'reclamation' of a magical object deemed too powerful to be loose in the world. Even though that would still piss off the sorcerers — and probably the vampire — no one could stand against me without standing against the guardians.

Yeah, I had it all worked out. I just hoped Blackwell was home when I knocked on the door of his freaking castle. I wanted to see his face when I 'officially' waltzed in and took the circlet from him.

Hell, I wanted him to try to stop me.

I was almost dozing by the time the portal behind me — the door that my father and the healer had exited through — opened in a wash of golden magic. I pivoted, standing in the buoyant power and facing the door just as Pulou the treasure keeper stepped through into the nexus. As I once again awkwardly curtsied, I noted that my necklace thrummed softly against my collarbone and that my neck felt normal once again.

"There you are, alchemist," Pulou said, his deep voice booming through the quiet of the room. "I've been waiting."

I opened my mouth to be all bitchy about the fact that I had been waiting freaking eons for him, but then he threw back his head and laughed.

Ah, dragons loved to laugh.

The portal closed behind Pulou. The treasure keeper was a dark-haired bear of a man who appeared to be in his mid-fifties, when in reality he was more than five hundred years old. He wore his typical full-length fur coat despite the fact it was late summer ... though I guess it wasn't summer where he'd just come from.

Anyway.

The fur coat was actually some sort of manifestation of the treasure keeper's magic, just as the sword was a manifestation of my father's warrior power. Pulou had taken a magical object I'd made ten months ago on the beach in Tofino, somehow shrunk it, and then stored it in an inner pocket of his coat. The magic that accompanied this feat had scrambled my brain, and left me with the impression that something extradimensional had occurred while I dumbly watched and didn't even remotely comprehend.

I was epically happy to never have to lay eyes on that object again, so I wasn't terribly desperate to wrap my head around the process. I'd twisted my katana — a gift from my father — into a circle around my sister's neck and filled it with all the magic Sienna had stolen from all the Adepts she'd killed and drained. Then I'd taken every last drop of her magic. Such a thing shouldn't have been possible. But I had done it, half dead and under great duress. It was a secret known only to the treasure keeper and me. An ability he thought too dangerous for anyone else to know of, and I agreed.

I was already unique enough when it came to power and heritage. I didn't need to be feared or even hunted by the Adept world. I just wanted to bake my cupcakes and steal Blackwell's circlet.

"Treasure keeper, I have a request," I said.

"Do you?" he asked, rather amused.

I nodded, and then launched into the speech I'd prepared. "Mot Blackwell, who's a sorcerer, houses an extensive collection of magical artifacts ..." — Pulou was frowning, just slightly, at me, but in a way that made me think I might be speaking gibberish — "… in his castle … Blackness Castle … in Scotland."

"That is the territory of the guardian Suanmi."

"Yes, but … he has this platinum and raw diamond circlet that's some sort of dampener, an inhibitor —"

"Dragons do not steal."

"Such an object should not be in the hands of such a sorcerer." I tried to retreat back to my prepared argument, but Pulou immediately derailed me again.

"Would this dampener work against you … or me … or any of the dragons?"

"Well … I … I'm not sure."

"The task I have for you is of much greater and immediate importance."

Ten months, I almost screamed. I'd been waiting for permission for ten months. I could have cracked Blackwell's wards — again — and waltzed in to lift the offending inhibitor months ago.

Pulou lifted one bushy eyebrow at me. I swallowed my inner brat, and when I could speak politely again I did so.

"It would be an honor, guardian, to hunt for treasure you deem of great importance."

"All sorcerers are tinged darkly," Pulou said. "That is just their way. Be sure that Suanmi has an eye on this Blackwell, if he is even worthy of such attention. I'm sure Drake has filled his guardian in on his escapade."

I nodded. "I was going to bring peanut butter and chocolate cupcakes, but I was worried I would be … incapable of getting them to you without interference."

"To bribe me with?"

"Yes."

"I will come to the bakery."

"Oh … I …" Visions of Pulou eating every last cupcake in the bakery flooded my mind. "I wouldn't want to impose."

"Nothing to it. I should check on the portal as well. Perhaps tomorrow?"

I nodded. Last time Pulou had used the word "tomorrow," the actual time lapse had been three months.

"Speaking of the portal —"

"We weren't."

"No, I … it's an expression."

"I know."

Right. No talking about the sword filled with Sienna's stolen magic — check. No talking about the portal in the bakery basement — double check. No going after Blackwell or his circlet without incurring Suanmi's wrath — triple check.

I fished around in my satchel and found the charmed gold Cartier pen by the taste of its sorcerer magic. I held the pen out to the treasure keeper, presenting it on my open palm. Dragons preferred to be formal about such things.

"As tasked, treasure keeper," I said. I neglected to mention that I hadn't fixed its little writing-on-everything-at-a-whim glitch, because I found it entertaining. Plus, I wanted to see if dragons were prankable.

"I propose a trade," Pulou said.

He pulled a folded piece of parchment — crumpled along with some candy wrappers — from his outer pocket and held it out to me. The candy wrappers fell to the floor and disappeared. Impressive cleaning spell. No wonder the nexus was always so pristine and practically ageless. Though how did it decide what was garbage?

I had to smirk at the presence of the candy wrappers, though. I came by my sweet tooth genetically. At least, that was how I currently justified my chocolate consumption levels.

The treasure keeper plucked the charmed pen out of my hand at the same time as I took the offered bundle from him. The moment I touched it, I thought — and immediately dismissed — that it might be skin. As in, human.

I ignored the bile threatening to rise at the back of my throat, unfolded the please-don't-be-human-skin parchment, and stared at all the pretty colors and shapes drawn on it. I had an inkling it was supposed to be a map — based on the plethora of green and blue — but I had no freaking idea how to read it. I thought the triangles were supposed to be mountains? Honestly, it looked like it belonged under glass in a museum, not in my hand and soon-to-be stained with chocolate.

"A task more worthy of the alchemist's skills," Pulou said. "A task more interesting." I wasn't a hundred percent sure he wasn't mocking me with the 'alchemist's skills' part, but I was too intrigued — in a slightly disgusted way — to fret about it.

"This ... this isn't a tattoo, is it?"

"Yes, from my predecessor. Entrusted to me when I assumed his guardianship."

The 'tattoo' was about as wide and long as my back, and undoubtedly that was where it had been placed ... you know, before it was ... removed. I was holding what was possibly a map previously tattooed on and then skinned from a guardian dragon. A flower-and-leaf motif along one side, multicolored striped circles in either corner, and what appeared to be interconnected blocks along the other side, blurred its purpose for me. It sleepily thrummed with magic.

"I must go. Bixi calls."

My meetings with Pulou were always exceedingly brief and usually ended with me firing questions at the treasure keeper's back as he was called away to open a portal for another guardian elsewhere in the world. Bixi was the guardian of North Africa. In human form she was the spitting image of Cleopatra, but her guardian-inherited ability was shapeshifting.

Pulou brushed by me. His magic was a far more bearable version of Suanmi's. It didn't constantly boil around him as the fire breather's power did.

"Should I come back tomorrow for further instruction? Will we hunt together?"

"My magic will not help in this hunt. You must go where guardians dare not tread."

Wait, what? Um, that didn't sound good at all.

" 'Dare not tread'?" I said. "But not like, 'cannot tread,' right? Not like this could kill me?"

"I do not hold you in such low regard, Jade Godfrey," Pulou said. His tone was as serious as I'd ever heard it. "But I have now given you access to all the knowledge I possess in the matter. Unfortunately, my predecessor's journals were lost in a fire before I had a chance to study them."

He gestured toward the tattoo that I continued to hold gingerly by the edges. "As I'm sure you can taste, the tattoo was created by an alchemist. Luckily for me, you're also an alchemist. Figure out how to read it, and then we shall talk about guardian myths."

The treasure keeper pulled open a door covered in hieroglyphics. Or at least hundreds of shapes that I was guessing were ancient Egyptian writing, based on my extensive film-and-TV accumulated knowledge. The portal magic flooded the nexus, making my brain momentarily stutter. I swore the golden magic reached out for Pulou, as if welcoming him home with a cozy hug.

Pulou stepped into the portal.

"Wait!" I cried after him — regaining the use of my tongue if not my brain — as he disappeared from my sight. "At least tell me if it's a map!"

The door snapped shut behind the treasure keeper.

I was once again alone in the nexus. Why did I have the feeling that I was the one who'd just gotten pranked?

It is a map.

I looked up. Pulou's voice echoed through the nexus, but he hadn't returned.

I sighed, carefully refolded the parchment along the lines that already creased it, and tucked it into my trusty Matt & Nat satchel.

Right. I finally got assigned a real treasure-hunting mission, but first I had to figure out how to read a map that even a guardian couldn't read … great. It was like being stuck in a high school geography class all over again when I'd never been better than a C+ student. And I'd really, really been looking forward to stealing the circlet from Blackwell's castle. Whoops, I meant reclaiming the inhibitor. Yeah, and kicking the sorcerer's ass if he tried to stop me. I had unresolved feelings for Blackwell. As in, I was really resolved he was evil through and through, but I didn't know what to do about it.

Okay.

If it was a map, someone should be able to read it. If Pulou thought that someone was me, then who was I to question one of the guardian nine?

I turned toward the First Nations-carved cedar door, through which I'd entered the nexus hours ago, and willed the portal to take me home.

"It's my belated birthday." Kandy the green-haired werewolf stood — arms crossed and glowering — in the middle of the bakery basement. She'd been waiting for me the moment I stepped from the portal onto the hard-packed dirt floor.

"I know," I answered, giving her a blazing smile. It was her belated birthday because she'd gone camping with her Norwegian buddy, Jorgen, on the weekend of her actual birthday, August 8th. I'd been invited, but I had a feeling that my and a werewolf's idea of camping were completely different. Plus, I still wasn't sure whether I would have been crashing a date or not. Kandy was super close-mouthed about anything remotely personal. Her personal. Not mine, of course.

I hadn't even known that Kandy was a physiotherapist until she got certified to work in Canada and started picking up shifts at the clinic a couple of blocks down the street. Even then, I thought she only told me because she needed a reference for work visa purposes.

I'd created four new cupcakes — *Sass in a Cup, Tease in a Cup, Flirt in a Cup,* and *Tart in a Cup* — with the taste of Kandy's dark-chocolate berry-infused magic in mind, though without the bitter finish. I'd given Kandy two of her birthday cupcakes for her camping trip, because my main gift hadn't been ready until today. My now-twenty-six-year-old werewolf best friend was perfectly happy to have two chances to eat cupcakes especially made for her, and I was more than happy to make them.

"You're late."

"Am I?" I said, as if I didn't know we had any plans at all. Then I dug into the inner side pocket of my satchel, carefully avoiding touching the dragonskin map, and pulled out a folded, printed piece of paper. I handed the paper to Kandy.

Her glower deepened as she snatched the paper from me. The green-haired werewolf was about two inches shorter than me, and favored tank tops and ripped jeans. But tonight she was dressed in sleek black pants that fit her lithe body like a rubber glove and rode almost embarrassingly low on her nonexistent hips. Her black satin halter top draped, rather becomingly, down to the small of her back. Her hair, which she'd been growing out, was gelled straight up in various three-inch spikes all over her head.

I was going to need to change.

Kandy unfolded the paper and read the tickets I'd printed. I'd bought us two spots in a truffle-making course at Chocolate Arts that night.

Kandy huffed, hiding her approval of the gift behind her grumpiness. "So that takes care of dinner. Then what?" she asked.

I laughed. "Oh, I've got a few ideas. There might even be dancing."

"You have exactly thirty minutes to look respectable enough to be by my side tonight."

"Aye, aye, belated-birthday captain," I said with a salute. Then I stepped past the werewolf to climb the wooden stairs that led out of the basement and into the pantry of my bakery above.

Kandy stopped me by wrapping her arm around my neck from behind, pressing her face into the curls at the back of my neck. It was like being held — carefully — by steel bands.

"Sometimes I worry you won't come back," she whispered. "When you go through the portal."

"I won't leave you."

I felt Kandy nod, but she didn't immediately release me. Ten months ago, she had chosen to stay in Vancouver with me instead of returning to the base of the West

Coast North American Pack in Portland, though she'd visited at least once a month since making that decision. She really wasn't a fan of the pack's new beta, Audrey. And I also thought Kandy held some guilt about the death of a fledgling werewolf, Jeremy, at the hands of my sister over a year ago. Guilt because she was technically a pack enforcer, and she should have protected him better. She swore she stayed for my protection, along with some political mumbo jumbo about alliances and whatever. Except Kandy was the least political person I knew.

She also might have stayed because she thought Desmond had broken my heart. He hadn't — we weren't meant to be together despite all odds or anything — but he'd dented it pretty good. No matter that Sienna had deserved it. I wasn't about to forgive him for killing my sister.

I hadn't heard from or spoken to Kandy's alpha since January, when I'd chosen to aid Rochelle instead of helping the pack get their collective hands around Blackwell's neck. The visit had resulted in claws and knives unsheathed and insults exchanged, and had probably widened the divide between Desmond and me rather than repaired anything.

I wasn't going to be a political ally — in or out of Desmond's bed — and that was all he wanted me in his life for anyway. It was time to move on. Didn't we all deserve to fall head over heels for someone who utterly adored us in return?

Sigh.

"I thought there would be more cupcakes," Kandy muttered into my hair.

"There will be cupcakes. Two new ones, plus the first two you already tasted."

"I looked everywhere."

I laughed. "I baked them at Gran's."

Kandy swore and released me. "What are you waiting for, then?" she growled. Then she dashed ahead of me up the stairs.

Not all werewolves kept their emotions so far in check as Kandy did, but tears and robust laughter were rare occurrences with my best friend. We were complete opposites that way.

I switched out my T-shirt for a light-blue silk peasant blouse with a drawstring neck, and my jeans for a black silk skirt. The skirt had the most perfect, subtly ruffled edge that fell just above my knees. I kept my necklace coiled three times around my neck, where it rested nicely on my collarbone, and strapped the invisible sheath for my jade knife to my bare thigh. The skirt was loose enough that it didn't show the outline of the knife when I was standing, but I'd have to be careful when sitting down. I usually left the unnerving of people to Kandy, and it was her belated birthday after all. I slipped on a pair of black Fluevogs — classic Gorgeous Minis — to complete the look. Thankfully I'd gotten my legs waxed last weekend, so I was good to go barelegged.

I hustled through the apartment to join Kandy in the living room, where she was sharing a glass of red wine with my mother, Scarlett. As I crossed by the kitchen, Scarlett smiled, her strawberry blond hair its usual perfect smooth wave down her back.

A plate of candied salmon, cream cheese, and onion-and-garlic brown rice crackers sat on the gray granite kitchen island, and I fell on this treat without a word. I had to compete with Kandy, though, and the salmon was already half gone. Scarlett laughed and touched my shoulder lightly. Her magic tingled through the thin silk of my blouse. She touched me every time she saw me these days, as if reassuring herself I was actually beside her. Gran as well. I'd scared them very badly in Tofino. Or rather, Sienna almost killing me in Tofino had scared my mother and grandmother terribly.

"Merlot, Jade?" Scarlett asked.

"No thanks, Mom. I think we're almost late as it is."

"The cab is waiting for us," Kandy said. She swallowed the remainder of her wine in a single gulp. Her wicked metabolism probably burned off all the alcohol before it even hit her stomach. I had found — since recovering from almost dying, and draining my magic so severely in order to take Sienna's — that I had to drink so much to get buzzed now that my stomach usually rebelled before my head did. Yeah, I'd tested it more than once. A girl had to try to have some fun, and Kandy was always up for a round of good pub food.

"It's like a four-block walk," I said.

"More like seven, and in those shoes?" Kandy said, a wolfish grin on her face. I took the grin to mean that my outfit was acceptable.

I laughed, and then cried out, "Let the revelry begin!"

Scarlett laughed. Kandy and I headed for the front door. As I passed the couch, I realized I'd forgotten to transfer my wallet and keys to a smaller, prettier bag, so I jogged back to my bedroom and grabbed my satchel instead. Thankfully, Matt & Nat satchels went with every outfit. At least every outfit I owned.

Chocolate Arts was on West Third Avenue between Pine and Fir Streets, just one block north and six blocks east of the bakery. The evening was clear and balmy. The sun still wouldn't set for a couple of hours. Though it would be the first day of fall next Tuesday, the glorious summer weather had held and the trees hadn't started changing color yet. The cherry tree and magnolia blossoms were months gone, but the air was still sweetly fragrant. Kandy could probably pick me up, throw me across False Creek, and I'd hit downtown Vancouver, but you'd never know that a big city was that near tonight.

We hopped into the completely unnecessary cab, which drove the half-dozen blocks and pulled up to double-park out front of the chocolatier. I passed the cabby a ten, happy that I'd thought to grab cash from the ATM yesterday when I dropped the deposit for the bakery. Kandy was on the sidewalk before the taxi had fully pulled to a stop. There was parking out back that led customers through the kitchen to the storefront, but the one time I'd entered through the back, I felt like I was totally invading the chocolatier's creative space.

Chocolate Arts specialized in decadent truffles using Valrhona and Cacao Barry chocolate, as well as their own line of chocolate and ice cream bars. Their salted caramels were the first I'd ever tasted, and the eighth-inch rectangles of chocolate-covered goodness were a go-to purchase for me. As in, every time I dropped by. Tonight, we'd be learning how to make some of their signature truffles, which meant Kandy and I would be guzzling melted chocolate while we rolled balls of variously flavored ganache into lumps of tastiness. I planned to be cocoa-buzzed and covered in chocolate up to my elbows within the hour. Too bad I didn't have anyone to lick it off me later … or I'd bring home a container cup.

Kandy, inches from opening the front door, turned back to grin at me as the cab pulled away. The green of her shapeshifter magic rolled across her eyes as she accessed some of her power — probably her sense of smell. Then she ducked inside the store with a husky laugh of anticipation.

Right. It was Kandy's birthday, not my pity party. I was damn lucky to have her as a friend, especially with all we'd been through in the last year. I would have abandoned my trouble-enticing ass ten months ago … well, that was a lie. I was loyal to a fault. But then, so was Kandy.

I knew the green-haired werewolf was still nursing the arm she'd injured ten months ago in Tofino — and then had injured again, by Audrey's hand, back in January. Werewolves healed quickly, so the lingering nature of the injury spoke volumes about its severity. The fact that Kandy remained in Vancouver with me — potentially unable to fully access the healing magic of the pack — meant the world to me. I could count my true friends on one hand.

No matter how many new cupcakes I created, how much chocolate I consumed, or how full I packed my days with treasure collecting and running a business, I just couldn't shake this feeling of being out of sync with my life. My normal life. Or rather, the new normal. I just wasn't quite sure what that was anymore.

Kandy poked her head out from the entrance and hissed, "We're late."

The only time the werewolf cared about being prompt was when food or lives were on the line.

I grinned and followed her as she ducked back inside. A double-masted sailboat made entirely out of chocolate occupied the window display by the front door. Even the life-rings, ropes, and pulleys were chocolate. The milk chocolate waves were capped with white chocolate.

Oh, yes. It was going to be a great evening.

Chapter Three

After way too much chocolate — and not a lot of actual learning — at Chocolate Arts, I seriously hoped that the chocolatier didn't regret not doubling the price of our tickets. Not bothering with a cab this time, Kandy and I headed up a block and crossed over to Fable Kitchen, which had opened two years ago a few blocks east of the bakery. I hadn't had a chance to check it out yet, but I really liked its 'from farm to table' mandate, and Kandy liked anywhere that cooked a great steak.

We shared mussels to start, and yes, we 'added' fries as the menu helpfully suggested. I had the halibut while Kandy got her red meat fix. But the shining glory of the meal was the s'mores for dessert. Yes, freaking s'mores. I tried to not look too closely at the bill when it came, reminding myself that the bakery was doing well and Kandy's birthday only came once a year. Belated or otherwise. Plus, it wasn't like I actually needed new shoes … or groceries next week.

We wandered home giggling and joking, cutting down to the alley behind West Fourth Avenue at Yew Street. I always preferred to use the back entrance of the bakery to come and go from my apartment, probably because I adored my kitchen, my haven, so much. Even just passing through it on the way to bed kept me grounded. The sun had set, but reds, pinks, and oranges still streaked the steadily deepening blue sky above the harbor. The colors even kissed the edges of the dark North Shore Mountains.

"You promised me dancing," Kandy said, then dissolved into a fit of giggles over something she only thought she'd said out loud. Giggling wasn't the werewolf's thing. She was more buzzed than I'd ever seen her, and I guessed that mixing drinks eventually had its way with werewolf metabolism as well.

"Tomorrow night. I have to bake in the morning," I said. "I also have mani-pedis booked at two."

"And Sunday? Brunch?"

"Only the best for my green-haired friend."

Kandy's snort dissolved into another round of giggles, and she threw her arm around my neck.

I laughed, feeling delightfully warm — inside and out — myself.

Then, steps from the bakery's back door, the shadow of the adjacent wine store's industrial-sized garbage can tried to grab me.

Seriously, it reached out as if it had actual fingers and tried to latch onto my left arm.

I shrieked, jumped sideways to free myself, and knocked Kandy flying across the alley. I willed my jade knife into my right hand, slashed at the shadow, and met absolutely no resistance.

I stood there, knife in hand, staring at nothing except the deepening shadows of the evening. The echoes of my scream rebounded off the buildings to either side, their presence making me feel suddenly claustrophobic.

"What the hell?" Kandy muttered.

I spared her a glance. She was sprawled on her ass on the asphalt, rubbing her arm. Her bad arm. Shit.

"The shadow ... Jesus, I'm sorry. I thought the garbage can shadow just tried to ... latch onto me."

The green of her magic rolled across her eyes as Kandy silently rose up and onto the balls of her feet without placing her hands down on the ground. She stared into the shadows behind the garbage can, then shifted her gaze to look behind the recycling bin. Every hint of the giggles was gone from her demeanor now.

"I don't smell anything," she whispered, her voice low and intense. "Magic?"

I shook my head but didn't sheath my knife. I couldn't taste any magic nearby other than Kandy's.

Great. Now I was hallucinating terrors out of thin air. Sure, it was shadowy air, but I'd ruined our buzz over nothing. "I'm sorry —"

Thunder cracked and a bolt of lightning split the air about twenty feet in front of us. The alley flooded with mind-numbing magic that somehow tasted of metal and electricity, along with the underlying spiciness that I always associated with dragons.

Kandy was growling beside me, leaning into the press of the magic as if fighting for her footing.

A dark figure of a man appeared — legs astride and arms akimbo — at the core of the light.

I felt Kandy's magic shift, two-inch claws appearing where her fingernails should be as she slashed at the magic still buffeting us. I stepped one pace ahead and shifted to place her just behind my right shoulder, shielding her from the bulk of the magic's force with my body.

The electric white magic — some sort of transportation spell, at best guess — disappeared with a snap.

The man was dressed in dragon leathers and easily over six feet tall. He was dark blond, broad shouldered, and unarmed as far as I could see. But with the amount of magic he wielded — especially if the transportation spell was of his own making — I knew that visible weapons meant very little.

"Dragon," I whispered for Kandy's benefit. "I ... think."

"You think?" she asked, her wolf growl infusing her tone.

The possibly-a-dragon-or-possibly-some-hybrid-I'd-never-met opened his eyes. With the dim light in the alley paired with the near dark of the night, I couldn't distinguish their color.

"Sie! Frau!" he shouted.

Immediately after the foreign words left his mouth, he threw back his head, arched his body forward, and screamed in agony. Then he collapsed onto the asphalt before us.

"That can't be good," I said.

Kandy had slammed her still-clawed hands over her ears at his scream, but she dropped them as we cautiously stepped forward. She prodded the possible-dragon with her foot, then looked at me.

I shrugged. "His magic is dim."

"Does your knife cut dragon flesh?"

"Haven't had a reason or a chance to try it yet."

Kandy raised an eyebrow at me. Yeah, dragons were pretty quick on their feet, even in training.

"Okay," Kandy continued. "Well, if he tries to kill me ..."

"I'll skewer him. Dragon or no."

Kandy grabbed his shoulder and rolled him over with a grunt. "Heavy."

"Dragons usually are."

We stared down at the black leather-swathed dragon at our feet. He was out cold. Everything about him was definitely broad — as in shoulders, chest, nose, cheekbones, and jaw.

"At least he's damn cute," Kandy said. "You know, if he's here to eviscerate us."

Kandy and I had very different opinions on what qualified as 'cute.' The man at my feet was dangerous. I could tell that by his magic alone.

Still, he was a dragon … I thought.

I sighed.

"We're going to have to bring him inside."

"Yep, that scream was crazy. I'm surprised the neighbors aren't swamping us yet."

"Friday night. Most of the nearest neighbors are still at work." Kitsilano was a pretty upscale neighborhood, but the bakery was backed by apartment buildings typically rented out to people who worked in the area. I was fairly certain we'd been served by a few of my neighbors at the restaurant tonight. Even Todd, my espresso wizard, lived a couple of blocks from here. His rent wasn't fantastic but he was only blocks from work and the beach, and what more did an early twenty-something want?

I grabbed the guy's wrists, thankful that he wore leather gauntlets so I didn't need to touch him skin to skin. Kandy grabbed his booted ankles and we dragged him to the bakery alley door. Yeah, dragged. He was too heavy to lift in heels.

We got him through the back door and situated on the tile floor between my stainless steel workstation and the oven. Oddly, getting him through the bakery wards took some extra thought and magic exertion on my part. The invitation to enter was usually made between two conscious parties. I hadn't known that made a difference until tonight. I thought about trying to lift him up onto the counter, just to be polite, but decided his weight might crush it.

"Should we tie him up?" Kandy asked.

"He is a dragon …"

"But not one you know."

"Yeah, but all dragons are supposed to be, you know, peacekeepers."

Kandy snorted. "Right. Your dad, the peacekeeper."

"I say we leave him here to sleep it off … I'm assuming the transportation spell drained him. And you stay with me tonight, behind the wards of the apartment."

"And when he wakes and we aren't here?"

"I'll feel him from upstairs," I muttered. "He packs a lot of magic."

"Seems risky."

"Yeah," I agreed, but I couldn't figure out what else to do. "I could take him to the nexus, if I could manage to pull him through the portal with me, but … I'm wary of dragging beings I don't know into the nexus." Yeah, I'd been there and done that … with a demon, the very first time I'd met my dad, actually. I was still on Suanmi's black list — and quite possibly the black lists of other guardians as well — because of it. Well, that was one of the reasons Suanmi hated me anyway.

"Sensible."

"Yeah."

I glanced at the digital clock on the oven. It was just after midnight. "I'll check on him on the hour. If he's not awake before I need to bake, I'm going to have to move him anyway."

Halfway up the back stairs to the apartment, I remembered I had the dragonskin tattoo map in my satchel.

Kandy insisted on coming down and keeping watch on the sleeping dragon while I slipped into the back office.

I'd bought a small fire safe when I opened the bakery, but I'd only ever used it to hold deposits that I couldn't immediately walk the block to the bank, as well as the cash float. After Tofino, I'd moved that safe underneath the front counter in the bakery and replaced the one in my office with a crazy expensive, bolted-into-the-floor model.

The installer thought I was crazy when he found out I was putting it in the back of a bakery and not in some six-thousand-square-foot Shaughnessy mansion, where I was probably planning on filling it with diamonds. It took up about a quarter of my office. In addition to the wards already on the bakery, I layered the safe with the same protection spells I'd placed on my apartment. Then I asked Scarlett and Gran to add their own protections. All the spells were keyed to me, and I was the only person who knew the combination. I didn't even write it down.

Yeah, it wasn't overkill.

Because after Tofino, I found myself in possession of two magical items that ... well, that scared me silly to possess them.

One was Blackwell's original leather-bound *Book of Demon History on Earth*. This wasn't actually a spellbook, but had enough information in it that my sister had managed to use it to raise two separate sets of demons — one in London and one in Tofino. The book itself wasn't powerful, but obviously the information contained in it could be dangerous.

The second item was of my own making. And it was far, far more terrifying. I'd taken a sacrificial knife that had previously been wielded by my sister to kill a teenaged werewolf in order to summon a demon. Then, using magic stolen from a sorcerer who my sister had also killed, I turned that knife into a weapon that could cut through any magic. Well, any magic I'd seen it tested against. A knife sharpened by blood magic and forged with my alchemist powers. A knife that had almost killed an ancient vampire, who I'd previously thought immortal.

Actually, I was pretty sure that the knife had killed Kett, and that only the intervention of his maker and an uber-powerful elder vampire had brought him back.

So, yeah. I didn't want either item in the hands of anyone. Not even me. But they were my responsibility now, and I wasn't going to shirk the duty even if it scared me silly.

I placed Pulou's map in the safe, two shelves down from the knife and the book. I didn't think the blood magic would leech out or anything. I just really, really didn't want to accidentally brush the cursed knife. I had tried to figure out what I'd created — and how to undo it — months ago, but the magic was tangled, fused. I could probably separate it from the knife, but into what? I didn't want to inadvertently create something even more terrible.

Sigh.

Pulou had called the knife a trifle when I tried to give it to him. The demon history book was so insignificant to him that he barely spared it a shake of his head when I tried to donate it to the nexus library. I needed to keep reminding myself of that. Of course, none of the nine guardians saw Blackwell as a threat either, but I knew better. Didn't I?

Anyway. With the map locked in the safe, I needed to get some sleep before I had to bake in four hours. I had a new recipe I wanted to test, a variation of Kandy's blackberry birthday cupcakes. The dragon was still out cold on the kitchen floor as we headed back up to the apartment and rolled into bed. Kandy took the couch. Scarlett wasn't home, so I sent her a text message as my head hit the pillow.

Beware of the sleeping dragon in the bakery kitchen.

I woke up suddenly and fully aware. What had woken me and whether I'd been dreaming, I didn't know. My bedroom was pitch dark. I reached over and tapped my phone on the nightstand to check the time. It was 4:21 in the freaking morning. I still had over half an hour until my alarm.

Then I remembered the dragon in the kitchen bakery. I stretched my dowser senses beyond the apartment wards, but didn't taste any magic other than Kandy's berry-infused dark-chocolate from the living room. The unknown dragon was probably still unconscious, because I was certain I would taste someone as powerful as him even through my wards.

Though, speaking of wards, something was off. I just wasn't sure what or where.

I slipped out of bed, wiggled my toes into some flip-flops, and pulled a hoodie over my tank top and cupcake-printed pajama bottoms. The PJs were a gift from Kandy for my twenty-fourth birthday last February. Yeah, I was a Pisces. Supposedly, that was why I had a thing for shoes — according to a local astrologer. I brushed my fingers over the hilt of the knife invisibly strapped to my right thigh, which I slept with most nights now. My comfort blanket was a knife, so no wonder I was imagining being attacked by shadows in the alley after a couple of drinks.

I wandered out into the living room, still not knowing what had woken me. All that remained of the dozen *Flirt in a Cup* — a blackberry cake with chocolate-blackberry buttercream icing — that I'd given to Kandy as a bedtime snack were the crusted paper cups strewn across my steamer-trunk coffee table. The green-haired werewolf was snoring and sprawled out on the couch, but she woke instantly when I lightly touched her shoulder. She rolled to her feet in a smooth, silent motion behind me as I crossed through the room to the back stairs.

I couldn't taste Scarlett's magic, so she hadn't come back to the apartment last night. I wondered if she was with my dad. She often came home smelling of sun and sand, but usually left me a note on the fridge. Of course, I hadn't checked for one last night.

At the top of the stairs to the bakery, I changed my mind about the flip-flops and shucked them off my feet. Then I sidled down the stairs with Kandy close behind me. I didn't turn on the lights. I couldn't see in the dark as well as Kandy, but I could see well enough by the digital light coming off the various appliances to note that the kitchen was empty. No sleeping dragon.

The light was on in the office, but the door was half closed.

The tile was cool underneath my bare feet as I slipped as silently as possible past my stainless steel workstation. Then, standing an arm's length away, I slowly pushed the office door all the way open.

The black leather-swathed dragon — if that was what he was — stood in front of my safe with his back to the door. The safe door was freaking crumpled and hanging off one hinge. He appeared to have effortlessly ripped through the multilayered wards along with the man-made steel. I seriously hoped the magical backlash had been a bitch. If it hadn't, I'd happily make him regret destroying days of work and hundreds of dollars. The nullification of the wards was probably what had woken me. Because, even standing this close, I could barely taste his smoky dragon magic.

He turned — almost lazily, as if he had all the time in the world — toward where Kandy and I stood in the office doorway. I estimated that there was maybe seven feet between us. I could have my knife in his heart with one lunge. Except he had my map — Pulou's map — draped over his hands. And I didn't go around stabbing people in the heart without some witty banter first.

He was glaring at the tattooed map as though it was the bane of his existence.

"That doesn't belong to you," I said. "And you broke my freaking safe."

"The freaking safe wasn't safe enough."

His English was heavily-accented with German, I thought. He spoke as if testing out the words.

"Hilarious, asshole. I could have left you in the alley."

"You couldn't have kept me out."

"I can kick you out now ... without the map."

Kandy shifted behind me.

The guy's gaze flicked to her and then back to me. "You going to set your wolf against me, witch?" he asked. "I will crush her skull with one hand."

Kandy started laughing. "I love it when they underestimate you," she said between chortles.

"Dragons are immune to witch magic," he snapped. Well, that confirmed the dragon identification. Oddly, his accent was easing with each word he spoke. "That I even have to explain such things confirms that you are in possession of something you have no ability to protect —"

"Wrong species," Kandy interrupted. "Dumb, dumb."

He looked confused. It was difficult to maintain intimidation when confused, but he pulled it off.

So I pulled my knife.

A smile spread across his face. I ignored how this transformed him from stern, grumbly dragon into a gorgeous creature of great power. Delicious, actually. Yeah, there was nothing cute about him at all.

"Alchemist," he whispered. His English was almost unaccented now, which was freaky weird but cool. Gold glinted across his could-be-green, but might-be-blue eyes. I'd never seen dragon magic manifest like that before. Man, his arrogance would give Kett a run for his blood money.

Kandy snorted. "Don't dragons usually call you 'warrior's daughter'?"

That wiped the smile from his full-lipped, wide-jawed face. He narrowed his deep-green eyes at me.

Okay, I got that I kept noticing he was hot. Forgive me. I hadn't had a good romp in over a year. Hell, I hadn't had a great romp in much, much longer than that.

"Remind me not to elect you secret keeper," I mock hissed at Kandy.

I felt her shrug behind me. "Fair fights are more interesting to watch."

"Yeah, but now he's not sure. Fight blocker."

Kandy choked out a laugh. "Fine. You want to ruin your bakery, you go for it. He'll hit back."

"I will," he said. Then he pulled the sacrificial knife out of the sheath on his right thigh.

He'd stolen my freaking knife as well.

"That's not yours," I snapped.

"It feels like mine."

"Really not a point in your favor, dragon. You know, on the good or evil scale."

"Come take it back, then."

So I did ... without taking a step. I'd been testing my alchemist powers for over a year. And I had specifically been working with the sacrificial knife, trying to figure out a way to neutralize its magic. When the neutralizing didn't work out, I'd installed a fail-safe.

The knife, like any other magical object I constructed, was made with my magic. And my magic was tied to me. I'd found I could call an object I made back to me with a single thought. Well, a super-focused single thought. Okay, some intense thinking and coaxing. The sacrificial knife was a bit pissy, actually. It didn't much like being held by me. Yes, it was an inanimate object, but that was what it felt like to me. Maybe I was just projecting because I was repelled by it.

Anyway, it had taken a bunch of coaxing and more applications of my magic. But the sacrificial knife came now at my call.

The dragon looked a little shocked to be weaponless. Then he looked more shocked to find my jade knife at his neck and the sacrificial knife poised at his heart. The fact that he had the capacity to be shocked humanized him. I tried to not notice the starburst of deep blue around his pupils.

"Not a witch, nor just an alchemist," he murmured. His throat moved against the blade of my jade knife. He needed a shave. The blade was helpful in that regard. I tried not to smirk and failed.

"That's my map, entrusted to me," I said.

"This?" He held the map with one hand so I could see it. "By whom?"

"Kandy?" I prompted.

The green-haired werewolf reached over my shoulder and flicked her claws in the guy's face before she carefully took the map from him. He flinched and looked like he was thinking about not letting go of it, but he did.

"You think that knife can pierce the heart of a dragon, warrior's daughter?" he asked, heavy on the sarcasm. For someone who might have just learned English, then adapted his accent to match mine, he sure picked up speech nuances quickly.

"You held it, dragon. You tell me."

He held my gaze for a moment. Then he leaned into me — pressing against both blades, the jade knife at his neck and the sacrificial knife at his heart. I ignored the instinct to back off even as the jade blade drew blood and the sacrificial knife cut through his dragon leathers like soft butter. He hissed and curled his lip at me.

Then he took a step back, his gaze still locked to mine. He lifted his hand and wiped the blood from his neck. Besides the blood, his skin was unblemished. He healed as quickly as Kett, and much quicker than I did. He let go of my gaze to stare at the blood on his hand. He looked bemused.

I lifted my jade knife vertically, drawing his attention as I watched a drop of his blood slide down the hilt. Then I reached out with my alchemist powers, and with a single lick of magic, I absorbed the blood into the blade. I felt the dragon's magic dissipate through the knife, then settle.

The guy grunted in surprise, but then tried to cover. Apparently, he'd never seen an alchemist in action before..

I took a step back, twirling the knife and its new pulse of power in my hand. Then I sheathed it. The dragon watched me, dissecting my every move. That was what Branson the sword master had trained me to do. I kept hold of the sacrificial knife in my left hand but allowed it to hang by my side.

Then I waited.

The dragon rolled his shoulders and his neck. Then, having made some decision, he huffed out an exasperated sigh.

"Warner, sentinel of the instruments of assassination, son of Jiaotu, guardian of Northern Europe," he said. His tone was formal but his bow was limited to a tilt of his chin.

I had no idea what 'sentinel' or 'instruments of assassination' meant. Sure, I'd been studying, but the nexus library was insanely huge. I could devote my entire life to it and still not get through a single row. Though, granted, I'd been rather focused on Blackwell and figuring out the proper way to 'reclaim' his circlet. Hell, figuring out how to seize the sorcerer's entire collection would have been even better.

Kandy stepped up beside me. "Kandy, werewolf, enforcer of the West Coast North American Pack." She snapped her teeth on the 'k' in pack and I stifled a smile. The green-haired werewolf had a real loathing of formalities.

Warner inclined his head in Kandy's direction but kept his gaze on me.

"Jade Godfrey, granddaughter of Pearl Godfrey, Convocation chair," I said. Then I raised my chin just a little more. "Daughter of Yazi, warrior of the guardians, guardian of Australia."

Warner started to sneer at this proclamation, but he managed to control his expression. "Child of a witch and a guardian?" he asked doubtfully.

"I was unaware that Jiaotu had any children," I countered. "You look nothing like him." Jiaotu was as white blond and almost as pale as Kett. He was also fast 'friends' with Suanmi. He'd witnessed me dragging a demon into the nexus, of course. Then he'd been an asshole to Kett and outraged over my heritage. Since then we hadn't spoken.

Warner's face blanked. "She and I are very alike," he said, enunciating his words carefully.

"She?"

"What year is it?"

I glanced at Kandy. She curled her lip at me questioningly.

"2014. September 19th," the werewolf answered. "You're crashing my belated birthday party."

Warner let out a pained breath. "Four hundred and fifty years," he whispered.

"That's a lot of time to be missing," Kandy said, putting together the pieces of the conversation quicker than I did. "Why show up now? Here?"

"It's my duty to protect the location of the instruments," he answered doggedly, as if he might be trying to convince himself. "No matter what year you claim it to be."

"Instruments?" I asked.

He lifted his hand and pointed a finger at the map Kandy still held. "Where did you get that?"

Kandy tilted her head, suddenly more interested in than wary of Warner. But I'd felt his magic spread through my knife. I wasn't so quick to relax around someone who held that much power in a single drop of blood.

"Tell him the rest of your title," she prompted.

I hesitated. Then, trusting the werewolf's judgement, I said, "Alchemist. Hunter for the treasure keeper, Pulou. Do I need to elaborate?"

He shook his head, clearly not happy with my 'job title.' "You're not powerful enough to hold such a thing," he said, referencing the map.

"I believe she just established her dominance, dragon," Kandy growled. Then, to prove her point, she turned her back on him and crossed into the kitchen. She rolled the map as she did so, tucking it into the elastic band at the small of her back.

Knowing a werewolf game when I saw one, I followed her, flicking on the kitchen lights as I did so.

"I would speak to the treasure keeper," Warner called after me.

"Go for it," I said as I crossed around the stainless steel workstation to the bakery fridge.

Warner followed us out of the office, his gaze sweeping the kitchen to identify the two exits. "You will take me to the nearest portal."

Kandy, her back still to Warner, climbed up on a stool that was reserved especially for her. She laid her head in her arms as if taking a nap.

I pulled butter out of the fridge.

"What are you doing?" Warner asked through gritted teeth.

"Baking," I answered. "It's my shift. And I'm already awake, aren't I?"

"Baking? Baking?" he echoed, getting angry now. "The warrior's daughter, the treasure keeper's hunter, bakes? Bakes what?"

"Tasty cupcakes." Kandy smacked her lips together for emphasis.

"Cupcakes!" he bellowed. "You have triggered the shadow scouts with your ineptitude and blatant disregard —"

"You think he'd be thanking us, hey alchemist?" Kandy said. Then she turned to sneer at Warner. "I get what 'sentinel' means. That's your job. You work for the dragons, and so does Jade."

Kandy was always quicker on her feet than I was. She figured people out by playing them. Warner went very quiet. I unwrapped the butter and dropped it into my standing mixer.

"I don't know where I am," Warner finally said, his tone quiet but strong. "I must speak to the treasure keeper."

I glanced over at Kandy. She shrugged, leaving the decision to me.

I looked at Warner. He was huge. I could barely see the doorframe of the office behind him. He was almost as wide at the shoulders as Desmond but was taller, so that his girth was proportional. Even weaponless, he was intimidating.

I brushed the fingers of my right hand across my knife, invisible at my hip. I called up his magic that now resided in it. Powerful dragon magic.

"Something tried to grab me in the alley," I said. "A shadow."

"You fought it off?" he asked. His tone of surprise irked me, but I just nodded.

Kandy snorted. "Shook it off, more like it," she said. It seemed the wolf wasn't interested in hiding power today.

"These shadows are after the map?" I asked.

Warner hesitated, his gaze dropping to the map tucked in at the small of Kandy's back. "It was likely a demon scout. A benign shadow form ultimately after the location of the instruments. Their detection is one of the ... functions of the sentinels. The map is dangerous in the wrong hands."

Yeah, I wasn't a complete idiot. 'Benign' meant something very different to a dragon than it did to the rest of us mortals. He'd hesitated to use the word 'function' as well. Maybe because he was still learning English. Or maybe he was just being guarded. Actually, I was surprised he'd offered as much as he had already. Dragons weren't all over the concept of sharing.

"Can you read it?"

"No."

I glanced at Kandy, who shook her head. The wolf could usually figure out if someone was telling the truth, but I took her head shake to indicate she couldn't tell with Warner.

"Will you escort me to the nexus, and present me to the treasure keeper?" he asked.

"You want me to come with you?"

Warner clenched and unclenched his hands at his sides. It bothered him to request my help. "2014," he murmured, not looking at me or answering my question.

"That's a long time for you?" I asked, suddenly feeling sorry for the displacement he must be feeling.

He nodded.

"I will escort you," I said. "After I bake, and …" — I glanced down at my PJs — "… and change."

"That would be wise," he said snarkily.

And I didn't feel sorry for him anymore.

"Though time is of the essence," he continued.

"Nothing is coming through the wards," I said.

"I countered your wards easily."

"Did you?" I asked. My tone was deadly quiet, but challenging. I knew there was no way he'd broken into my safe without getting some backlash. In fact, I wondered now if that was why he'd been slow to engage me further.

He didn't answer.

Kandy flashed her nonsmile at Warner and laughed huskily. "This is going to be fun."

"Only you would think so, werewolf," I answered.

"Nah, you love this part. You just don't like to admit it because it clashes with your image of yourself."

I snorted, and applied myself to baking cupcakes.

Warner took a few steps farther into the kitchen, glowering distrustfully at the overhead fluorescent lights. He touched the edge of the stainless steel workstation tentatively, as if concerned it might bite him, but then didn't seem to know where to place himself. "I'm rather hungry," he finally admitted.

Kandy chortled, slipped off the stool, and grabbed a liter of milk out of the fridge along with some eggs.

She passed the milk to Warner and went hunting for a frying pan.

Warner popped the cap off the glass milk container and smelled it. "I'd prefer mead," he said. "Milk is for babies."

We ignored him. He tilted back his head and drank the entire container of milk in one long swig. I realized I was watching the muscles move in his neck, and tore my gaze away to find Kandy smirking at me.

"I like my eggs scrambled," I said.

"I like my cupcakes by the dozen," she retorted.

I laughed. What the hell, hey? This wasn't any crazier than my life usually was.

Chapter Four

Bryn, my full-timer, showed up for her shift early. After giving Warner an eyeful, she was happy to oversee the bakery setup and the last of the baking. I was fairly certain she thought Warner had spent the night, and she seemed to accept his leather getup with nothing more than a saucy grin.

Kandy grabbed a tray of her birthday cupcakes — *Sass in a Cup,* chocolate blackberry cake with dark-chocolate blackberry buttercream icing — and hustled Warner out into the bakery storefront to wrestle coffee out of the espresso machine while I hightailed it upstairs to change. I seriously hoped the werewolf didn't break my La Pavoni Bar-Star, because the purchase of it had badly dented my business credit card last spring. The swanky new machine featured a copper boiler with an auto shut-off and two group heads — yep, I had no idea what that meant, except it was a classy red and crazy expensive. My espresso wizard, Todd, insisted it was the best, and totally kiboshed the idea of trying to buy a refurbished unit.

I dashed into my bedroom, where I pulled a royal-blue 'Zombie Survival Plan' T-shirt over my tank top, swapped out my PJs for an older pair of Seven jeans, and laced on my 7th Heaven 8 Eye Fluevog boots. I opted for flats, not knowing if I should expect to be attacked every time I went into the nexus now or not. Branson had been pretty huffy yesterday, so he might be giving me the silent treatment ... again.

I grabbed my satchel and headed downstairs to get the map from Kandy. The green-haired werewolf distracted Bryn while I pretended to slip out the back door into the alley, but actually tugged Warner into the pantry instead. He covered his confusion at this maneuver pretty quickly. But then, all the chocolate the pantry held usually distracted me as well.

"That's not for you," I snapped as he reached for a two-pound box of 75 percent single-origin from Tanzania that I used in my gluten-free chewy chocolate cookies. He snatched his hand back as I opened the door to the basement, then looked pissed at his own reaction.

Yeah, that tone — completely ripped off from Gran — totally worked with Drake as well. But then, the fledgling was fourteen years old, not over five hundred years old like Warner. Though I was a little fuzzy on whether he should count the years in 'stasis,' so maybe he was actually much younger. Now really wasn't the time to ask.

I'd be prickly about waking up a few hundred years in the future as well. What if all my favorite things no longer existed? I shuddered at the thought. My needs might be basic — family, chocolate, and fabulous, functional shoes — but they were necessities.

We descended the stairs and hit the dirt floor of the basement storage room. Not that I actually used it for storage. I didn't bother turning on the single bare bulb that hung from a wire in the middle of the room. We weren't staying.

"Why are we here, alchemist?" Warner asked.

"You wanted a portal," I said.

He glanced around the concrete-patched brick walls, as if he couldn't see the portal sleepily thrumming away on the east wall. He was slightly hunched, his head just clearing the concrete ceiling. I could see him by the light of the pantry. He hadn't closed the door behind him. I sighed and climbed the six stairs to pull it shut.

Turning back and descending again into the dark, I reached out to the magic of the portal and willed it to open for me as I brushed by Warner. Golden light flooded the tiny room.

He grunted in surprise. "Well hidden," he murmured, intrigued.

I wondered if Pulou would be pissed at me for bringing Warner through this way. I got that the portal was some sort of secret, but when a mysterious dragon shows up, mystically transported — according to him — from another time, and his magic doesn't feel malicious … well, I couldn't think of what else to do but take him to the nexus. I wasn't driving eight hours to the Sea Lion Caves outside Florence, Oregon, just to use the next nearest portal.

That was pack territory, and I didn't want to ask Desmond — aka my-alpha-status-makes-killing-your-sister-okay — permission for anything. Plus, I was never, ever setting foot in that cave again. Ignoring the fact that I'd used it last January when Desmond had dangled Blackwell in front of me. I had thwarted destiny once — the vision that Chi Wen had shown me of Sienna's death by my hand hadn't come to pass — but I wasn't going to play with fate … well, not willingly.

Assuming that Warner didn't need his hand held, I stepped into the golden, pure magic of the portal. I felt that moment of suspension, a brief but blissful hesitation of step, before my forward foot hit the white marble floor of the nexus on the other side. The crossing was effortless for me now.

It took Warner longer.

The dizzily gilded circular room was empty, and the other eight doors were firmly closed. I couldn't taste Drake's or Branson's magic anywhere near, though that didn't mean I wasn't going to be attacked at any moment. Drake moved particularly fast, especially for a fledgling dragon. I got the feeling that even the other guardians saw something special in him, though I hadn't met many other fledglings. None of the other guardians had selected successors, as far as I knew.

Interestingly, after my last face-to-face with Suanmi, I found the normally brain-warping magic of the nexus easier to handle. Perhaps I'd inadvertently absorbed some of the fire breather's magic into my necklace. I had felt her intense power settle around me to a bearable level, and the necklace naturally functioned as a portable personal ward, so that did make some sense.

Warner stepped out of the portal behind me just as Chi Wen the far seer wandered into the room.

Ah, damn. I'd been trying to avoid destiny today.

Chi Wen, the eldest of the guardians, appeared to be an ancient Chinese gentleman. He loved to smile. As in, constantly. I wasn't sure he was capable of any other expression. All gray hair and wrinkles, he came up to my collarbone, though he wasn't particularly wizened.

As best as I'd guessed, he wielded oracle and telepathic powers. The oracle magic was like calling 911, except he was the only operator sifting through visions of disasters and pending worldwide destruction. He then tasked these imminent catastrophes to various guardians depending on their particular power sets. I wasn't completely sure about the telepathic part, but I was fairly certain he could at least communicate with the other guardians without vocalizing his thoughts. Which was probably a good thing, because I rarely understood a word that came out of his mouth. And that had nothing to do with his heavy accent.

Chi Wen grinned at me like I was his own child safely home from the demonic wars ... and in his mind, maybe I was. I curtsied with much more reverence and grace than I had for Suanmi.

I always tried to clear my mind in the far seer's presence, but today I found myself repeating *Please don't touch me, please don't read me* in my head. The far seer scared me way more than any of the other guardians. Sure, they could all end my very existence with a single glance. But Chi Wen could show me my future, and that was utterly terrifying. Completely soul shaking.

Warner stepped up beside me. He wasn't a stand-just-behind-my-shoulder-person like Kett, or even Kandy. With him being a mighty dragon — with obvious prejudices against my heritage — I was surprised he didn't stride completely past me.

"Hello, dragon slayer," Chi Wen called cheerfully as he shuffled toward us.

Warner cranked his head to look at me, actually taking a step away as he did so.

"Don't look at me," I said. "The far seer was obviously addressing you."

"Yes," Chi Wen said agreeably. "Every blade needs a solid hilt."

Err ... yeah, I had no idea what that meant. But I kept my mouth shut and tried to not flinch when Chi Wen patted my shoulder as he passed.

As he touched me, I suddenly realized I was drowning — and had been drowning for some time — surrounded by crushing water. I started to panic, to thrash, to die — but then I broke the surface, my mouth full of salty water and the warm sun on my face.

I gasped for air, realizing I was in the nexus — that I'd never left — as I filled my lungs with as much oxygen as they could hold.

Chi Wen was gone.

Warner was looking at me like I was a ticking time bomb.

"What?" I asked, as snarky as I could be to cover my near drowning in the middle of a waterless chamber.

"What did the far seer show you?" Warner asked.

Well, that was a rude question.

A jet-black cat sauntered through the far archway. Its casual gait was insufficient cover for the cunning betrayed by its yellow eyes. Its sleek fur shone among all the gold of the decor, not a hair out of place.

Warner, still frowning at me, followed my gaze. Then he went utterly still and pale.

"A black cat in the heart of the guardian temple," he murmured. He reached for a weapon that he didn't actually have, then held his hands before himself, wary. "Doom crosses our footsteps."

I snorted out a laugh. "What century are you living in?"

Spicy dragon magic — all apricots and smoky syrup — gathered around the cat along with a haze of golden light. The creature transformed amid a wash of intense magic, as the shapeshifters did. Then Bixi — doing her best Cleopatra impersonation — stood before us. White dress, gold armbands, heavily kohled eyes and all. She obviously didn't have to stash extra clothing everywhere like Kandy did when she changed back from her wolf form.

Logically, I knew Bixi wasn't actually Cleopatra, since she was supposedly only around seven hundred years old. But still, I wondered if there wasn't some deep ancestral connection going on with the guardian of North Africa. And again, when did 'seven hundred' become an 'only'? It was also interesting that the guardians seemed to decide what physical age suited them best. Suanmi was technically younger than Bixi but appeared to be a youthful forty-five. Bixi looked to be about my age at the most. My father Yazi, the third-youngest of the guardians, appeared to be thirty-five.

Warner dropped into a deep bow beside me.

"Hello, warrior's daughter," Bixi said, completely ignoring Warner.

"Hello, guardian."

"What earthly delight have you brought with you this time?"

Warner started coughing — no, choking — beside me.

I reached into my satchel, fished around, and pulled out a simple yet modern, yellow-papered Sirene chocolate bar. As far as I knew, this was the only bar that the newly established company produced out of Victoria, on Vancouver Island. It consisted of a tasting pair made from 72 percent Ecuador and 67 percent Madagascar cocoa. It was a new purchase I'd acquired downtown last weekend at Xoxolat — a mecca of earthly delights that carried a vast selection of single-origin chocolate bars from around the world. I hadn't even tried a single square of the Sirene yet, and I'd really been looking forward to it. Normally, I tried to distract chocolate-questing dragons with cupcakes or cookies, but in my haste to get Warner sorted out I'd forgotten to pack a box.

Bixi came just short of snatching it out of my hand. "I enjoy your visits, alchemist," she said. Then, pressing the bar to her nose and smelling it through its wrapper, she sauntered off in the direction she'd come. Her thin, gold-strapped sandals made no sound on the stone floor.

Dragons had a strong sense of smell and great taste in chocolate. Though regrettably, they never seemed to have any around.

Warner straightened as she left, and stared after her long after she'd gone.

"You've never met Bixi?" I asked.

"No."

I wasn't exceptionally skilled at math, but if the Jiaotu I knew was four hundred years old and Bixi was seven hundred, there should have been room in there for Warner to have crossed paths with the guardian of North Africa. Though I didn't know how old Jiaotu had been before assuming the mantle of guardian of Northern Europe. I didn't know how long Warner's mother had been gone. The dragon had whispered 'four hundred and fifty years' when Kandy had told him what year it was.

In retrospect, I'd been pretty heartless telling Warner his mom was flat-out dead. That hadn't been my intention, but …

"I'm sorry," I said.

"What?"

"I'm sorry. All this must be confusing and sad —"

"It's my job, alchemist."

Right. Dragons and duty went hand in hand.

"Fine." I shrugged. "I can mind my own business. I hang with an ancient vampire who doesn't like to chat about his past."

"If I was a vampire," Warner said, somehow infusing his voice with utter loathing without actually sneering, "I wouldn't want to talk about my despicable and devious life either."

Right. Kett and Warner were so going to be bosom buddies. I'd almost forgotten how enlightened dragons were — not. I guessed I'd been hanging out with the easygoing ones. Now that was a laugh.

Choosing to ignore Warner and get this party started before we ran into anyone who might try to kick my ass — which was a rather long list when I was in the nexus ... or Europe — I slowly rotated to look at the nine doors surrounding me. They were all still closed, but I thought I might try Suanmi's trick of simply calling to Pulou.

"Pulou? Treasure keeper? Ah ... the alchemist attends you?"

Nothing happened.

"Err ... Jade Godfrey paging Pulou the treasure keeper. Paging Pulou."

"Irreverent behavior isn't going to get you —" Warner began. Then the door carved with wolves and white-capped mountains clicked open a couple of inches. Golden portal magic spilled out from around its edges. Then it snapped shut.

"Northern Europe?" I mused.

Warner didn't answer, but he did stare at the wolf-carved door for a long time. I wondered why he didn't just walk through it and confirm that his mother had relinquished her guardian mantle. Except, of course, Europe was huge and he'd have no way of knowing — as far as I could tell — where Jiaotu was on the other side. Each door of the nexus could lead to many different portal exits, as long as you knew where you were going before you stepped into the golden magic.

Actually, now that I thought about it, I had no idea what special ability came with the guardianship of Northern Europe. What powers Jiaotu wielded beyond his dragon strength, agility, and invulnerability. I hadn't stumbled across a guardian manual in the library yet. Or better still, a clearly outlined flow chart. Yeah, guardians were a cagey bunch about magic. But then, so were most Adepts. I opened my mouth to ask Warner, then quickly decided against it. I didn't want to appear more ignorant than I probably already did. Plus, it was just plain rude to ask about an Adept's magic.

I sat down in the center of the room, crossed my legs, and retrieved a second treasure from my satchel — a 75 percent Madagascar raw chocolate bar from Raaka Chocolate in Brooklyn. Oh yes, lovely. This was also a new treat. I carefully opened the package, attempting to preserve the paper as I always did. Then I promptly ripped it, as I always did.

"We just wait?" Warner asked.

"Usually."

The sentinel kept his back to me, standing with legs spread wide and arms crossed. Settling in for the long haul, I thought, and definitely setting down a no-chatting zone. Fine by me. I had new chocolate to savor, and I wasn't keen on sharing with grumpy dragons.

Just as long as I didn't start feeling sorry about Warner being way out of his own time ... and his dead mother ...

"You want a piece?" I asked.

"No."

Jerk.

I wasn't going to ask a second time.

Pulou didn't make us wait long, though he seemed less jovial than usual. In fact, his welcoming smile disappeared and didn't return the instant he assessed Warner. The sentinel had bowed as the guardian stepped through the portal from Northern Europe. I'd already curtsied too many times in the past couple of days, so I didn't bother. I figured my deference from yesterday still stood.

"Treasure keeper," I said. I stood and tucked the remains of my chocolate back in my bag.

Pulou nodded, though his gaze remained on Warner. Bowed head or not, something about the set of Warner's shoulders screamed defiance. And oddly, I found I liked that about him.

"This is Warner, son of Jiaotu ... well ... the former Jiaotu. He says he's the sentinel of the instruments ..." I stumbled with the formal phrasing. "Oh, I don't freaking know. He appeared in the alley behind my bakery last night in a blinding flash of ridiculously powerful magic, right after some shadow tried to grab me. He collapsed and I hauled his ass into the bakery to sleep the transportation spell off. He says he's a sentinel, and he's pissed you gave me the map."

Warner shifted awkwardly after this less than proper introduction, but he didn't look up. His hands were firmly clasped behind his back.

Pulou didn't speak.

"Treasure keeper," Warner finally said, eyes still cast down somewhere around Pulou's feet.

"Sentinel," Pulou said. "I do not know you, and have only heard of your kind. My predecessor put you on task?"

"Yes, guardian," Warner answered. "In the mid-fifteen-hundreds by my best reckoning. Much time has passed." He glanced at me.

I grinned wickedly. Yeah, I imagined I was very different from women in the sixteenth century.

Pulou's laugh felt quick and cursory. "The warrior's daughter is unique, no matter what the time period. If she consents to your presence on her hunt, you are fortunate indeed."

"So it is true?" Warner asked, looking Pulou fully in the face. "You have tasked a half-blood to hunt down the instruments of assassination?"

"Err …" I said, attempting to interrupt the power play that was brewing before swords were drawn and I got caught in the backlash. "No one mentioned the assassination part."

They ignored me. Yeah, I saw that slight coming a mile away.

"The half-blood — as you so arrogantly refer to her — wields remarkable magic."

"Dragons —"

"The warrior's daughter is not bound by that which binds us," Pulou interrupted. "I have set the task. Do you question me further, sentinel?"

Warner didn't answer right away. When he spoke, he did so like a man heavily editing himself — short and to the point, so as to not chance further words leaking out. "No, guardian."

"That is best," the treasure keeper said. "As far as I know, you are the last of your line. Unique, as Jade Godfrey is unique. I wouldn't want to subdue you."

Subdue you? That didn't sound like a great option. Actually, I wasn't too sure that wasn't code for 'kill you.'

I watched Pulou as he stared at Warner. The sentinel didn't look away, but he also didn't speak. The treasure keeper's magic rose up and around his fur coat in a golden aura with a flood of spicy dragon magic — this with hints of black tea and heavy cream.

"Not only is Jade Godfrey the child of the warrior, she is also under the protection of the nine." Pulou's voice was a dead-low whisper I'd never heard from the guardian. He loved to laugh almost as much as my father.

Warner nodded once. "I would never —"

Pulou's magic pressed toward the sentinel, who leaned into it with a grimace. He stood at least four inches taller than the treasure keeper, but Pulou easily had eight inches of width on him. I'd never seen a power play between dragons before. It was rather uncomfortable, for my dowser senses and my sense of individuality.

I wrapped my fingers through the wedding rings on my necklace in an attempt to draw on more of its shielding magic.

"We are contemporaries, yes?" Pulou asked. "Warner, son of Jiaotu-who-was, sentinel of the instruments of assassination."

"No, guardian," Warner said. His gaze remained locked to the treasure keeper's, but his voice was strained.

"Why not?" Pulou's voice was still pitched low. "Were we not born of an age?"

"I have no desire to challenge you or any guardian. I chose my task willingly, gladly …" Pain laced Warner's words. He shifted toward me — involuntarily, I thought — but this caused Pulou's magic to brush against me.

I cried out from the sudden scrambling of my brain. My eyes were momentarily unable to focus.

Pulou immediately dampened his magic. I swayed forward, as did Warner, at the loss of it.

"My apologies, alchemist," Pulou murmured. "I forget how young you are." He shifted his gaze to Warner once again. "We understand each other now."

Warner nodded.

I really had no freaking idea what was going on, and now I had a splitting headache. "Someone needs to fill me in."

"Unbeknownst to me, the sentinel was tasked by my predecessor to protect the instruments of assassination whenever they are sought," Pulou said. "If there is no incursion, he sleeps, yes?"

Warner nodded. His shoulders were slumped wearily. Standing up to the intimidating magic of the treasure keeper was impressive but obviously draining.

"And the map, like, triggered him ... ?" I asked, starting to put things together for myself.

Pulou looked to Warner for confirmation. The sentinel nodded.

"And the shadow that the alchemist mentioned?" Pulou asked. "Was it a demon scout?"

"I believe so," Warner answered.

"Such beings shouldn't be able to come through in any amount of force," Pulou said. "Nor should they be any match for your knife, alchemist."

Well, that was good to know, and nice to hear that Pulou had such confidence in my abilities. A little ego stroking was always welcomed and appreciated. Pair it with chocolate and you could get almost anywhere, anytime with me.

"And the instruments of assassination?" I asked.

"Have you unlocked the map?" Pulou asked instead of answering me.

"Not yet."

"By the time my predecessor chose me as his successor, he was ... ready to relinquish his mantle. My time with him was short. I didn't even know of the tattoo until after I had taken his seat among the guardians. He kept journals spanning almost nine hundred years, as most guardians do. But, as I mentioned yesterday, the bulk of this knowledge was lost in a fire only a few years after I assumed the mantle of the treasure keeper."

Warner made a pained noise.

Pulou acknowledged this with a curt nod. "If you had asked me yesterday if such a thing existed, I would have said the instruments were a myth, dragon lore."

"They're not," Warner said.

"As is made obvious by your presence, sentinel," Pulou said gruffly. The treasure keeper really wasn't a fan of Warner waltzing in and questioning his directives. "Have you laid eyes on the instruments? Do you know their form and function? Do you know the location of the items I seek?"

"No, guardian," Warner answered, his tone edged with frustration. "Just that they are best left hidden, as your predecessor deemed."

"I might not have absorbed his memories when I absorbed his powers, sentinel," Pulou said. "But I can read what little survived the fire. The treasure keeper left what was untouchable where it lay. Not because he thought it was safer there, but because he had no means to reach it." Pulou turned to deliberately look at me. "I do."

Warner didn't answer, though he did glance at me before he once again looked to the ground at Pulou's feet.

"To whom do you owe your allegiance, Warner, son of Jiaotu-who-was?"

"You, guardian, and the nine."

Pulou nodded, his amiable grin returning. "Your hunt is still afoot, Jade Godfrey," he said. "Enjoy the chase. Luckily, Warner, sentinel of the instruments of assassination, will now be by your side if you so wish. I imagine you will find his experience with the shadow demons who apparently also seek this treasure valuable."

"Yeah, some heads-up on that shadow demon part would have been cool."

Pulou snorted. "For both of us. Unlock the map, alchemist. Find the instruments and bring them to me. Tread carefully, but quickly. I will inform the guardians of the sentinel's return and his ... insight."

The treasure keeper turned and walked away. From the back, he totally looked like a grizzly bear, except with a shiny coat.

Pulou paused beneath the far archway, then turned to look at Warner. "I am sorry for the loss of your mother, sentinel. She was a strong, capable guardian to her final years. Wearing such power can be taxing on a dragon, but silver-tongued Jiaotu never faltered."

"Thank you, guardian," Warner said.

"We will speak again," Pulou said.

"I'm forever in your service," Warner said, bowing far deeper than he had when first meeting the treasure keeper.

Pulou nodded and then walked through the archway that led to the dragon residences.

I turned to Warner. "So ... are you coming with me, then?"

He eyed me. "You would fail without me, and most likely die. Allowing an item such as this —"

"Yeah, yeah," I interrupted. "I get that, like a lot. What I don't get is why I'm constantly saddled with old men."

Warner frowned. "I'm not old. And you're not a horse."

Okay, this conversation was going somewhere rather raunchy rather quickly. "I'm not saying I'm a horse. I'm saying you were born in 1500."

"I was born in 1507. I have slept four and a half centuries."

"Don't try to play me, Warner, son of Jiaotu-who-was. Everyone has a sob story. Hell, my sister just spent the last year trying to kill me and drain my powers —"

"Impossible."

"Ah, don't be that guy."

"That guy?"

"You've forgotten your training in the execution of your task. Listen, dragon."

Warner fell silent, staring at me. Then he nodded. "I hear you, alchemist. I'm sorry your sister tried to kill you."

"I'm sorry you woke up, like, four hundred and fifty years into the future and your mom is dead."

Warner nodded. I ignored the fact that, when agreeable, he was awfully gorgeous in a manly, chiseled way. I'm not attracted to grumpy older men … I'm not attracted to grumpy older men … I'm not attracted to grumpy older men. Yeah, I'd just keep telling myself that.

"Let's get out of here before we bump into any more guardians."

"That's a good plan."

I smiled at him. "Yeah, I'm cute and quick. Just not particularly smart."

"Indeed," he agreed. "You should have left me in the alley. You're foolishly fearless, Jade Godfrey, warrior's daughter."

"See?" I said flippantly as I crossed back to the native-carved cedar door that led to the bakery. "We're getting to know each other already. I'm cute and fearless, and you're obsessive and grumpy … in really tight leather pants."

Chapter Five

By the time we returned to the bakery, it was after closing, though it felt like we'd only been gone an hour or so. The more guardians I interacted with in the nexus, the worse I found that time differential. Evidently, three quick conversations with three guardians equaled approximately ten hours.

I stepped through the portal and made a beeline to the stairs up to the pantry with Warner trailing behind me. The sentinel hadn't spoken a word. He didn't come across as the thoughtful type — more like the break-and-tumble-and-figure-shit-out-later type — but he was obviously working through centuries of shock now.

I could taste Kandy's distinctive berry-infused dark-chocolate magic in the bakery storefront. I'd completely missed our mani-pedi appointment, but found the green-haired werewolf contentedly mowing her way through leftover cupcakes and playing chess on her iPad.

I normally donated the day-olds to the daycare at the Kitsilano Neighborhood House. But apparently not on my best friend's belated-birthday weekend. And yes, the green-haired werewolf was crazy good at chess. She was a complex person. I adored every inch of her every quirk.

The green of her shapeshifter magic rolled over Kandy's eyes as Warner and I crossed around the empty display case and joined her in the small seating area by the French-paned front windows. She had about two dozen cupcakes arranged by frosting color on one of the tall, circular tables. Her legs were curled around the legs of the high stool she was perched on to overlook her purloined loot. Kandy, the cupcake pirate.

"He's staying?" she asked with her mouth full of the first bite of a *Tart in a Cup*, a mouth-watering blackberry cake with blackberry buttercream icing, which also happened to be another of her birthday cupcakes.

"Pulou thinks he might be helpful," I answered.

Kandy snorted. "Dragons use that word too loosely." She stuffed the rest of the cupcake in her mouth and then licked the icing off her fingers.

"The practically immortal often do," I said as I sat down at the empty table next to her. I pulled the map out of my satchel and unrolled it before me.

Kandy snagged two more cupcakes, then wandered over to stand by me, peering down at the tattooed dragonskin. She handed me one of her birthday cupcakes — *Tease in a Cup*, a delectably moist chocolate blackberry cake with blackberry buttercream. Sharing food was a pretty big gesture from a werewolf, especially as I'd pretty much missed the second day of her belated-birthday weekend. But I figured creating four cupcakes in her honor was the same as banking a bunch of IOUs.

"He's catatonic now?" Kandy asked.

I glanced up at Warner, who had followed me only as far as the first set of windows and now seemed to be mesmerized by the trinkets hanging there. Before I'd known I was an alchemist, I used to collect bits of natural or residual magic — stones, jewelry, sea glass, broken china — and fasten them together into pretty wind chimes or window decorations. I had no idea at the time that I was actually making magical objects capable of holding various spells or charms, if the holder knew how to work an object's magic that way. My sister Sienna had figured that out, not me. She'd used my trinkets to hold or focus the magic she stole from other Adepts. She killed three werewolves and her own boyfriend — a latent necromancer — using my trinkets as magical anchors before anyone figured out what she was doing.

"He's absorbing, I think," I answered Kandy. Dragons were fascinated by magic, and often got caught up watching it for hours. Even I, who saw and tasted magic more intensely than anyone else I knew — except perhaps Pulou — grew bored more quickly. "He's slept for four hundred and fifty years." Then I lowered my voice out of respect, though not secrecy. Dragon hearing was even better than that of a werewolf. "And his mom is definitely dead."

Kandy grunted sympathetically, then said, "He's going to need new clothes."

I shook my head. Werewolves didn't have a deep well of empathy to draw on. Life was pretty cut and dried, black and white to them. Eat or be eaten. That sort of thing. Whether you needed it or not, Kandy was always ready with a kick in the ass.

Though she did have a point. Warner drew a lot of attention, and I imagined he would even without the leather getup. Then I stopped myself from attempting to figure out what sort of chest — hairy, smooth, somewhere in between — his leather vest covered. I was going to have to take him clothes shopping. There was a Mark's Work Wearhouse just down the street. And now I was trying to visualize him in 501s and an unbuttoned blue plaid work shirt. The blue would bring out his eyes …

"Can he read it?" Kandy asked, referencing the map.

"He says not," I answered, though I wasn't completely sure. Warner, despite Pulou's suggestion, didn't seem like the helpful type. His current introspection could totally just be passive resistance in disguise.

I peered down at the tattoo. As before, I found the mix of images baffling. Branches of flowers and leaves, circles slashed with colored stripes, and interconnected blocks that looked vaguely mechanical ringed the edges. The center of the tattoo was filled with splotches of green and blue, and with the tiny black triangles that I still thought might be mountains or other geographical indicators.

Warner, still completely ignoring us, reached out and ran his fingers across the five trinkets hanging before him. They clinked together, sending a sweet chime through the room. The dragon breathed in deeply, almost as if he was inhaling the sound. Then his body settled. I hadn't noticed that he'd been tense before. But then, I didn't know him at all.

I returned my attention to the map. "Maybe the symbols on the outside edge are clues to the object, not the location?"

Kandy shrugged and retrieved another cupcake.

My stomach grumbled. I was starving. Warner turned his gaze on me. I couldn't read anything in his look, but I wasn't going to be embarrassed about a rumbly tummy.

"Do you know what we're looking for or not?" I asked him.

"Not," he answered, terse but not angry.

"You've been guarding this thing for centuries, but you know nothing about it?"

"I know it needs to be protected." If Warner had been a werewolf, he would have bared his teeth at me. As a dragon, he kept his tone evenly aloof.

"Rainbows," Kandy said. Her mouth was now full of *Sex in a Cup*, a cocoa cake spiced with cinnamon and topped with dark-chocolate buttercream. It was a standby favorite of mine.

"What?"

"Well, almost rainbows." The green-haired werewolf pointed at the striped circle in the top right of the map. "See? Just missing green." She moved her hand diagonally to point at the striped circle in the bottom left corner of the map. The colors of the thin stripes ran red, orange, yellow, blue, and violet, skipping the green that would normally sit between yellow and blue in a rainbow.

"Maybe the circle represents the earth?" Kandy said. "You know, with the rainbow arching over? Everything in the middle is just mumbo-jumbo, though. Doesn't look like a map to me at all."

I stared at Kandy.

"What?" she snapped. "Don't you go to grade school in Canada?"

"We call it elementary here," I murmured as I transferred my attention back to the map.

"Well, if you'd had to be graded, maybe you would have recognized a half-assed rainbow when you saw one."

I didn't correct Kandy on the grades/grade school versus no grades/elementary school thing. Warner had stepped closer to peer at the map just over my shoulder, but he didn't contribute to the conversation. I wasn't sure that the rainbow notion helped to decode the map, but I had an idea about who could.

"You know who we need."

"Don't say it," Kandy said. "We don't need an old, long-toothed xenophobe."

"I could at least text him," I said.

"If he wanted to hunt treasure with us, he'd be here," Kandy snapped. "Plus, no one wants him around anyway, Mr. Icy Know-It-All."

"A vampire?" Warner asked. He didn't sound overjoyed. But then, Drake was the only dragon I'd ever met who didn't loathe vampires, and the fourteen-year-old just wasn't completely indoctrinated yet.

"Yeah," Kandy answered. "An older-than-your-ass, too-powerful bloodsucker who collects knowledge and people like Jade collects magical bits."

Warner glanced over my head at the trinkets in the window, then looked back at me. It had been a long time since I'd wondered if someone found me attractive — me, not my magic — and I found myself wishing I'd put on lip gloss. Just a sheer pink that would pop against my tanned skin. Warner's brow creased, and I realized I'd been staring at him.

Damn it. He was a freaking dragon. I wasn't lusting after someone more powerful than I was. That was just asking for trouble. And I was really, really tired of trouble.

"Other than Pulou," I said, putting myself back on point, "Kett's the oldest Adept we know … well, at least of those who've been roaming the earth for centuries. It isn't like Chi Wen gets out much. This could be a map of someplace we just don't know. Which, honestly, could be a lot of places."

I took a picture of the map and texted it to Kett. Kandy stuffed an entire cupcake in her mouth. She seriously liked to pretend she hated Kett, but was actually upset that he'd been gone for so long. I don't think the werewolf was accustomed to her pack being so tiny. It pretty much consisted of Gran, Scarlett, and me when she was in Vancouver.

"Maybe he'll recognize it. If not, we'll have to start randomly clicking around on Google maps."

"Forget that." The werewolf wasn't a fan of computers. They were too sedentary for her.

"Kett?" Warner prompted. He looked as though he completely expected us to dutifully spill every little thing we knew.

Kandy narrowed her eyes at the dragon. "None of your beeswax, buddy," she growled. "We don't need the vampire or you — except if the bloodsucker knows how to read the map. You're just prettified, useless muscle."

"Excuse me, wolf?" Warner's voice was suddenly low and dangerous. Kandy had plucked him out of whatever funk he'd been burrowing into as easily as she now picked up another cupcake and idly licked off the icing.

I unsuccessfully suppressed my smirk. Werewolf games were always amusing — unless you were the besieged puck at center ice. Unsurprisingly, Kandy was a hockey fan. She'd been seriously pissed when the Canucks hadn't made the playoffs last April, and had actually forced me into a sports bar to see LA take the Stanley Cup.

My cellphone pinged.

"Quick," Kandy said. "Where is old fangy anyway?"

"You know," I said, "if you really miss him, you could call."

"I'm going to have to hurt you for that crack."

The text message on my phone read:

> *What is this?*

I typed back: *A map?* I hit send.

> *Where is the key?*

The key?

> *Every map needs a key.*

"He says we need a key," I said.

"He doesn't mean an actual key," Kandy said, peering over my shoulder at my phone. "He means, like, a legend. You know, something that tells us how to decode the symbols."

Like a decoder ring?

Kandy snorted at my text.

"You're communicating with the vampire now?" Warner asked. "Through that? It's not magical." The centuries-old mighty dragon was baffled by a cellphone.

"It's a phone. We're sending text messages."

"Human technology," Kandy offered.

"Don't touch it," I said.

Warner frowned at my warning, like a toddler about to dispute his bedtime. No matter how young the sentinel claimed to be, all ancient beings hated being told what to do.

"Your dragon magic will break it," I said, hoping to stop the tantrum before it began. My cellphone pinged.

> *Perhaps.*

I smirked. Yeah, the vampire didn't know what a decoder ring was, but he wasn't about to clarify and lose face. My phone pinged again.

> *There appears to be too many layers. You must look at it a different way.*

Helpful.

The vampire didn't get sarcasm when it was directly in his face. I was fairly certain he'd miss it in text form as well.

> *You're welcome.*

Yep. I was brilliant at being right about all the little things.

Layers, Kett had texted. Maybe that was why the green and blue and black marks didn't actually look like a map? Maybe they were all jumbled up and on top of each other? I touched the edge of the map. I'd avoided doing so before, not because it thrummed with dragon magic but because it was just plain icky to touch dried skin.

I could tap into and pull out this magic. I could transfer it or meld it with other residual magic. Or with another magical object. But I couldn't pull off layers and look at them like … a picture.

Layers of pictures.

"Wisteria," I murmured.

"The reconstructionist? From London?" Kandy asked.

"Yeah," I answered. "That's what she does, isn't it? Pulls images out of residual magic?"

Kandy shrugged. I wasn't clear about how Wisteria Fairchild's magic worked either, though I'd seen the results of it two times now. She worked as a reconstructionist for the witches' Convocation — or, specifically, for the Convocation's investigative teams. Yeah, the witches had formed and employed supernatural investigative teams. Who knew? Not me.

The reconstructionist's job was to go to scenes of magical crimes or mysteries and collect the residual magic into something that resembled a video playback without a computer or TV, which she then stored in a cube thingy. I'd seen her recording of my sister — along with her boyfriend Rusty — murdering Hudson, a werewolf who'd been the beta of Kandy's pack and someone I'd seriously considered seriously dating for far too brief of a moment. Then I'd seen a similar reconstruction of Sienna murdering Rusty.

I'd avoided viewing Wisteria's reconstruction of the triple demon summoning Sienna had engineered in London. My sister had murdered three sorcerers and tried to murder Mory — a teenaged necromancer friend of mine, and Rusty's sister. Then she had kicked Kett's, Kandy's, and my asses to get away unscathed … with the sacrificial knife that I'd thought was carefully hidden until Warner busted into my safe.

"Reconstructionist?" Warner asked. "Witch magic?"

"Yep," I said. "You got a better idea, leather pants?"

Warner screwed up one side of his face at this terrible attempt at a nickname. Unfortunately, this quizzical look made him adorable. No one needed an adorable, dangerous dragon grumping around the bakery. Least of all me.

"We aren't allowed in London," Kandy said.

It was kind of Kandy to say 'we,' though it was really only me who was banned from London. Maybe even all of England. Yes, I wasn't allowed to enter an entire country, based on the say-so of one uber-powerful super-old vampire. A vampire I hadn't even met. I had, however, seen his magic running through the veins of his blood grandson Kett, who had returned from true death a second time through the intervention of his grandsire.

When vampires shared blood, they literally gave away part of their magic to make fledglings — or, as in Kett's case, to resurrect other vampires. The big bad of London was seriously pissed that he'd had to divide his power because I got Kett killed … yeah, with that same knife I was trying to keep locked away.

"Wisteria doesn't live in London," I answered. "Gran might know where to find her."

I'd only spent about two hours in Wisteria Fairchild's presence, and I was concerned that she wouldn't be receptive to repeating the experience. I scared her, like the guardian dragons scared me. I also had a habit of dragging mayhem and chaos in my wake, and Wisteria had intimate knowledge of the end results.

Though I was seriously hoping that had just been one bad year that was way behind me now.

Kandy pushed her second-to-last *Flirt in a Cup* across the table in Warner's direction with a wolfish grin. He regarded her with narrow-eyed suspicion, but didn't even blink before consuming the cupcake in three big bites. Kandy, still grinning, wagged her eyebrows at me.

I couldn't help but laugh as I peeled the paper off a *Rapture in a Cup* myself. Werewolf games were always more fun when paired with a swirl of yellow and chocolate cake with cream cheese chocolate icing.

Gran entered the bakery kitchen, her fresh-cut-grass-and-lilac-scented magic sparking behind her eyes in a way I'd never seen. Warner immediately slid from his stool, but he didn't move out from behind the stainless steel workstation. I'd texted Gran right before ordering Chinese food from Connie's Cookhouse. We had spread just about every dish of takeout we could order on the workstation, because I wasn't interested in bringing Warner through the wards up to my apartment. Not yet, anyway. I was especially a fan of Connie's cod in black bean sauce, and Kandy had a bit of an obsession going with their ginger beef. Warner wielded his chopsticks as if he'd grown up using them, even with the gai-lan in garlic that I had to be taught how to eat — thick end up — by a friend.

"Gran," I said. I stood for a hug as she set her purse on the steel counter between the fridge and the ovens. "Everything okay?"

"Yes," Gran replied. Her eyes flicked over my shoulder to Warner. I had the same color eyes — indigo blue — as Gran and my mother, Scarlett, but that was where the resemblance stopped. As it was today, Gran's silver hair was usually pulled back in a long braid, but like Scarlett's, it had been strawberry blond. Neither my mother nor grandmother had my height or ... other assets. No matter how many yoga classes or how much dragon training I did, 'petite' would never be a word used to describe me.

I stepped to the side to introduce Gran to Warner. "Pearl Godfrey, Convocation chair —"

"Grandmother of Jade, alchemist and slayer of demons," Gran said. She raised her chin with pride.

Emotion momentarily stopped my words. I'd never heard Gran title herself that way. It was a prideful acknowledgment of my accomplishments, and also a thinly veiled warning to Warner. Kandy must have given Gran a blow-by-blow account of the sentinel's appearance in the alley while he and I were in the nexus. Normally, the werewolf wasn't so verbose.

I nodded, then continued. "Meet Warner, sentinel, son of Jiaotu-who-was." I deliberately didn't mention the 'instruments of assassination' part of Warner's sentinel title. After London and Tofino, I figured Gran was looking for any hint of a reason to lock me away in a protection circle and never let me out.

"Tasked by the treasure keeper to aid, not hinder, the warrior's daughter," Warner added. Then he inclined his head toward Gran.

She nodded in return but didn't smile.

Well, that was tense.

Gran finally turned to me. "Wisteria Fairchild is in Seattle ..." — her eyes flicked to Warner and then back to me again — "... on Convocation business."

"Ah. There isn't a portal into Seattle," I said as I turned to look at Warner as well. Still swathed head to toe in black leather, he looked completely out of place in my bakery kitchen. He hadn't returned to eating.

"Then you will have to wait a few days until she can come here," Gran said.

"We could drive if we borrow Gran's car. It's spell protected," I said, though I wasn't jazzed about it. "There's no way we can fly, not with a dragon." Not with a dragon powerful enough to rip through the reinforced door of my safe and my wards like they were made of marshmallows, at any rate. Warner's magic would disable the security scanners way before he got anywhere near enough to mess with an airplane's electronics.

"Yeah, I'm not getting on a plane with him," Kandy said as she slathered a package of plum sauce on a spring roll. "Hell, I'm not going into Seattle with him dressed like that."

"We will make a request of the treasure keeper," Warner said. "And how should I be clothed?"

"I can't just ask Pulou to open doors on a whim," I said.

Kandy sucked plum sauce off her fingers, then reached for her iPad.

"You indicated that this witch in Seattle ..." — the city name was unfamiliar to Warner — "... could read the map."

"I said I thought she might be able to."

"We'll buy you something like this," Kandy said. She was holding her iPad up for Warner to look at.

"The treasure keeper will oblige," Warner said as he reached for the tablet.

"Don't touch ..." Too late.

Warner frowned at the iPad for a moment, then handed it back to Kandy, who was grinning rather manically. Oddly, the iPad seemed unscathed, though it had flicked to sleep mode before I could see what Kandy had shown the sentinel.

I sighed. "Kandy ..."

The green-haired werewolf turned the smile on me. "Captain America on his day off."

What? Oh, no.

Dragon magic — spicy, dark chocolate with a smooth, creamy, sweet cherry finish — rose to tickle me along my left cheek, shoulder, and ribcage. Oh. My. God. Chocolate cake, whipped cream, and cherries ... Warner's magic tasted exactly like the black-forest-cake ice cream they served at Mario's Gelati, which I had yet to replicate to my satisfaction in a cupcake. I hadn't realized how much he'd been dampening his power until now.

My stomach fluttered in anticipation and my heart rate picked up a few beats. I slowly turned to look at Warner as his dragon magic settled around him.

He was wearing a dark gray T-shirt, cut low enough at the neck that I could see a patch of chest hair and the edge of a tattoo across his collarbone that had been hidden by the leather vest. My mouth ran dry, and I inhaled deeply instead of giving in to the appreciative moan I could feel aching at the back of my throat. The tight T-shirt stretched over a muscled physique that I would have sworn had been Photoshopped had I seen it on Facebook, then tapered down into low-slung dark blue jeans. A distressed leather jacket hung off Warner's broad shoulders like it was tailored to him ... and I guess it was.

Oh. My. God. Times two.

Kandy whistled. "That's a useful talent."

Warner shrugged, perfectly mimicking the green-haired werewolf. Then he flashed me a movie-star grin that turned my knees to goo. Thankfully, I was leaning back against the counter.

I checked my chin for drool, then crossed my arms and tried to look unimpressed. "Fancy, but what else can you do?"

Warner's grin widened into a smile. He didn't answer. Instead, he took off the jacket, flexing biceps the size of my freaking thighs as he did so. Oh, God, really? How the hell was I going to be at all effective with that around? Then he reapplied himself to the Chinese food with a renewed vigor.

Ever since seeing the latest Marvel Comics box-office hit, I'd had this ongoing fantasy that involved a certain muscle-bound superhero, a motorcycle chase, then an alien brawl that ended in a steaming shower for two.

"That was not helpful," I hissed at Kandy.

"Really?" She eyed Warner appreciatively. "I think it was very helpful."

"Wisteria Fairchild?" Gran called my attention off the suddenly too-accessible sexy dragon scarfing Chinese food in my bakery kitchen. She was genuinely unimpressed. She had eyes only for beautiful Brazilian guardian dragons. Qiuniu was an impossibly high bar for any man ... you know, if you were into that sort of thing.

"Right. Seattle. Treasure keeper," I said.

"The reconstructionist is prepared to meet you," Gran said.

"Prepared? Had to twist her arm, did you?"

Gran offered a tight smile but no reply. Yeah, Wisteria Fairchild was probably as reluctant as I thought she would be. "Tell her I'll double her fee."

"She agreed to triple, plus expenses, and a healer on call."

Jesus. The witch really didn't like me. And I really, really couldn't blame her. Though the healer provision smarted.

"Tell her we'll meet her at the Bacco Cafe in two hours, depending on how long we need to wait for the treasure keeper to open a direct portal. Though without mentioning the portal or treasure keeper part of that. So … just two hours, Bacco Cafe."

"For triple, she'll wait all night." The blue of her witch magic rolled over Gran's eyes. I wouldn't have risked pissing off the head of the Convocation if I were Wisteria Fairchild. But then, I'd seen Gran in action.

"You ready for your first trip to the nexus?" I directed this question to Kandy, who answered with her patented nonsmile.

Nothing daunted the werewolf.

I wished I could say the same.

Warner wiped his mouth with a paper napkin. Then he carefully started replacing the lids on the containers that still had food in them. I turned away to retrieve the sacrificial knife and some American cash from the broken safe, pushing away thoughts of strong fingers doing delicate tasks. With the safe broken, I couldn't leave the knife here if I wasn't going to be back soon, even if the bakery was closed tomorrow. Maybe I'd finally convince Pulou to keep it.

I rolled the knife in a red-and-white-striped tea towel, then tucked it into my satchel while I paused in the office doorway to look back into the kitchen. Gran was picking at some Szechuan green beans and texting. Kandy was looking up maps on her iPad.

Warner looked up from wiping the workstation and snagged my attention with his green-blue eyes. The knife made my bag feel epically heavy hanging off my shoulder. It felt filled with all the guilt I carried over the blood magic I'd practiced to save Mory's life. It reminded me of the darkness that had swallowed my sister … that had entered the perfect life I thought I'd been building. Now, arrayed before me — only steps away in my bakery kitchen — was another glimpse of that unattainable, perfect life. A life that the darkness that had taken up residence within me would never let me have.

I dropped Warner's gaze and tugged at my necklace, willing it to buffer me from the power of the knife. The shielding magic of the wedding rings responded instantly, but the weight of the bag didn't change.

"Ready?" I called to Kandy and Warner as I turned to the pantry. What the necklace couldn't fix, chocolate would always soothe. And I just happened to have about ten pounds of the good stuff on hand.

To that end, I tucked a couple of Valrhona chocolate bars in my satchel as I crossed through the pantry. The satchel pretty much operated as a go-bag for treasure hunting now, rather than just a fashion accessory. I even had one of those hotel sewing kits in it, along with cash, a lead-lined case to protect my phone from the magic of the portals, and chocolate. But extra chocolate was always a smart idea and never went to waste.

As I jogged down the stairs to the basement and reached out for the magic of the portal, I reminded myself that there was no such thing as a perfect life, and it didn't do me any good to stare after something I could never have.

Chapter Six

I pulled Kandy through the golden magic of the portal from the bakery basement. Warner had preceded us. The green-haired werewolf stumbled forward, though her footing should have been solid on the white marble floor. She grabbed my shoulder for extra support as she gasped, her eyes blazing green. Claws appeared at the ends of her fingers to dig into the flesh of my shoulder.

"Ouch."

"Easy, wolf," Warner said as he turned back to us. His tone was kinder than I expected.

"The magic," Kandy muttered. Her voice was pained. I could feel her attempting to rein in her shapeshifter magic as it rippled down her arms and across her body.

The portal closed behind us and Kandy half straightened, though she was still gripping my shoulder. My first visit to the dragon nexus had been overwhelming as well ... and I'd had the magic of all nine guardians to contend with then. I still wondered how I survived that first onslaught. Now, of course, I'd built up a tolerance.

Pulou strode into the circular room underneath the archway that led to the dragon residences. I instantly knew that his presence wasn't a coincidence.

"The far seer sends his greetings to Kandice Tate, enforcer of the West Coast North American Pack, friend and bodyguard to Jade Godfrey, the warrior's daughter. I am Pulou, the treasure keeper of the guardians. One of the nine."

Kandy pushed away from me, as if to force herself to stand without assistance before Pulou. She nodded her head in a brief bow, but then kept her gaze downcast somewhere around Pulou's chest.

"We are well met, treasure keeper," the green-haired werewolf said.

Pulou shifted his gaze from Kandy to me, and then to Warner. "Alchemist. Sentinel."

"Treasure keeper." We all spoke in unison.

"Are you ready for what lies ahead, Kandice Tate?"

Kandy squared her shoulders and lifted her gaze to meet Pulou's. "I prefer to be called Kandy, treasure keeper," she said. "My mother was Kandice."

Pulou grinned at the green-haired werewolf. "We all have our ancestral burdens to bear."

Kandy nodded. "I'm always ready, guardian," she said. "Just don't tell me I'm going to die."

Pulou lost the smile.

"I know who the far seer is," the green-haired werewolf continued. Kandy was always quicker at putting things together than I was. Dread ached through my chest, momentarily taking my breath away.

"It is indeed a great and terrible thing to be seen by the far seer," Pulou said. "But it is not to you his gaze falls, werewolf."

Then he looked at me.

"Are you going to tell me not to go?" I asked.

"No. You will proceed as tasked," Pulou answered. "I have a gift for your companion." He reached into the pocket of his fur coat and pulled out two gold bracelets. "At the behest of the far seer."

The twin bracelets were carved with runes I had no ability to read. Actually, they were thick — over three inches wide — and more like cuffs than bracelets. They were edged with a raised lip that was speckled with tiny, densely clustered diamonds.

With no hint of hesitation, Kandy held her arms out to Pulou as if she were about to be arrested.

Something about the gesture struck me. "Wait …" I murmured.

"Indeed," Warner said. "Beware of dragons bearing gifts of gold and gem." There was nothing accusatory in the sentinel's tone. He spoke as if discussing the weather, though he avoided Pulou's gaze when it turned toward him.

My stomach churned uncomfortably. I had always trusted Pulou without a second thought. I didn't want to question that, not for one moment.

"I'm not an idiot," Kandy snapped. Then she took a step toward Pulou. "I accept that the far seer believes these will help me protect Jade Godfrey on her quest."

Pulou nodded, then carefully slipped the cuffs over Kandy's hands and onto her wrists. When he let go, the magic of the cuffs — by their dense, earthy taste, they were of sorcerer design — flared and then constricted. The cuffs tightened on Kandy's thin wrists. I had no idea how the werewolf would get them off without a blowtorch now.

"I take half-form," Kandy said.

"They will adjust." Pulou placed three of his fingers on the runes on the tops of the cuffs. Each glowed briefly at his touch. "Now only removable by you. But if I may offer a caution?"

"Don't take them off," Kandy said. "Ever."

"Yes," Pulou said. "You have learned to temper your strength before, but these will offer a new series of lessons."

Kandy nodded. Pulou removed his fingers from the cuffs and the werewolf withdrew her arms solemnly.

The magical cuffs were completely incongruent to her obscenely printed T-shirt — this one featured a banana and what appeared to be grapes, but I didn't look at it too closely — and torn jeans. For some reason that disparity made my heart even heavier.

The treasure keeper looked to me. "You are traveling?"

"Yes, but —"

Pulou turned his head as if listening to something only he could hear; then he frowned. "Where?" he asked curtly.

"Seattle, but —"

"Turn around, warrior's daughter, and the door will take you there."

I hesitated, a ton of questions poised on my lips and in my mind. Questions about the far seer's vision and about the cuffs. But Pulou's expression was stern and unyielding. I turned to face the door from which we'd come only a few moments before.

Most secondary portals led only to the dragon nexus or to the grid point portals, which were kind of like the spots where lines of latitude and longitude intersected, if those were lines of magic. Because natural magic percolated — or maybe 'leaked out' was a better way to put it — at these places all over the world, the guardians had anchored their portal system at each grid point.

Conversely, the nine doors of the nexus were each keyed to a different territory, and — if you knew how to use them — led to anywhere within that territory a guardian wished to go.

Or, in this case, anywhere Pulou wanted to send us.

"Hold a location in your mind, alchemist, and then take your companions there."

Ah, I loved it when super-powerful beings simplified magic like it was at their beck and call. And maybe it was — for them — but it certainly wasn't for me.

I linked fingers with Kandy on my left and Warner on my right.

Behind me, the magic of a portal flared. Another guardian coming through ... a dozen to one, and based on Pulou's brusqueness, it was Suanmi.

"Go now," Pulou said.

"Inn at the Market. Suite 401," Kandy muttered. "I booked us a room. You know, just in case."

I stepped into the golden magic of the portal just as I felt the fire breather step into the nexus behind me. I cleared the thought of Pulou's frown out of my mind, trying to focus solely on Suite 401 of the Inn at the Market in the very heart of Seattle. I'd been at the hotel two years ago for the chocolate festival, and had planned to go again this October. I'd stayed in a suite that had a living room overlooking the Chocolate Box, with the bedroom up a set of stairs ...

Kandy bore the magic of the portal better on her second passage, though it probably helped that we were stepping out of the nexus and into a hotel firmly set in the human world of Seattle, Washington. Yes, the United States of America. Rather belatedly, I realized I'd forgotten my passport.

I'd also forgotten to ask Pulou again about taking the sacrificial knife. Double damn.

The one-way portal snapped shut behind us. As in, completely shut with no hint of its magic remaining. I'd forgotten to arrange transportation back. That was really going to make the lack-of-passport situation worse.

And Warner wouldn't have any identification at all, though I doubt that was ever a problem for the dragon-born, who appeared to walk through the world unhindered by mortal restrictions.

Okay, so maybe dragons weren't the only prejudiced ones.

We arrived in the living room of the hotel suite, landing only inches from the back of a plush-looking, dark-beige couch. A couple of matching chairs with dark-brown stained wooden arms and a glass coffee table framed in the same dark wood created a cozy seating area before us. Fresh paint was the only obvious indication that the hotel had recently undergone renovations.

The door of the cabinet that held the TV broke off in Kandy's hand, hinges and all. The green-haired werewolf glanced over in surprise. "I was looking for the minibar," she said.

"The cuffs," Warner muttered as he moved from window to window to look out at the well-lit city. We were on the wrong side of the hotel for a water view, but Pike Place Market, which ran along the edge of Seattle's downtown waterfront, was only a block west of here.

"No wards," Warner said.

"Why would there be?" Kandy was unsuccessfully trying to reattach the cabinet door. If the skyscrapers and the throng of humanity Warner could see from the windows confused him, he didn't mention it.

"We should probably check in," I said. I pulled a hinged case out of my satchel. Originally, the navy-blue quilted box had held an expensive pen set of Gran's, but I'd borrowed it and lined it with lead before I started treasure hunting for Pulou. I opened it, retrieved my phone, and muttered a prayer while I booted it up. So far, the lead had protected the phone from the magic of the portal and the dragon nexus, but I was still waiting for the day it didn't work.

"I used the gold card number and booked under your name," Kandy said as she strode toward the suite door. The werewolf was referring to the credit card that was also permanently tucked into the lead-lined case with the hope of protecting its chip and magnetic strip from nexus and portal magic. The Scottish witch, Amber Cameron, had secured the credit card for me in exchange for a purse of dragon gold. I hadn't realized the worth of the coins when I'd given them to the witch, but she'd exchanged them and opened a bank account that automatically covered the monthly payment on the credit card. I even got the statements by email, though I'd set that up separately. I only used the card on official dragon business.

My phone booted. Yay, me! I quickly texted our location to Gran, and then sent a text message to Wisteria.

We're here.

Kandy flung open the door to the hotel corridor with much more force than was necessary and then grumbled under her breath about "dragon gifts" and "stupid learning curves."

"First stop, Fran's Chocolates," I said as I followed Kandy out the door. The warm cream, brown, and beige decor continued through the corridor.

"They'll be closed."

My phone pinged.

> *You're early. It will take me ten minutes to get to you.*

"Right. Tomorrow morning, first thing." I sent Wisteria a smiley face text. "Second thing, See's Candies. They're both walking distance."

"Everything is walking distance for you, Jade."

Kandy's tone was serious, but she smirked and playfully tapped the back of my calf with a flick of her foot when I turned to look at her. Her hand-painted Chuck Taylor Classic Hi Tops were brand new though, and decorated with what appeared to be a native-inspired design. In green, of course.

I could taste Warner's magic behind us as the dragon stepped from the suite to follow us out. I still wasn't completely sure whether or not the sentinel was my babysitter or my teammate.

"Wolves?" I asked, referencing Kandy's runners as we turned down the hall toward the bank of elevators.

"B-day gift from Desmond," she replied.

Ah, Desmond Charles Llewelyn. Lord and Alpha of the West Coast North American Pack. It had been ten months since Tofino, and yet when I thought of Desmond, I couldn't remember anything except his hands — and seeing them close around Sienna's head far too quickly for me to do anything but watch. Watch as he snapped my sister's neck ... watch as her body fell lifeless between us.

Sienna — whether deserving of execution or not — would always be standing somewhere between Desmond and me.

Kandy slapped her hand over the elevator call button and managed to crack it.

We both watched as half the button fell to the ground. The other half lit up helpfully.

"Maybe no more touching things ... just for a bit?"

Kandy grumbled. The elevator doors open as Warner joined us. We stepped in and waited for the dragon to do the same.

The sentinel's eyes darted around the interior of the elevator.

"No," he declared.

Kandy snorted, but then stepped out from the elevator and crossed to the stairs without further comment. I wondered if it was the human technology or the confined space that bothered Warner, but decided it was the cramped space when his step faltered at the top of the stairs. The hotel hadn't wasted any square footage in their stairwells, though the paint and carpeting were obviously new.

Of course, I wouldn't have noticed Warner's hesitation if I hadn't been looking back over my shoulder and staring at the patch of chest hair that edged his T-shirt collar, right above the notch at the center of his collarbone.

I tore my eyes away and jogged down the stairs to catch up with Kandy, continuing down to the lobby. The dragon would follow or not. I certainly couldn't force him or assuage whatever concerns he had. He'd made it very clear where I ranked in his worldview ... somewhere just above Suanmi's classification of 'abomination.' Okay, maybe I was being dramatic, but dragons weren't forward thinkers, and old dragons — excepting Chi Wen and maybe Bixi — were especially mired in their prejudices. And dragons who had 'slept' for the past four hundred and fifty years? Well, I actually wasn't sure where Warner fell on the prejudice scale yet.

While Kandy checked us in, I headed out toward the courtyard that the Inn at the Market shared with a wine bar bistro and a sushi place. The front desk clerk made no mention of us arriving from within the hotel, as opposed to through the front door. Nor did she blink at the fact that we didn't have any luggage. She simply welcomed us back — I imagined she could see on her computer that this was my third stay — and then dealt with getting Kandy the requested key cards.

When I realized Warner was watching me exit the lobby, I resisted the urge to go around and around in the revolving door. It probably freaked him out, though he was currently inscrutable. And really, I didn't need to be any more childish than normal. The sentinel continued to check out the lobby as if sniffing for bombs, and maybe he was. But I could tell without even trying that there wasn't a drop of magic within the hotel — not even a tiny tint of residual magic on any of the floors. Not even from the magical portal that we'd just walked through four floors up. Yeah, my dowser senses were that sharp now.

Which was why I didn't bother to cross right and around the corner to see if Wisteria was in the cafe yet. I knew she wasn't anywhere nearby — not on foot, anyway. I imagined that if she came by car, I wouldn't pick up her sweet nutmeg magic as readily.

Instead, I stepped left, crossed out of the courtyard, and down the stairs to the sidewalk. If I looked west, I could see Pike Place Market at the base of the hill. The valet stand stood empty to one side. The street was cobbled, and currently clear of vehicles. I was a huge fan of the Granville Island Market in Vancouver, but it was obviously an idea ripped off from Seattle years ago. Old wooden buildings, once used for shipping and fisheries and industrial stuff, stretched along the waterfront here.

The red paint of their shiplapped siding was faded perfectly to my mind. Though I couldn't see it from this vantage point, I knew a large brass piggy bank sat at the main entrance a block south. I always made sure to drop a donation in the brass pig for the market's social services whenever I visited.

Unfortunately, along with most of the restaurants within the neighboring buildings, the market was currently closed. No five-dollar bouquet of flowers for me tonight, or mini frozen cheesecake bombs from —

Minty magic tickled my taste buds, and it certainly wasn't emanating from the dragon who had just stepped out through the stationary glass door beside the revolving front entrance of the hotel.

An involuntarily smile spread across my face. I didn't bother looking around or questioning this sudden development.

The peppermint taste intensified. He was dampening his magic as much as he could, trying to sneak up on me. But sneaking up on me was no longer in his power.

I laughed. "Kett," I whispered. "I can taste you."

A breeze buffeted my face and I reached out to grab it — only to have Warner knock me spinning to the side. My right ankle twisted on the edge of the sidewalk, though I was normally very sure-footed in my 8 Eye boots, and I fell onto one knee.

A boom resounded like two cars crashing, and then the pavement underneath my hands cracked. I turned my head, my curls obscuring most of my vision, but I could see that Warner had Kett pinned to the pavement by the neck.

"No!" I cried. But even as I straightened, Kett smashed his double-fisted hands up underneath Warner's broad chin, driving the dragon's head backward with a sharp crack.

I gained my feet, but Kett was gone before I closed the space between us. Warner was still crouched as if he had hold of the vampire, but he was looking around, confused.

"Vampire," Warner hissed.

"Duh," I replied.

My ankle was killing me — it was the same foot I'd mangled in London on Sienna's delayed booby trap spell — so I rotated it while I looked around. I spotted Kett in the deep shadow beyond the overhead light placed over the hotel's subtle signage. His eyes were blood red, but he didn't attack further. Warner obviously couldn't see him, and I — again, childishly — couldn't contain a smirk.

"He's after the map," Warner hissed as he straightened.

"He's not after the map, loser," I said. "And you hurt my ankle."

This threw Warner momentarily, though I wasn't sure it was concern for my health and safety that gave him pause.

"The vampire is my friend," I added.

"Vampires don't have friends, especially not dragons. They're evil incarnate —"

"Wake up, sixteenth century, and smell the progress. It kind of tastes like freedom, doesn't it?"

"Freedom is just the moment before disaster falls."

Kett started laughing. Warner whirled to look behind him, but he still couldn't see the vampire.

"Not helping, Kett," I called. "And Warner, I'd be careful. Talk like that will only endear you to the vampire."

"Kett." Warner spat the vampire's name like it was a wad of tasteless bubblegum. "The vampire you were

... texting." 'Texting' was given the same treatment as the name.

Kettil the executioner, of the vampire Conclave, stepped out from the shadow. Warner flinched at his appearance. The vampire hadn't changed — not a single hair was different than the last time I'd seen him. He was all ice ... skin, hair, and demeanor. Only his eyes — gone back to blue now — offered any color in the dark of the late evening. He was easily four inches shorter than Warner and half as broad, though I knew from experience that he was muscled granite underneath his lightweight tan cashmere sweater and designer blue jeans. The V-neck was his only nod to the warmer weather.

"I should have snapped your neck," Warner said.

"Hey!" I cried.

"And yet you couldn't, dragon," Kett answered.

"Why was your so-called friend stalking you?" Warner said to me. His sneer was impressive and seemed utterly natural on his face, which made me wonder if he was sneering underneath the inscrutability all the time. It made me wonder if I could actually trust him.

"I know nothing about you," I said, voicing my thoughts out loud. "Neither does Pulou, really. Other than who and what you claim to be. And being a mighty dragon, I'm sure the treasure keeper gives little thought to the frailties of the merely mortal."

"Your point?" Warner snapped. If words could break bones, he'd be good at it.

"You tossed me aside like —"

"I was protecting you —"

"I don't need your protection."

"She really doesn't," Kandy called. Her dry tone cut through the tension building between Warner and me. I looked up to see the werewolf leaning against the valet desk. "Hey, vamp," she said.

"Werewolf." Kett nodded to Kandy over his shoulder.

"You're here to help me treasure hunt," I said to Warner, attempting to keep my tone measured and even. "No more or less. Do not step between me and another again. Never again."

"You're only half-dragon —"

"Yeah, I'm tired of that. I know I should give you leeway, what with the deep sleep, dead mom, and skewed sense of —"

Warner turned and walked away.

" — duty."

I watched his broad shoulders, noting how stiffly he held himself, as he turned the corner and walked out of my sight and into the market.

"I like him," Kandy declared.

Kett laughed.

"That's a lot of laughing for one day, vampire," I grumbled. Man, I hated it when people walked away from arguments. "I guess I was a little ... hasty."

"Yep, like the pudding," Kandy said.

I stared at her.

"Porridge," Kett said, as if he was clarifying.

Kandy waved him off as she bounded down the stairs.

"What? Is that an American saying?"

"And British," Kett answered.

"Shut up," Kandy said gleefully. Then she playfully punched Kett in the shoulder, knocking him flying a half block down the sidewalk.

I glanced around to make sure there were no accidental witnesses of this feat of strength. The street and sidewalks were still clear.

"Ow!" the werewolf cried, woefully holding up her hand. Her forefinger and middle finger were hanging slack.

Kett was back beside us and peering at the cuffs Kandy wore before I could speak.

"Intriguing," he murmured. Then, quick as anything, he reached up and snapped Kandy's fingers back into place. She yowled.

Jesus. I'm surprised we hadn't attracted a crowd yet.

"You should be more careful, wolf." Kett was, as always, completely unruffled by being tossed down the sidewalk.

"Keep your opinions to yourself, vamp," Kandy snarked back. But she turned and grinned at me. The werewolf — whether she'd admit it or not — had a missing member of her pack back, and this pleased her. I wished I could be so ... easily anchored.

Usually fretting wasn't my thing, yet I seemed to slip into it any time life paused these days. I couldn't even get through a yoga class anymore without my mind drudging up mini panic attacks about black magic and dead sisters, rather than the peace I desperately sought on the mat.

"I'll look after Warner," the green-haired werewolf declared. Then she took off at a trot, calling back over her shoulder. "You never know what a dragon is going to do next." Yeah, that was manically gleeful as well. I worried that Kandy was mixing up Warner's grumpiness with Drake's playful energy. She was an adult, though. And admittedly, she could read people way better than I could.

"You have dented the dragon's ego," Kett said. He was watching me watch Kandy.

"You think?" I laid on the sarcasm.

Kett touched his neck thoughtfully, though no mark or bruise appeared where Warner had held him. "His magic is different than that of the fledgling's or your father's."

"Yeah. Same underlying spice, but he can adapt. Like, change his accent and clothes at will."

"Ah, a chameleon."

"Yeah, I guess so." I met Kett's ice-blue eyes and smiled. "I've missed you."

"Have you, warrior's daughter?" He showed no trace of humor in his face or tone, but I was fairly certain he was amused.

"Yeah, I guess if you're old as hell, a couple of months means nothing to you."

"Interesting word choice."

"Let's not play games, vampire."

Kett inclined his head. "You're here to see the reconstructionist."

"And how do you know that?"

The vampire didn't answer. He just slipped back into the shadows, then moved east up the hill to disappear around the corner of the hotel.

I sighed and followed him. If I looked up from here and counted floors, I'd be able to pick out the windows of our suite. Instead, I scanned the main street, which was empty to the north but full of people a block or so south. Even though it was almost eleven o'clock at night, people were still coming and going from restaurants or pubs. All the stores were closed. Others, clustered in groups farther south, seemed settled in for the night.

Seattle was still mild this time of year, similar to Vancouver, and sleeping in the streets was a viable option … you know, if you didn't have any other options.

Given the choice, I know I'd choose to curl up on my couch and watch an old movie on Netflix at this time of night any day of the week. At least then the only demons I saw were trapped on my TV screen.

Man, I was in a mood tonight. Something about Warner really set me off … in a bunch of different directions.

Still, as the scent of Wisteria's sweet nutmeg magic filtered in on the slight breeze, I couldn't deny the tiny thrill and the grin that spread across my face as I turned north toward the cafe on the next corner. I actively denied this part of me — tried to bury it in cupcakes and chocolate. But, with the vampire in the shadows somewhere nearby, each step I took toward solving the mystery Pulou had handed me felt solid and sure.

I liked the unknown chaos coming my way. It filled all the dark, empty places.

Chapter Seven

The cross streets in this section of Seattle — including Pine Street, where the front entrance of the Inn at the Market was — all dropped off steeply to the market and the waterfront. Along with the fact that all the neighboring stores and restaurants were closed and therefore dark, this gave the impression that the brightly lit Bacco Cafe was perched on a precipice.

I could see Wisteria settling into a table at the farthest corner of the cafe and ordering something from the server. A tea, I guessed. Oddly, the chairs closest to her had been lifted and flipped onto their tables as if the floor was about to be scrubbed.

Wisteria's dark blond hair was pulled back into the perfectly smooth French twist she had worn the last time I saw her. Her cornflower-blue, pristinely pressed cotton dress was belted in white to create an empire waist. She looked as if she were about to attend a wedding, but this was everyday attire for the witch. The blue of the dress was a couple of shades lighter than the magic I could see pooled in the palms of her folded hands.

Kett was somewhere in the shadows of one of the storefront stoops just ahead of me. I could taste his magic rather than see him. "Why are you hunting the reconstructionist?" I whispered into the dark night.

"Why do you assume I'm hunting anyone?" Kett murmured back without revealing himself.

"Well, you aren't working together. Are you? Or dating? Do vampires even date?"

"Your words indicate jealousy, warrior's daughter."

"But my tone sounds concerned."

"Indeed." Kett laughed. "I would not be hunting a Fairchild witch without permission."

"Whose permission? And do you have it?"

Kett didn't answer.

"Have you even met her?" I asked.

"Not officially."

"And this isn't any of my business."

"Not even remotely."

I sighed. I had my own reasons for being in Seattle, for meeting with the reconstructionist. I wasn't here to police Kett or Wisteria, if she'd done something to get on the Conclave's radar.

"She saw you die in London," I said.

"Yes," Kett answered. "Perhaps it is best left at that."

I nodded into the darkness and continued up the sidewalk toward the cafe. I could taste Kandy's magic no more than a few blocks away, but I wasn't familiar enough with Warner's magic to pick up his whereabouts. Or perhaps he was just really good at concealing his magic.

Still tasting the vampire's peppermint magic somewhere behind me, I stepped through the door. The cafe had a midcentury feel to it — black and white linoleum, Formica tabletops, wire condiment holders — but didn't go overboard with the aesthetic.

Wisteria looked up as I entered, and I involuntarily flinched from the raging pool of witch magic that overlaid her eyes so densely I had no idea of their actual color. The reconstructionist frowned, but then immediately smoothed the expression from her face. I'd forgotten that the witch held her magic so intensely concentrated behind her eyes, and then in her hands. I imagined it had something to do with how she utilized that magic, but I had never seen witch magic held this way. By taste, Wisteria was nowhere near as powerful as Gran, or even my mom, Scarlett. But as I had the first time I met her, I understood that as tightly coiled as Wisteria Fairchild kept her magic, I didn't want to be the one to see it all unravel.

"Jade Godfrey." Wisteria's American accent was subtle beneath the measured, polite tone that I imagined she had learned in some high-priced private school.

"Wisteria Fairchild. Thank you for meeting me." I offered her a broad grin as I sauntered over to the table. The cafe was completely empty, and oddly tidy.

"As requested."

Right. Boundaries erected and acknowledged.

I settled into the seat across from Wisteria, which placed my back to the entrance. No one with a drop of magic in them was going to sneak up on me even if they got past the vampire outside — which I wouldn't hesitate to say was pretty impossible. Not that I had anything I knew of to worry about in Seattle. Like Vancouver, the Pacific Northwest in general wasn't a hotbed for magic beyond the witches of the Godfrey coven. A coven that claimed me as one of their own, though I was only half-witch and effectively nonpracticing.

Wisteria changed the position of her folded hands. On first glance, her fingernails were tastefully French manicured. But with a closer look — beyond the magic that coated my human vision — I could see that her nails were painted a shimmery light blue beneath their white tips, rather than the traditional pink.

"Nice manicure."

"I like yours as well." Wisteria actually smiled. Well, the edges of her lips quirked upward.

I grinned and tapped my jade-green nails on the table one at a time. "They match my knife."

Wisteria lost the half-smile, and I instantly regretted my flippant words. I didn't want the witch to be any more scared of me than she already was.

The server crossed out of the kitchen and quickly unloaded her tray onto our table. She had a ring of pink roses tattooed around her right wrist that matched the pink streaks in her hair. She was also about one-quarter witch, her magic so diluted — just a hint of the grassy tone that told me she was of witch descent — that I hadn't noticed it until she'd entered the room.

I glanced at Wisteria, who was gazing steadily at my left shoulder. Treating me as if I were a shapeshifter or a vampire, taking direct eye contact as some sort of power play — or an invitation to a power play.

The waitress placed a hot chocolate in front of me, and some sort of floral mint tea by Wisteria. The hot chocolate smelled divine, though slightly sweeter than I usually made it. Then she placed a plate of what looked like mini cheesecakes in the middle of the table.

"Um, hello," I said.

The server laughed. "Not ours. Fortunately for me, or I'd be three hundred pounds easily."

"I brought them," Wisteria said but then didn't elaborate.

The server placed a fork in front of Wisteria, and another in front of me. "Anything else?"

"No, thank you," Wisteria said.

The server retreated back behind the front counter and through the swinging door to the kitchen.

I gestured to the plate of sweets. "You're not trying to woo me, are you? Because for these, I might consider it."

Wisteria barked out an involuntary laugh, which seemed to surprise her as much as it did me. A slight smile remained on her face as she gracefully lifted a hand to point at individual treats. I imagined it would be terribly painful to be Wisteria Fairchild's full-time friend. I could pretend that all her apparent perfection was a learned facade to try to make myself feel better. But I could tell as easily as I could see her coiled magic that Wisteria Fairchild was a well-educated, cultured, and thoughtful woman. Around her, all my imperfections would be glaringly and constantly obvious to me.

"The cafe closes every day at three," Wisteria said.

"I could have chosen another place."

"Everything in the immediate area closes at or before 10 P.M. But a quick phone call here and a quick trip to the Confectional was easy enough."

"You obviously know me too well."

"The Confectional is actually one of my favorite places in Seattle. Shall I enlighten you?" she asked, referencing the mini cheesecakes.

"Please do."

Wisteria pointed to a cheesecake wrapped in crinkly brown paper with a hint of a green swirl in its topping. "Key lime white chocolate. Usually only available for the summer season, but I managed to grab one before they changed their menu for the fall." She tugged at the paper edge of another treat to reveal three layers. "Peanut butter and chocolate."

I let out an involuntary groan.

Wisteria laughed under her breath. "Wait for it," she said as she pointed at the final cheesecake. "The quadruple chocolate. Dark chocolate blended into the batter with chunks of milk-, white-, and extra-dark chocolate in the center."

"Chocolate in the batter and extra-dark chunks mixed in?" I moaned. "I love you."

"They have cheesecake truffles —"

"Enough," I cried as I lifted my fork eagerly to the dessert before me. "I already don't know where to start."

Wisteria laughed quietly again, unfolded her paper napkin, and spread it across her lap. Then she lifted her eyes to me. I didn't flinch when I met her gaze this time. She chose to dig into the key lime treat first. I managed to get a quarter of the peanut butter and chocolate onto my fork and into my mouth without salivating too unbecomingly. I never was one for delayed gratification. The peanut butter was smooth and creamy.

"Lovely," I said.

Wisteria nodded. She was still savoring her first bite. I ruthlessly attacked the quadruple chocolate and immediately decided to somehow steal the idea — in cupcake form — for the bakery. Though the creaminess of the cheesecake might not translate ... maybe in a thick cream cheese frosting —

"You have something you would like me to look at?" Wisteria asked, reminding me — very politely — that this wasn't a play date.

"Yes, a map."

"You think I can reconstruct the magic of a map?"

"I hope so."

I glanced around. The cafe was still empty.

"The server will not return until after we leave. I've already paid her for opening and for her time."

I reached into my satchel, which I still wore slung across my chest. I hadn't even thought to hang it over the back of the chair, not with the knife and the map in it.

I nudged the plate of desserts and my ignored hot chocolate to the right edge of the table, against the window. I rolled out the map on the left.

Wisteria gasped and dropped her fork. It clattered against the lip of her tea and then flipped off onto the floor. "The magic …" she moaned, then clamped her mouth shut.

"You can see magic without a circle?" I asked. Most witches could feel magic, but very few could see it — like I did — without casting a circle.

Wisteria nodded, then shook her head to deny her involuntary admission. Her lips were so tightly pursed that I could see the outline of her teeth beneath her skin. Most Adepts were cagey about their abilities. It was probably rude that I had asked in the first place.

I looked away, directing my attention to the map before me and giving the witch some time to control her reaction. The tattoo map thrummed with spicy dragon magic, but it didn't look any different in the lighting of the cafe than it had in the golden wash of the dragon nexus or the track lighting of the bakery. It was still a jumbled mess of green, blue, and black lines, surrounded by striped circles, leaves, and industrial blocks.

"It's skin?" Wisteria asked. Her voice was pitched a little higher than normal, but she was obviously attempting to get down to business.

"Yes."

Wisteria stared at the map, not speaking. She was clutching her hands together against her chest, her knuckles white.

"Is it ..." She cut off her own question, then started again with her voice more modulated and muted. "Is it dragonskin?"

Smart witch. As far as I knew, she'd only met one half-dragon — me — in person and only seen one fledgling guardian in action — Drake.

"Yes —"

Something hit the window beside me. Wisteria flinched. It sounded like a bird, but when I turned to look, I couldn't see anything but the deep shadows of the buildings across the street.

Then the shadow shifted where no shadow could be. It pressed against the window, spreading like stumpy fingers along the edges of the glass.

"What ... is ... that?" Wisteria murmured.

"What color is it? To you?" I wanted a confirmation of the black seething mass I was seeing.

Wisteria shook her head, but I wasn't sure if she couldn't see its magic or was refusing to look.

The black mass, a deeper black than any of the other shadows on the street, suddenly peeled back off the window. Warner was standing on the other side of the glass and holding the seething mass aloft. It was writhing in his grasp, attempting to grab on to his arm, shoulder, and hip. Or more specifically, I could see it attempting to adhere itself to Warner's magic.

The sentinel locked his gaze to mine. Then, with a grim sort of satisfaction, he grabbed another section of the black, roiling mass and ripped the shadow in half. The dark magic disintegrated into nothing. No ash or sand was left behind, as it was with the demons I'd seen vanquished. Vanquished, not killed, because my father had informed me that demons were from another dimension. Though that was only relevant if the shadows were some sort of demon. Warner and Pulou thought they were demon scouts, but now I wasn't so sure.

Warner flicked his green gaze to Wisteria, who was staring at him with wide eyes. Then he turned on his heel into the shadows beyond the streetlights, disappearing as thoroughly as the vampire usually did.

"Well, that teaches me," I muttered.

"What?" Wisteria asked breathlessly.

"Warner is pissed at me."

Two bright pinpoints of red light across the street winked out. That was the only hint I had of Kett's location. He was watching us from the stoop across the road, the red glow emanating from his eyes indicating that he had been powering up somehow.

"Warner?"

"The dragon, you know, hanging around outside the window, ripping shadow demons in half."

"Dragon? Window? Shadow demons?"

The witch was shaken, still staring out the window and attempting to see the unseeable. But instead of feeling badly for her, all I could think about was her demanding triple pay, expenses, and a healer on call in order to meet with me. I imagined her inputting the receipt for the mini cheesecakes on an expense report, carefully broken out with the tax in a separate column.

"You still have that healer on call, don't you?" I'd meant to be sarcastic but the question came out angry instead.

Wisteria cranked her head back to look at me, some retort — or maybe an apology — on her lips. But then she swallowed whatever she was going to say and stiffly nodded.

"Can you cast in a hotel room?" I had no idea how Wisteria practiced magic. Except she had to be able to do so on call, and on location, in order to execute the duties of her job.

The witch nodded, rose gracefully to her feet, and pulled her too-large designer bag off the back of her chair. With the bag hung over her shoulder, she stood waiting for her orders like a good little soldier.

I grabbed what was left of the desserts and walked out of the cafe, expecting the witch to follow.

She did.

Yeah, we weren't going to be friends anytime soon.

I could feel shadows shifting around us as we hustled along the sidewalk back to the hotel, but I couldn't taste any new or different magic in the darkness. Wisteria clutched her huge purse to her chest, kept her eyes straight ahead, and her pretty pumps firmly planted in the pools of light emanating from the street lamps. Pretending that dangerous magic didn't exist wasn't the best MO. But it seemed to work for the reconstructionist, because we made it to the hotel without incident.

If the shadows were seeking the map like Warner thought they were, I wasn't sure why they'd pressed against the window in the diner but didn't try to grab me on the street.

I couldn't tell if Kett and Warner followed Wisteria and me around the block and back into the hotel, but Kandy joined us in the lobby. She quickly relieved me of the half-eaten mini cheesecakes.

"Witch," the green-haired werewolf said to Wisteria.

"Kandy," the reconstructionist replied coolly.

We paused before the elevators. Kandy was grinning at Wisteria in a way that was sure to end in someone getting hurt. Probably me.

"Cool in here, hey?" Kandy asked me.

"Warner and the shadow thing freaked the reconstructionist out," I replied.

"Shadow thing?"

"Demon or whatever. Warner tore it up."

"Really? I just saw him twisting his hands in the air. I figured it was some sort of weird dragon sign language."

I laughed, then focused on the pertinent part of Kandy's statement. "You couldn't see the shadow move across the window?"

Kandy shook her head. "The air was a bit musty, but I couldn't see anything."

Interesting. A shifter should be able to see demons. Even partly manifested ones. But typically they couldn't see magic, only scent it. So did that mean the shadows were some sort of magic? And not demon scouts?

The werewolf then eyed Wisteria, who stoically didn't meet her gaze. "She doesn't look freaked."

"Yeah. She and Kett should play poker."

"That would be insanely boring."

"Agreed."

The elevator announced its arrival with a cheerful ping as its doors slid open. We stepped inside in two strides, Wisteria between Kandy and me. The werewolf hit the button for the fourth floor and popped the last half of cheesecake into her mouth — the quadruple chocolate. I was momentarily sorrowful to see the end of its creamy goodness.

As the doors of the elevator slid closed, Warner stepped inside at the last possible second, angling sideways. He brushed between Wisteria and me to fill the spot behind us. He'd clearly gotten over his trouble with confined spaces. That was quick.

"Chameleon," I muttered to myself, repeating Kett's word.

Warner didn't speak. I could see his reflection in the polished steel, or chrome, or whatever of the elevator door. Standing sternly behind us — and despite the sexy leather jacket, tight T-shirt, and low-slung jeans — he looked exactly as advertised. A sentinel. A soldier whose job it was to stand watch over something precious, or sacred, or vulnerable.

Wisteria took a step away from Warner and me, closer to Kandy. She was almost the same height as the werewolf, and easily two inches shorter than my five feet nine inches.

And now I was suddenly feeling like the heel I was. I sighed.

"And what is up with you, alchemist?" Kandy asked.

"Wisteria thinks I'm going to get her killed, and Warner thinks I'm completely incapable ... of anything."

"Killed is a strong ... word," Wisteria said.

"But probably pretty close to the truth," Kandy said — again, far too gleefully. "But think of how much fun we'll have first."

"I doubt that'll help, Kandy," I said. "Note how the sentinel here remains silent."

"I do as tasked, warrior's daughter. No more, no less." Warner's tone was deliberate and flat as he threw my own words back in my face ... well, at the back of my head.

The elevator bumped to a stop. I noted Warner gripping the handrail that ran around the interior, and hoped he didn't dent it. We were already going to have to confess to the broken cabinet door and elevator button.

Kandy stepped out into the hall. Wisteria followed her. I looked back at Warner and whispered, "I know you were just trying to take the piss out of me, but you probably didn't need to mention the warrior's daughter part in front of the reconstructionist."

Warner had the decency to look chagrined. Dragons were all about containing deep, dark secrets, but not fantastic about keeping their mouths shut. I didn't know Wisteria very well — as in, not at all — but she wasn't a witch in my coven. And my parentage drew too much attention already.

The doors started to close and I stopped them with a thrust of my arm.

Warner stepped out of the elevator and nodded to me formally. "My apologies, alchemist."

"And mine," I said. "Why don't we reboot?" Off Warner's frown, I added, "You know, like you waking up from the deep sleep."

"Ah, yes. I understand … reboot. Start again."

"Yep."

"I'm … taking longer to adapt than usual," he said, casting his gaze around the short hall that branched off for the elevator and stairs.

"I imagine the world is a very different place."

He locked his gaze to mine, his eyes more blue than green in this light. "I will persevere."

"Yeah, I'm guessing that's your middle name, sixteenth century." I turned to follow Kandy and Wisteria back to the suite. "Warner Perseverance Jiaotuson."

"It doesn't help that your idiom is all at once playful, esoteric, and, at times, bemusing."

I'd have to look up two of those words in a dictionary later — just for clarification — but I got the gist. "Yeah, I get that. Like, a lot."

Back in the suite, Wisteria gestured toward the glass coffee table that sat directly in front of the dark-beige couch. I thought the couch folded out into a bed, but was fairly certain we weren't going to be testing that assumption during this trip.

I gathered that the witch wanted me to place the map on the table, so I did. Kandy retreated to the far side of the room and found the minibar in a niche I hadn't noticed tucked underneath the stairs.

Warner paced the windows, closing all the curtains but leaving himself a couple of inches to peer out. The air was a bit stale in the room, but I didn't mention it. I figured Warner would have a heart attack if I tried to open a window, and I really wasn't a fan of air conditioning.

Wisteria pulled four pillar candles out of her huge bag — white, green, blue, and red — which she placed at north, south, west, and east points around the map.

"I'm still not exactly clear what you want me to do here." The reconstructionist spoke to me, though she was watching Warner as he paced the edges of the room.

"We think the magic is layered," I said. "Maybe with a different map on each layer." Then, exploring the idea out loud, I continued. "Or maybe it's like a puzzle and the layers just need to be shifted."

"You can see that?"

"No. It just looks jumbled to me."

Wisteria peered down at the map and then nodded. "You think I can pull a picture from the residual magic."

"That's what you do."

Wisteria looked doubtful. "I reconstruct magical events."

"And this is full of magic."

Wisteria's gaze flicked to Warner and then to me. "So is the room."

I nodded toward the coffee table and the witches' circle she'd started to construct with the candles. "You have your boundary. We won't cross it."

"I'm guessing you want to see what I see."

"Is that possible? Without you storing it in one of your cube things? It shouldn't be stored anywhere."

Wisteria nodded, but she didn't look happy about it.

Something buffeted the windows to the east. I took a couple of steps back from the coffee table to look out. Warner crossed to stand beside me. I could still see the block letters spelling 'chocolate' in the sign for the Chocolate Box up the street.

"The wind?" I murmured.

"No," Warner replied. Then he spoke over his shoulder to Wisteria. "Close your circle, witch." He lifted the curtain just enough to look south up First Avenue.

Wisteria, who'd been circling the table, didn't respond. But she did begin lighting the candles as she passed them a second time. Her shoes and lightly tinted stockings were tucked off to one side, next to her massive purse. I hadn't seen her remove them to walk barefoot on the carpet. Most witches preferred to cast outdoors, closer to the earth magic they summoned and controlled. I liked the dirt floor of my bakery basement.

Something crept across the glass of the window next to me, but when I looked out, I couldn't see anything moving in the dark. The exterior lights of the hotel only illuminated the first storey, and there weren't any balconies on this side of the building. So the night could be filled with shadow demons and I wouldn't know it. It was odd to be possibly surrounded by nasty magic and not taste it.

I willed my jade knife into my hand from the invisible sheath at my hip. "Why didn't they attack on the street? When we were out in the open?" I asked.

"I don't know," Warner muttered. He sounded epically frustrated.

Wisteria's sweet nutmeg magic swirled around the candles, and I wondered if the reconstructionist fed the spell with her own power. That seemed like a risky thing to do, and even more draining than a regular casting. But then, Wisteria Fairchild had a lot of magic held in reserve.

Kandy wandered back into the living room, a cola in one hand and a half-eaten milk-chocolate-and-nougat Toblerone bar in the other. She lifted her chin and scented the air. The green of her shapeshifter magic rolled across her eyes.

The windows started rattling ... one at a time, then all three at once. Wisteria let out a quickly suppressed hiss of fear, but kept her attention on her candles and the magic she was wielding.

"Close the circle, witch," Warner repeated. He stepped back from the window as if expecting something to come through it at any minute.

The reconstructionist sank down with her back to Warner and me, sitting on the floor at the edge of the coffee table. As she settled, her magic gathered through her and into the circle as if called back to task. The circle snapped closed abruptly, taking most of the sweet nutmeg taste with it. Wisteria had sealed her magic in with the residual magic that constantly thrummed from the map. At least I thought it was residual. It was kind of like snapping a lid closed on a snug Tupperware container.

The rattling of the windows ceased.

Warner was staring at my chest, and I could feel a blush rise to my cheeks before I realized he was looking at my necklace.

Right.

Silly me.

"How long were you outside the wards of the bakery that night in the alley?" he asked. It was obvious he was piecing something together.

"Hours."

Wisteria held her hands palm forward toward the map and the circle of magic that now surrounded it. If anything shifted in the circle at this gesture, I couldn't tell. I couldn't see or taste any magic beyond the circle at all.

"The necklace you wear is a shielding artifact? A personal ward?"

"Sure."

"It must be helping to keep the shadow scouts at bay."

"One showed up in the alley, right before you did."

"Perhaps after hours of trying to pinpoint you, and perhaps traveling from a great distance."

"Pulou carried the map for centuries, without a necklace."

Warner laughed. "The treasure keeper is as his title implies. He has no need for such devices."

"When I took it out in the cafe, the shadow appeared."

"Or simply gained strength. Here as well." He gestured to the windows.

I lifted my fingers to thread them through the wedding rings of my necklace. Warner started pacing the windows again, systematically checking them.

Kandy climbed up on the back of the couch and perched there, peering down at the map and the witches' circle. Her eyes still blazed green, but by her expression, she couldn't see any more than I could within the closed circle.

Wisteria held up her hand, as if expecting it to be taken.

I hesitated. I wasn't big on touching other Adepts. I tasted their magic much more intensely when I was physically connected.

Wisteria half turned her head to me and widened her fingers impatiently.

I stepped forward and took the witch's hand as I sank cross-legged beside her at the coffee table. Her magic instantly tingled through my fingers and up my arm, but it wasn't overly intense. I assumed she had her magic concentrated on the witches' circle before her.

Now that I was touching the reconstructionist, I could see what she saw within the circle.

I leaned forward. She had managed to pull a sort of 3D rendering off the map, but the image was still all jumbled.

Warner stopped pacing and stepped up behind me. Wisteria squeezed my hand, involuntarily I thought, at his closeness. She made no comment, though, nor did the magic in the circle waver.

Kandy came off the couch to crouch down on the other side of the coffee table. Looking across the circle at her, with the 3D map hovering between us, it appeared as if the map was projected onto her face, and that a ghostly version of the tattoo had been transferred to her skin.

"Can you see anything?" the green-haired werewolf asked.

I shook my head, then clarified. "Same map. Just 3D and hovering about a foot above the actual map." Then I spoke to Wisteria. "You can't, like, shift it? Or section off magic?"

"This is what the residual wants to be. There is nothing else here," Wisteria answered. "I thought I might be able to pick up an image of the tattoo artist, assuming he or she contributed their own magic to the well of magic that exists in the tattoo. But no. Just this."

"Can you rotate it?"

"Sure, but I did do so before I joined you to the circle." Wisteria gestured toward the circle with a flick of her fingers, and the image slowly spun as if a camera was circling it. The reconstructionist was careful to not let her fingers touch the edges of the witches' circle.

I watched the ghostly image as it slowly rotated before me. I was hoping that if I looked closely enough, I might see something from another angle that looked like an actual map.

"Wait," I murmured. "Go back a couple of inches."

Wisteria gestured again. The hovering projection paused and then rotated back a couple of inches. I leaned forward, practically pressing my nose to the outer edge of the magic of Wisteria's circle.

"What's that?" I asked. I was looking at the side of one of the two circles that were intersected by the five-colored lines. The would-be rainbows, as Kandy had called them. From this angle, the now three-dimensional circle looked thicker — almost as deep as the cuffs that Pulou had given to Kandy.

"Where?" Wisteria asked.

"There." I pointed. "Can you rotate forward to the other intersected circle?"

Wisteria beckoned the map to turn a hundred and eighty degrees until I was staring at the second circle. This one had no thickness other than the tattooed line.

"Go back?" I asked. Wisteria obliged. I was once again looking at the first circle — the one that would have looked like a cuff or bracelet, except for the five-colored lines crossing and blocking the opening on one side. "Does that look thicker to you?"

Wisteria nodded.

"And more substantial, yes? Not as ghostly as the rest of the image."

I didn't wait for Wisteria to confirm my observation. I lifted my hand and reached for the image hovering before me.

"No — !" the reconstructionist cried, but I was already crossing through the barrier of the witches' circle, coaxing the magic to allow me passage and to seal over my hand as it passed.

I reached for the intersected circle. My fingertips almost brushed its edge.

I wasn't in the hotel room anymore.

I was crouched in what appeared to be a treasure trove of some sort, peering at the jeweled hilt of a sword that was leaning against a three-foot-tall Buddha carved out of some sort of tusk. Some sort of massive tusk, stolen from a massive tusked animal. PETA would freak out if they ever laid eyes on it, though the Buddha was cheerfully smiling and holding his ample belly.

My hand was still moving — as if in slow motion — toward the five-colored intersected circle, which now appeared to be a rune-etched banded artifact made out of gold. Thin strips of gold inlaid with gems stretched across its open interior to form the colored lines. The artifact was hanging haphazardly off the cross guard of the sword, like a coat about to slide off a coat rack.

My fingers closed over the edges of the gold and gem band. Earthy sorcerer magic flooded my mouth.

Still caught in this same breath — this same endless motion I'd begun in the hotel and was continuing in the treasure trove — I lifted the circle off the cross guard of the sword. Holding it aloft before me, I started to straighten and look around. I could feel the press of magic from all directions, tasting the fact that I was surrounded by thousands upon thousands of magical objects.

The Buddha was wearing my mangled katana like a crown. The sword — which I'd twisted around my sister's neck ten months ago and used to drain every last drop of her magic, stolen and natural — sat lopsided on the statue's head. Swirls of magic — blue, green, and black — rolled through the folded blade. Dried blood had flaked from its edges to rest on the Buddha's shoulders like horrific dandruff.

"What?" I cried.

I was back in the hotel room.

I was sitting cross-legged by the coffee table as before. My arm was extended into the witches' circle, hovering in the 3D image of the tattoo. I was holding the banded artifact.

" — don't!" Wisteria cried.

Not even a second had passed.

"Oh my God," I breathed.

"What's that?" Kandy asked cheerfully.

"Was I here? Am I here?" I asked. "Did I go?"

"You have your arm jammed into my circle," Wisteria snapped. So she could be bitchy when pressed. Good to know. "And you just plucked something out of the residual magic."

"But I didn't disappear?"

"Nope," Kandy said.

"Where did you find yourself, alchemist?" Warner asked. His voice was soft, so as not to startle me.

I pulled my hand out of the witches' circle. A little abruptly, perhaps, because the magic collapsed with a pop of blue and gold.

Warner hunched down beside me, his gaze on the artifact in my hand. "You reached into the witches' circle," he prompted.

"Yes. Then into the residual magic."

"And saw … this?" He gestured toward the artifact I still held aloft on the fingertips of my right hand.

"Yes, and … other treasure." I corrected myself before mentioning my katana. The sword, what it contained, and what I had the ability to do — drain all the magic from an Adept — was a secret between Pulou and me. Pulou was of the opinion that I would be feared — maybe even hunted — if that little trick of mine became general knowledge.

"You reached into the residual magic of the former treasure keeper and pulled out treasure," Warner said. He wasn't speaking to me, but that was a fairly succinct way of putting it. Except …

"I pulled out this treasure," I said. "I'm not sure I could have grabbed anything else. The former treasure keeper obviously left this, somehow, in the magic of his tattoo."

"He left that thing in his skin?" Kandy asked. "Seriously disgusting."

"That's pretty judgy coming from a werewolf," I said.

"Hey, I don't go around embedding metal objects into people … not unless they really deserve it. I have these."

She flashed her claws. The rest of her hand remained human.

Wisteria flinched. She'd been so still and quiet I'd all but forgotten she was here.

The windows began to rattle. Now that the witches' circle wasn't cloaking the magic of the tattoo anymore, I gathered the shadow demons were looking for entry again.

I passed the artifact to Warner, who took it from me, but only after he'd deliberately placed his fingers exactly where I'd held mine.

Then I pulled off my necklace and untwisted it to its full length. I laid the thick gold chain with its wedding ring charms on the coffee table so it encircled the tattoo.

The windows stopped rattling.

"Now that's interesting," Warner murmured, far more intrigued by my necklace than he had been by the ancient artifact he held.

Wisteria stared at me. Her wide eyes and carefully measured breathing betrayed her usual poise. I imagined that Kandy could probably smell her fear.

"Thank you, reconstructionist."

Wisteria nodded stiffly and started shoving her candles back into her purse. She obviously wasn't going to be sticking around for a chat. I assumed that seeing someone pull a physical object out of residual magic had freaked her out. It certainly freaked me out, but I had a better understanding — in my limited capacity — of how the treasure keeper's magic worked.

In Tofino, I'd seen Pulou somehow shrink down my sword and tuck it into an inner pocket of his fur coat. By the haphazard look of the treasure trove I'd just seen, a lot of objects were likewise tucked away there. The banded artifact had obviously been specifically tied to the tattooed map.

Wisteria skipped the stockings and slipped on her shoes. "I have an apartment in town," she said. "But I fly out in the morning."

"Thank you for casting for me, reconstructionist," I said.

"It's my job," Wisteria said. "And your grandmother has been supportive of my career for a long time."

Kandy padded over to the door and Wisteria followed. Witch magic boiled out of her eyes and hands, telling me that despite her outwardly calm demeanor, she was absolutely desperate to get out of the room — but far too professional to flee.

I realized I was the big bad in the room now. That was odd, and disconcerting. I didn't feel dangerous or especially powerful. Not compared to everyone else ... Kett, Warner, all of the guardians ... even Drake. They were way scarier than me. Weren't they?

Chapter Eight

Kandy shut the door behind Wisteria, then whirled back into the room. "It's the key," she hissed.

"What?"

The green-haired werewolf pointed to the artifact Warner still held. I'd stood to say goodbye to the witch, but Warner was still hunkered down over the coffee table and staring at the map thoughtfully. "Kett said we needed a key. That's it. Like, literally."

I really wasn't following. The banded artifact looked nothing like a key. Plus, how the hell was a physically manifested key supposed to help us unlock a map?

Kandy squatted down next to the coffee table. "Look," she said, pointing at the upper right-hand corner of the tattoo. "Red, orange, yellow, blue, violet. And missing green."

"Right. I already pulled the artifact out of that part of the tattoo."

Kandy, ignoring me, shifted her gaze to the tattoo of the intersected circle on the bottom left corner of the map. The one that had appeared as a 3D tattoo in Wisteria's reconstruction, not a thicker line like the one I'd pulled the artifact from. "This one is red, orange, yellow, green, blue. Missing violet. Interesting."

"Okay, I'm missing it all."

"The color sequence of the stripes is a clue."

"To?"

Kandy shrugged.

"To unlocking the map," Warner said.

"Yes!" Kandy exclaimed. "Gimme, gimme." She extended her arm, then opened and closed her hand.

"Can you be gentle?" I asked.

The green-haired werewolf growled.

I grinned as I dropped the artifact into Kandy's open palm. The werewolf held it by the edges gingerly. I supposed she could have removed the cuffs, but if I'd received a gift at the far seer's behest, I'd never take it off either. The concept of fate or destiny was much scarier when you actually knew someone who saw the future.

Kandy lined up the color sequence with that of the intersected circle in the top right corner. They matched perfectly — which made sense, since I'd just pulled it from there. Then she carefully placed the artifact gently down on its tattooed counterpart.

Nothing happened.

Kandy frowned. "I thought …"

"What about the one missing the violet?" Warner prompted. Suddenly someone was actually interested in treasure hunting and attempting to be helpful. Though I had to begrudgingly admit that he had also ripped a shadow demon in two earlier, so that had been plenty helpful.

As Kandy reached to remove the artifact, it occurred to me that no one but an alchemist — or Pulou himself — could have seen and then removed the object from the map in the first place.

"Wait," I said. "Leave it for a moment."

I knelt between Warner and Kandy, then reached across the map to touch the edges of the artifact where it sat lined up with the tattoo. I didn't pick it up. I just let my fingers — and my magic — rest there lightly.

The magic of the map shifted. The center of the tattoo blurred, then swirled, and then solidified into something that looked a lot more like an actual map.

All three of us leaned forward, so that we smacked our heads together.

"Ow!" I cried, lifting my hand to my forehead.

Kandy snickered. Warner remained his stoic self, of course.

The magic of the map shifted back to its multilayered aspect, rendering the map unreadable once again.

"You have to hold it," Kandy said helpfully.

"Got that, Einstein."

"Hey! Who figured out the whole key thing being an actual key thing?"

"You." I spoke as if pained to admit it, but I was only playing at the begrudging tone. I touched the key a second time. The magic of the map percolated, then settled.

"What does that look like?" Kandy's voice was cast low, as if she was worried about frightening the magic of the map. I looked to where her index finger hovered just above a low point on the map.

"To me? As incomprehensible as before."

"Think alligators, hurricanes, and white sand beaches."

I peered at what appeared to be a pinky finger jutting into the sea. You know, if green was land and blue was water. "Florida?"

"Hell, yeah. That's Florida." Kandy moved her finger slightly. "But here ... all the little green dots and that black square thing? That looks a hell of a lot like Bermuda."

The 'black square thing' Kandy referred to glinted gold around the edges when I tilted my head to look at it.

"Green for land," I murmured.

"Blue for water," Kandy said. She grinned at me toothily. "I always love a reason to wear a bikini."

"Of course you do."

"Bikini?" Warner asked.

"Never mind," I answered. "You don't wear a bikini on a work trip."

"I ain't getting paid," Kandy said.

"You get paid in cupcakes, chocolate, and cookies."

"Yeah? I'm good with that."

"The square," Warner said. "Did you see it glow, alchemist?"

"Yeah, weird huh? What do squares mean on regular maps?"

"It's a grid point portal," Warner said, answering my question by not directly answering it. "The most southern in Haoxin's territory, I believe."

Still operating on pure instinct — because the accumulation of actual knowledge took way too long — and keeping the fingers of my right hand touching the key, I pressed my left forefinger to the black square. The magic of the map tingled, actually making my finger ache. Then the map blurred and reformed into a swath of green and blue, similar to how zooming in worked in Google Maps.

Kandy placed her palms down on either side of the map, then rose up to lean all the way over the coffee table. Warner did the same. My arms and the map were sandwiched between them like a weird game of Twister, where I was the only one touching the board.

"No landmarks?" Kandy asked.

"Perhaps we're too far away," Warner said. "Once we step through the portal, the magic may register the proximity of the instruments of assassination or the fortress that hides them."

"Fortress?" I asked. Even with my head canted to the right to make room for him, my left cheek was hovering up against Warner's right shoulder. His magic — all black forest cake, whipped cream, and cherries in deep, dark chocolate — emanated off him in a layer of heat. Or maybe the heat part was just the blush slowly spreading across my face.

Okay, admittedly it wasn't just a blush … it was a flush of desire, which also happened to be slowly uncoiling in my lower belly like a sleeping … dragon.

Warner shrugged. His shoulder touched my cheek and his tasty magic flooded through my mouth, causing me to actually salivate. I flinched away, losing contact with the map. I really, really didn't want to be sitting here lusting after a five-hundred-year-old dragon who was prejudiced … elitist … massively hunky —

"It's an assumption," Warner said. "Wars have been fought over less. An item such as this would be respected and feared. Hence, a fortress."

"You said you didn't know what we were looking for."

"I don't, not specifically." Warner shifted back on his heels, then rose to pace the room. I could almost see the gears turning in his head. "But I understand its significance."

"You're worried about something. Something other than the instruments of assassination."

"The shadow demons are not … what I expected."

"That's okay, neither am I."

Kandy snorted.

Instead of answering, Warner leaned over me to press his hand in the middle of the map. The magic of the map shifted underneath his touch. Actually, it appeared to writhe as if attempting to reject him.

"Of all dragons, I was uniquely qualified to be the sentinel of the instruments of assassination," he said. "Had I not accepted the duty I might have worn the mantle of a guardian one day."

I kept my eyes on the tattoo, worried that if I questioned Warner, it would interrupt his hushed confessional.

Runes appeared on the top edge of the map. No, not runes. It was more like ornate but blocky-looking calligraphy.

"What's that?" Kandy murmured. "English? I can't read it."

"Where dragons dare not tread," Warner said.

"I'm not a dragon," I said. I was being flippant, but then unknown magic and uncertain circumstances brought that shortcoming out in me.

Warner lifted his hand off the map but remained standing behind me. The letters disappeared. I didn't look up at the sentinel.

"When did you see this?" I asked. "After you pulled the map from my safe?"

"Yes."

"I've already been warned. Pulou told me when he gave me the assignment. That's why he gave it to me."

"My magic is adaptive, but I'm not sure I will be able to protect you all the way," Warner murmured.

"Good thing that isn't your job," Kandy said snarkily. She held up her arms to display her cuffs and looked at Warner as if he was a massive moron.

I stifled a laugh and ended up snorting like a pig instead — so not sexy.

Kandy mimicked my snort three or so times and then laughed her ass off.

"Pulou wants us to check in," I said, attempting to maintain a serious tone against Kandy's peals of laughter. "We'll see the treasure keeper, then figure out what's going on."

Warner didn't answer.

I looked at Kandy and raised an eyebrow.

She smirked at me, then rather mournfully said, "Fortress probably nixes the bikini idea, hey?"

I laughed. "The bigger issue is getting back to the nexus."

Then, as if I'd said the magic words, a portal opened behind me.

As I stepped through the golden magic of the portal with Kandy death-gripping my left hand, I realized I was leaving Seattle and Kett behind, without figuring out what the vampire was doing there or why he was following Wisteria. I ignored my immediate concern for the reconstructionist. She was a big girl and well versed in the Adept world, unlike me. Plus, Kett wasn't evil. Just … morally challenged. Though I felt like a heel even admitting that to myself. Kett's business was Kett's business.

Kandy's cuff kept zapping me with tiny electrical shocks whenever it came into contact with the skin of my wrist. It was like getting poked by some obnoxious kid in school. Poke. Hey, pay attention to me. Poke. Hey, why do you think the far seer thought Kandy needed extra strength? Poke. Hey, I thought you were tired of walking into unknown situations and having information withheld …

Except no one was withholding information. No one actually knew what was going on. And they still expected me to pull this hunt off.

Well, that was a first.

"How did you know to open the portal?" I asked Pulou two seconds after Kandy and I stepped into the nexus. I was seriously hoping we were psychically linked because that would be super cool and useful.

The treasure keeper was hustling toward the door that led to the territory of Australia — my father's territory — but he paused to look back at me.

"The far seer's gaze still rests on you," he said. He sounded as heavy about it as I felt. He lifted his eyes to look at Warner as he walked through the portal behind me.

It was exceedingly daunting — crushing, actually — to go from no expectations to being under the gaze of the far seer. As in, I was never going to do anything more than run a cupcake bakery, but suddenly I was hunting treasure referred to as the 'instruments of assassination' where 'dragons dare not tread.'

The portal behind us snapped shut before the treasure keeper spoke again. "I didn't know that the task I set before you was so potentially perilous, alchemist. But I must ask you to continue forward."

I nodded. "Does Chi Wen … does he …" I couldn't bring myself to finish the question about my own mortality, or the mortality of my companions. It had been obvious since Warner showed up in the alley that this wasn't some ordinary trinket collection. But it freaked me out to think I was walking some path that had already been foreseen by the far seer, and that what I was doing was important enough for him to notice from among all the things he must see in his day-to-day existence.

Pulou cast his unusually stern gaze across us all — first Kandy, then Warner, then back to me. "There is another who also sees."

"Rochelle," I whispered, thinking of the charcoal drawings stuffed in the sketchbook that Rochelle — the Oracle who'd sought haven from Blackwell with the pack last January — carried with her everywhere. A sketchbook I'd had no desire to even glance inside. That sketchbook, and whatever it contained, was at least one of the reasons Chi Wen had begun mentoring Rochelle.

"We don't want to know," Kandy blurted.

I nodded in agreement.

Pulou looked to Warner for confirmation.

"The fact that the far seer's gaze is upon us speaks of the significance of this mission," the sentinel said. "And is reason enough to continue."

"It's what Chi Wen doesn't see that is always a concern," Pulou said.

"That's okay," I said with more bravado than I felt. "I prefer it that way. At least then no one knows what's going on, and it's not just me ... in the dark ...wallowing in fear and distrust."

Pulou raised his eyebrow at me.

Yeah, I could have kept that last part to myself.

"I think I was in your coat earlier," I said. "Just in case an alarm got set off or something. That was me."

"Pardon me?" Pulou asked. His English accent always made it difficult to tell if he was pissed off or not. "My coat?"

I fished the gold and gem banded artifact out of my satchel and held it aloft.

"It's the key to the map," Kandy said proudly. "I figured out that part, but Jade pulled it out of the tattoo."

"You retrieved this from the tattoo?" Pulou asked. He stepped forward to look closer at the key, but didn't attempt to touch it. "You've unlocked the map?"

"Partly."

"I must return now," Pulou said with a nod toward the door that led to the territory of Australia. "I can't allow your father to have all the fun."

He meant guardian 'fun.' AKA vanquishing demons and saving the world. Whatever had been going on in my dad's territory a couple of days ago was obviously still happening.

Pulou looked at Warner. "You'll go as far as you can?"

"I will."

"Shall I open a portal?" Pulou said. It was obvious he wasn't happy about leaving us, but that he felt like he didn't have another choice.

"We're heading to a grid point," Warner answered.

Pulou turned away before I could mention I didn't actually know anything about the grid point that led to the Bahamas. I had uncovered the location of the portal in Scotland while researching Blackwell. So I could try to find this one the same way ... except the books in the library had a tendency to move around.

Pulou opened the door to Australia and disappeared into the golden portal magic. Kandy shuffled her feet, and I could feel Warner staring at me ... waiting on me. I guessed it was time to go.

I turned around to face the door that led to every grid point portal in North America, which happened to be the territory of Haoxin, the youngest of the guardian nine.

I stood staring at the native-carved cedar door, weighing my options. Warner, who stood to my left directly in the line of my vision, felt very tall all of a sudden. Brick wall-like, actually. Kandy shifted on her feet behind my right shoulder.

"So, here we go off to the Bahamas," I said.

"Sun, sand, and … some sort of girly drinks," Kandy said gleefully. Though I could hear her gritting her teeth from the intense magic of the nexus. "Margaritas in Mexico … mai tai's in Hawaii …"

"I have no idea what you're talking about, wolf," Warner said. "Why are you hesitating, alchemist? This deliberation seems out of character."

"I've never been to this grid point," I said. "I also feel … unprepared."

"You have your knives and necklace. The wolf has her strength and claws," Warner said. "And I'm a dragon. What more do we need to prepare?"

"Proper shoes?" I said snarkily.

Kandy snorted.

Warner looked down at my 8 Eye boots, then raised his eyebrow. "Shall I lead?" he asked. The sentinel held his hand out to me, elbow bent and palm up. An offering.

Kandy wove her fingers through my right hand. "Go, go, go," she muttered through clenched teeth. The excitement of the adventure obviously overrode the pain of the portal passage and the pressing magic of the nexus for the werewolf.

I turned to lock gazes with Warner. I had to tilt my chin much farther up than I thought naturally becoming. The blue starbursts around his pupils were a sharp contrast to the deep green of his irises.

He frowned and glanced down at the hand he still held out to me. "I will not harm you, alchemist. Or the wolf. We are compatriots, are we not?"

I nodded, though I had only a hazy idea of what he meant by 'compatriot.'

Then Warner smiled. He might not have my father's easygoing charm or Pulou's booming laugh, but the grin transformed his face, making him more than tempting. He lifted his hand higher and wiggled his fingers.

Tempting was exactly what he intended to be.

I shook my head at my hesitation, and — after urging my necklace to amp up its shielding — I placed my hand in Warner's.

Without another word, he reached over and opened the door before us. Kandy gasped as the golden magic flooded around us. Warner stepped through, tugging at my arm only lightly before I followed.

As always, I stepped into the blinding magic with no sense of space or grounding. This time, I also had no idea where we were going to end up. I blanked my mind, just in case the portal picked up on my ignorance over Warner's direction, and willed myself to also not think of the first and last time I'd stepped into a portal without direction.

That time, I'd ended up in the dragon nexus with a demon crushing me.

I took a second step. Warner's grip was firm on my hand. His skin was even warmer than the portal magic, and his black-forest-cake magic teased my taste buds. The sentinel bothered me ... put me on edge. I didn't like being afraid of anything. I didn't like being afraid of myself, specifically my desires. My hormones had driven me into a pile of pain and trouble over the past year, and Warner looked like a bruised ego and wounded heart delivered in a mug of tasty hot cocoa with whipped cream and a cherry on top. So because of that, I would shove those thoughts and feelings far —

The bottom dropped out underneath my feet. I fell — without even having a moment to flail — into cool and very, very deep water.

Warner let go of my hand as the water closed over my head.

Kandy, who was still clinging to my right hand, started dragging me down like a lead weight ... a hundred and twenty pounds of lead.

I opened my eyes, feeling the sting of salt water as I did. I was surrounded by blue that thrummed with magic. If I looked up, I could see sunlight glinting on the surface and a trail of air bubbles. Warner was above me, probably with his head above water.

I'd felt this sort of intense natural magic once before, at the grid point portal in Scotland. This magical reservoir was the reason guardians tied their portal system to the grid points. Well, at the points that intersected over land ... at least, I'd assumed that to be the case.

Kandy panicked. She wrenched her hand out of mine, still sinking as she began to thrash and scream. More air bubbles streamed by me. She knocked my leg with her hand. Her three-inch claws, manifested in her terror, ripped through my jeans. I tried to grab for her but she was out of reach.

Ignoring my instinct to surface in order to breathe, I twisted, swimming downward after my drowning friend. I'd swum in the ocean my entire life, but I'd never tried to swim down — or while wearing boots — before. Thankfully, the water was warmer than I was accustomed to, and Kandy's thrashing was slowing her descent.

I grabbed one of the green-haired werewolf's outstretched arms. This time, instead of fighting me off, she grabbed my wrist in return.

I changed direction, attempting to pull Kandy up. For a moment, we simply hung there suspended, even though I was kicking for all I was worth.

Kandy wrapped her other arm around my waist, and then got both arms around my shoulders, freeing my second hand.

I swam. Black dots obscured my sight as my oxygen-deprived brain started to shut down, and I closed my eyes in order to ignore them. My lungs screamed and I released the air I held, even though I was pretty sure that was the wrong thing to do.

Warner grabbed the back of my T-shirt — and painfully, a handful of hair — and hauled me to the surface.

I gasped, filling my lungs with sweet, fragrant air over and over.

Kandy's arms hung limp across my shoulders, her head lolling backward. Warner, swimming in place beside us, slammed the palm of his hand between her shoulder blades. The werewolf spewed a lungful of salt water all over me. Then she started coughing.

"Sorry," Warner said. "I didn't know about that last step."

I squinted at him through the glare of sunshine on the vibrant blue water. He was soaking wet, his hair plastered to his broad face. I could see prisms of natural magic everywhere, glinting off the water, the waves, and the droplets on Warner's face. The early morning sun was low in the sky behind me.

I started laughing. The seawater was salty on my lips — even saltier somehow than on the west coast.

Kandy groaned, then tried to laugh but ended up coughing again.

"Wolves don't swim," she croaked.

"I got that," I said. "Where the hell are we?" I couldn't see anything but blue water no matter what direction I turned.

"Off the coast of the Abaco Islands, I would guess," Warner said. "If the Spanish didn't destroy the land along with their extermination of the Lucayans."

"Pretty strong words for someone who rips shadow demons apart with his bare hands," I said, jumping to the conclusion that the Lucayans were the first inhabitants of the Bahamas.

"The Lucayans posed no threat to the invading force. As far as I remember, the Spanish didn't even want the land."

"That was a long time ago."

"Not for me."

"Dragons aren't usually so concerned with human history."

Warner didn't answer. Instead, he reached out to Kandy, offering his arm. I was surprised when she took it. She divided her weight between us, then started attempting to kick.

"You really can't swim," I said. "I'll have to book you some —"

"Forget it," Kandy snapped. The wolf was made of steel — literally, judging by the way she'd freaking sunk.

The magic of the portal bloomed above us, spilling light even more deeply golden than the sun. We paddled out of the way, waiting for someone to drop out of the sky.

Instead, a pretty, petite blond poked her head out of the doorway, hovering about three feet above us. Her dragon magic was a spicy combination of sweet, creamy tomatoes with a hint of basil. Only guardian magic was potent enough for me to taste it over the power of the portal. I'd never formally met Haoxin, the guardian of North America. But I'd caught a glimpse of her through the mind-scrambling magic of the nexus the day I pulled a demon through a portal to save my friends. At just over a hundred years old, she was the closest dragon in age to Drake and me that I knew of. Not that I was considered a dragon by everyone.

Haoxin scanned the horizon, then spotted us in the water below her sandaled feet. "Oh, it's you, alchemist," she said. Her accent was light-touch American. I would have guessed Californian if pressed, but her silky, straight blond hair and perfect tan might be cause for bias on my part.

"Guardian," I answered, as dignified as I could be when paddling around in the middle of the Caribbean Sea with a green-haired werewolf clinging to my shoulder. "May I introduce —"

Haoxin's gaze shifted to Warner and she smiled. This reminded me that she was also known by a secondary title — 'reckless and adventurous.' Guardian magic was divided among the nine by specific gifts — such as my father's sword — and characteristics. Though why the attributes of 'reckless and adventurous' were an important component of how the nine guardians of the world functioned, I didn't know.

"Hello, sentinel," Haoxin said. I swore her eyes were suddenly bigger, bluer, and her lips fuller, pinker than they had been moments before. I was fairly certain her guardian magic didn't have anything to do with shapeshifting, though, so maybe I was just seeing her through envy-tinted glasses.

"Greetings, guardian," Warner said affably. His grin was effortless and welcoming. Charming, even.

Lovely.

"We seem to have made a misstep," the sentinel continued.

Haoxin laughed softly, the sound raining down over we peons in the water like perfectly tuned chimes. "Shall I help you up, sentinel?"

"Thank you, but we must proceed."

A light wind moved across the sea to dry the droplets on my cheeks. This breeze caused Haoxin's blue silk dress to dance around her smooth, unblemished thighs, but she ignored it to point over our heads. "Land is that way, my friend."

"Thank you, guardian." Warner gave a nod that had to take the place of a bow, seeing as he was still treading water. He reached for Kandy and the werewolf wrapped her arms around his neck from the back.

Haoxin lost her sunny smile as she watched this exchange. Then she looked at me. "Alchemist," she said. But then instead of continuing to speak, she bit her lip and glanced back into the portal.

"You will find the island friendly," she finally said, though I got the sense she was editing herself. "Though I don't usually use this portal when I walk here."

"Yeah, I can see why."

Haoxin grinned fleetingly in a rote response to my sarcasm. "I hadn't thought … I would go with you on this adventure, alchemist, but I understand you tread where I may not. It bothers me that there is such a spot in my territory. Do you have your knife?"

"Yes, guardian."

Haoxin grinned again, her seriousness dissipating beneath a gleeful, almost mischievous, anticipation. "It's a brilliant blade. Wield it well. I look forward to the tale and … the cupcakes I'm told I've been missing."

Before I could answer, she stepped back into the portal and it snapped shut behind her.

"Haoxin?" Warner asked.

"Pretty, pretty," Kandy said. Despite the fact she was clinging to the sentinel, her predator nonsmile was firmly back in place.

"Yeah," I answered both of them. "Can you read their identities by their magic? I mean, when a new guardian ... ascends? Do they retain or embody the magic of their predecessor along with their names and titles?"

"Some. Enough," Warner answered. "Though I'd never met Haoxin before."

I opened my mouth to question him further, but he turned and began swimming in the direction Haoxin had indicated. I couldn't see any land. I wondered if the guardian's eyesight was just that much better than mine, or if she simply knew what way to head through experience.

Warner, who carried Kandy on his back as if she weighed no more than ... well ... a bag of cotton candy, was quickly outpacing me. His long arms and strong legs cut through the blue water with minimal backsplash. I sighed. I wasn't such an accomplished swimmer, but I could stay in the water for hours without much effort.

Pushing thoughts of what else long arms and strong legs would be good at out of my mind, I followed Warner. Haoxin had taken an immediate shine to the sentinel, so at least lust-wise, I was in good company. Though, after spending ten months or so in and out of the nexus — as well as in and out of conversation with Drake — I'd ascertained that there weren't exactly dozens of eligible dragons hanging around, so maybe Warner was just fresh meat to the guardian ... as maybe I was to Qiuniu.

I wasn't sure when all my relationships had gotten so complicated, though it might have been when the vampire had shown up outside of my bakery. More likely, it had been the moment Sienna had walked into my life. Problem was, I didn't think I could survive without people to care for. So, all I could do was what everyone else did — cherish the good relationships and attempt to avoid the bad. I didn't have a great track record doing either, but I was sure as hell trying.

Chapter Nine

Swimming wasn't exactly conducive to conversation, but after what felt like an hour — though was probably just ten minutes — I started to feel a little lonely paddling along after Warner. Granted the sentinel wasn't big on chatting in general … or rest breaks, it seemed.

Still, the ocean felt very, very vast, and that vastness was isolating. Vancouver wasn't exactly a bustling metropolis, but it wasn't tiny either. I was constantly surrounded. By magic, by people — human and Adept. But here, if I fell far enough behind Warner, I might get lost and never, ever be found.

Then I began to wonder what was swimming beneath me, and what sort of strange fish the ocean's denizens thought I was. Then I started to fret.

"What about sharks?" I asked, getting a mouthful of salty water as an answer. I'd never learned how to properly front crawl with my face in the water. "Are there sharks in these waters?" I couldn't remember if sharks preferred warmer or colder water. "Great whites?"

"What would sharks want with you, alchemist?" Warner called back as he lifted his head to one side to breathe. He didn't bother pausing. He was also getting far too accomplished at the art of snark.

"You don't think they'd at least try a test bite?"

Kandy laughed. She was clinging to the sentinel like a freaked-out barnacle, but still, she had the gall to giggle at me.

"Glass houses, wolf."

"You're the biggest predator around here, Jade," Kandy said. "Except maybe the dragon here. I haven't formed an opinion about him yet."

Warner stopped swimming. Kandy's head momentarily went underneath a wave. Hacking and spitting out water, the green-haired werewolf clambered up onto the sentinel's shoulders, even as I realized he'd managed to touch ground.

I hadn't thought we were anywhere near land. In fact, I still really couldn't see anything ahead — but then, I was madly squinting from the sun reflecting off the water.

I kicked my feet down but went under when I didn't touch the anticipated solid ground. Warner widened the gap between us as he pushed through the water like an army tank, or whatever the waterborne equivalent would be. My arms were screaming with the effort of the last few strokes, the pain made worse because I knew the ground was so near.

Warner was head and shoulders out of the water by the time I got the tips of my toes to touch. I didn't even want to think about how utterly destroyed my boots were. I was fairly certain the leather wouldn't bounce back from a saltwater bath. Warner's jacket, too … though seeing as his clothing was somehow a manifestation of his magic, maybe he was actually walking around naked all the time —

A wave crashed over my head. I choked on a mouthful of water before I realized I needed to spit it out. The surf picked up strength, and I had to fight against it to retain my footing. But even like this, walking was quicker than swimming.

I was up to my waist before I actually saw land. The white sand was difficult to distinguish in the bright morning light, but the greenery beyond made it obvious we were walking toward an island. I'd never known a beach to taper like this. The beaches I knew dropped off deeply after a dozen feet or so, depending on the tide. But then, I usually couldn't see all the way through the water either, like the clear view I now had of my ruined — but still pretty — black boots.

Kandy jumped off Warner's back, landing up to her knees in the water, and then made a mad dash for the beach. Her green hair was fluffier than I'd ever seen it. It also looked practically dry. Though it was early in the day, it was still warm. If I let the sun dry my hair and didn't tug on the curls too much, I shouldn't look like a complete wreck. I wasn't sure about my outfit, though.

The beach stretched for miles and miles in either direction, without a single rock or shell that I could see. A dense forest stood a dozen or so feet from the sandy shore. Well onto the sand now, Kandy tugged her T-shirt off over her head to reveal a sports bra. She then yanked off her jeans, one soaking, clinging leg at a time. Thankfully, the werewolf had excellent balance.

Between Kandy and me, Warner was almost clear of the water himself. Until he suddenly whirled around, stumbling as he looked at me ... or rather, turned his back on Kandy's striptease. He looked so utterly aghast that I had to laugh.

"That's a lot of skin for a five-hundred-plus-year-old dragon," I called to Kandy.

The werewolf barked out a laugh, but continued to unabashedly wring the water out of her jeans. She'd already jogged over to the nearest tree she could find and hung her T-shirt over a branch. Which was odd, because I thought tropical trees were all supposed to be palms. The forest behind Kandy had some palms along its edge, but most of the trees looked a lot like super-skinny pines.

Warner didn't seem to want to look at me either. Still ankle deep in the water and utterly soaking wet, he cast his gaze left, then right as if determinedly scoping out any possible security issue on the beach. This was an attempt to cover his obvious embarrassment.

"If you hang out with shapeshifters, they get naked," I said. "Often. You'll get used to it, sixteenth century." I stepped by the sentinel and finally got my wet ass out of the water.

I, at least, would find a stand of trees to strip behind. Not that I was sure I could call the jungle that spread out before me simply 'trees.' For that matter, I wasn't sure it was actually a jungle either. Where was Wikipedia when I needed it? Oh, yeah. With my utterly waterlogged phone in my completely ruined, beloved satchel.

The entire area thrummed with the wild, natural magic I associated with grid point portals, but I was surprised to feel it this intensely this far away from the portal. Oddly, with every step I took I felt like I was somehow crushing microbes of magic underneath my feet.

Unstrapping my knife was easy enough, though the leather of the sheath was stiff. But I absolutely loathed taking off wet jeans. It was the most undignified, ungraceful, and frustrating thing in the world of clothing. And I knew. I owned and operated a lot of bras — aka torture devices — and wet jeans were worse. By the time I got mine off, I was covered in freaking sand — me and the jeans. It was even in my hair and mouth, though how that had happened, I had no idea. I might have lost a bit of time to my white-hot rage.

"You okay in there, dowser?" Kandy called from somewhere deeper in the forest. She was obviously already patrolling. Half naked. Warner was probably about to have a heart attack. Though, it was sort of lovely that a man —

"You didn't get bit by a snake or anything, did you?" Kandy continued.

"Snakes!" I shrieked. "There are freaking snakes in here? And what do you mean by 'or anything'? What else is there in here to bite me?"

Kandy's laugh faded as she continued to scout farther into the trees. The fact that the werewolf just casually expected there might be snakes hanging around didn't help my mood.

After I got the jeans off, I realized my mistake. Was I just going to wait around here for my clothing to dry? Freaking hell, use your freaking head, Jade. Damn it.

I stopped to breathe deeply. Why the hell was I stressing out about such a stupid thing? Because I couldn't freak out about the treasure hunting mission that had become super intense super quickly? Because I had to prove I was brave and capable? And therefore something else had to snap?

I asked for this responsibility ... well, at least sort of. I'd asked to police Blackwell, at least. To be judge and jury in regards to the sorcerer. And Pulou deemed this more important. Hissy fits about wet jeans really weren't becoming. Thank God I was currently surrounded by trees and not judgement-happy vampires and dragons.

I started wringing my clothing out. I was going to have to put it all back on, wet and covered in sand.

Kandy appeared before me wearing a new blue tank top, green Lycra shorts, and holding a swath of red and orange material. Material that turned out to be an ankle-length sarong.

"Umm, you went clothes shopping in the jungle, and orange was the best you came up with?"

Kandy snorted and tossed the skirt over my wet head. She'd found me an orange tank top and flip-flops as well.

"The town is, like, literally ten steps over that ridge."

I pulled the skirt off my head to see Kandy pointing off into the jungle. "Literally?"

"Well, I jogged."

"So like a thirty minute walk for a normal person?"

Kandy bared her teeth at me.

I laughed. "And what about being half naked with crazy green hair and wet American dollars?"

"They didn't even blink twice," Kandy said. "I got this for the sentinel." She held up a T-shirt that was painted in a swirl of blue and greens.

I was fiddling with threading the ties of the skirt through its holes around my waist. "That's at least a size too small —"

"Exactly." Kandy flashed me her predator grin and took off toward the beach.

Damn it. I tugged the orange tank top on over my still-wet bra. Like I needed to see Warner in clothes any tighter than what he was already wearing. And the swirl of green and blue would only emphasize his eyes …

Damn, damn, damn it.

"Are you having some trouble, alchemist?"

I spun around to find Warner watching me as I strapped my knife to my right thigh. "No trouble." I shook my head, straightened to let my skirt fall back into place, and very deliberately did not check him out. He was wearing the T-shirt Kandy had found, along with a pair of beige shorts. Warner's gaze lingered on my leg, but I was fairly certain it was the knife that had caught his attention, not my thigh. All dragons could see magic, even through Gran's invisibility spell.

Warner lifted his gaze to meet mine, and I realized that I'd been staring at him despite vowing not to.

"You are beautiful, warrior's daughter," he said.

My mouth literally dropped open at this admission. Then I noticed he looked displeased, so I snapped it shut.

"It's perturbing that something so beautiful could be so deadly," he continued as he closed the space between us. "But that's how nature works, isn't it?"

"Perturbing?" I mocked, holding my ground at his advancement. "Also, Mr. I-tear-demons-in-half-with-my-bare-hands, who are you calling deadly?"

"It was the combination I was remarking on," he answered. "All dragons are deadly. You more so, and not just because the far seer referred to you as 'dragon slayer.' "

"He was talking about you," I said.

"He didn't even notice I was in the nexus."

"He sees all."

"Exactly my point."

Okay, I'd been lost since the beginning of this conversation, and was only more so now. Bravado didn't seem to be getting me through this time. "Just what are you accusing me of?"

He looked surprised. "Nothing, warrior's daughter. I was simply putting the pieces together. You, the map, the knife, the werewolf, the vampire, the witch ... and now here we are."

"Doing our duty, like good dragons."

He inclined his head. "I'll need a weapon."

"You could have mentioned that the three times we've been in the nexus in the last twelve hours."

He shrugged. I ignored the way this gesture tightened the T-shirt across his pecs. I was pissed at him. I didn't really know why, but I wanted to be pissed at him, so I clung to the feeling.

"Why? You already have a blade perfectly suited to me." He cast his gaze to my ruined satchel, which I'd propped on a tree root in the hopes of keeping it out of the sand. I hadn't opened it yet, because I was afraid to acknowledge the extent of the ruin.

"That blade is not for you," I said.

He looked at me, all dark and serious. "The knife scares you, alchemist. I can take it off your hands."

"I take responsibility for what I make," I said. "You seem to do fine with just your hands."

"The knife would do even better."

"I don't trust it."

"You don't trust me."

I couldn't deny that — not with utter truth — so I spun away, grabbed my satchel, and headed toward the beach, following the taste of Kandy's magic.

The map had led us to the Abaco Islands, a group of small islands within the Bahamas. Apparently, the grid point portal dropped us vaguely near the village of Hope Town, which we reached after much swimming and some walking, of course. While I'd been wrestling with my jeans, Kandy had done some quick but thorough scouting. The green-haired werewolf was currently poring over a pile of tourist brochures she'd picked up along with the clothing.

I pulled out the map and tried Kandy's trick of placing the key over the tattooed image of the key, carefully aligning the colors so that the missing green line was accounted for. The magic of the map shifted underneath my fingers again, but with more flash this time, and a mouthful of smoky dragon magic.

"We're closer," Kandy said as she peered over my shoulder.

"Yeah, if we're reading it correctly at all."

"We are." Kandy pointed to a small black rectangle that had now appeared on the green portion of the map. "That's the lighthouse."

"Once again, if we weren't just superimposing our guesses on a bunch of pretty green and blue blobs that were once tattooed on the back of a guardian dragon."

"Not a lighthouse," Warner corrected Kandy. "A doorway."

I flinched. That was the second time the sentinel had snuck up on me. He was good at muting his magic, but not that good. It was the natural magic that thrummed sleepily around me that dulled my dowser senses.

"Yeah," Kandy countered. "A doorway in a lighthouse."

"A lighthouse?" I asked, just to get in on the conversation like I was an active participant and all.

"On the other side of the island, see?" Kandy unfolded the tourist map she'd picked up along with the brochures. "The island is long and skinny, and we're currently here on the other side of this low ridge." She pointed to a specific spot on her paper map. "The lighthouse is in the middle of town here, on the beach opposite and a bit north of us. There's a path just over there." She pointed toward the trees farther up the beach.

She placed the tourist map alongside the tattooed map so we could compare them. They weren't identical, but the tourist map was obviously intended to be easy to read rather than overly detailed.

"That's how this stuff works, right?" Kandy asked. "Treasure hidden in landmarks or monuments? Like in Indiana Jones."

"If this were a movie, I wouldn't be wearing orange."

"It looks great on you."

"Funny how you found green Lycra shorts for yourself."

Kandy shrugged, then grinned at me wolfishly. Great. It seemed that if Kandy had her way, I'd be adorned in pretty skirts every day.

"Show us this lighthouse, wolf," Warner demanded. Well, it sounded demanding to me. Kandy didn't seem to mind.

The green-haired werewolf took off across the beach as I rolled the map and tucked it back into my ruined, waterlogged satchel. I'd dumped the contents and most of the water out, then repacked it with what I could fit. Thankfully, I could lace my boots to the strap, but I couldn't do anything about the sand that now permeated every inch of everything I owned. And the chocolate was gone. Melted away, I guessed, seeing as all I'd found were waterlogged wrappers. I really didn't want to deal with that reality at all.

Kandy disappeared into the pine forest. I followed with Warner at my heels, still feeling like I was crushing the natural magic underneath my feet as I walked. I remembered Gran saying that magic was dying as the earth was slowly being polluted and destroyed by humanity. Here, that didn't feel like the case at all.

I wondered how many witches lived near grid points. At least the grid points that connected over or near land. Witches borrowed magic from the earth. Well, when they weren't ripping it from other Adepts through bloody sacrifices as Sienna had done. Thankfully, black witches were rare. The Convocation made sure of that.

Or maybe witches would find it too intense, and the magic difficult to harness, this close to a grid point. For me, this magic didn't come with a specific taste or color. Just a freshness that made the natural hues of the vegetation surrounding us seem brighter and more intense.

We crossed out of the pine trees and onto a paved path that was too narrow to be an actual road.

"We haven't seen any animals," I murmured. "I can't even hear any nearby."

Kandy turned back to flash me a grin. The green of her shapeshifter magic rolled over her eyes. "They're near. Just not stupid enough to move when greater predators tread the earth."

We rounded a slight curve in the path, and I could see the top of the red-and-white horizontally striped lighthouse through the trees.

Then a golf cart tried to run us over.

Literally.

It zoomed up behind us and cut around as I was gazing up at the lighthouse. The cart actually brushed my skirt as it passed by.

"Hey," Kandy snarled as she stepped off the path.

"Sorry," a young woman cried as the cart sped away. "It's our honeymoon!"

"That's no excuse!" Kandy yelled after the speeding, swerving cart.

"The cart explains the narrow roads, though," I said.

"Honeymoon," Warner mused behind me. "The first month of marriage is the sweetest."

"Yeah?" Kandy asked. "Because of all the mead?" The green-haired werewolf chortled at whatever joke she thought she'd made. Though Warner snorted like he found her amusing, so maybe I was missing something.

"Do Adepts still practice the marriage ritual, then?" he asked me as he stepped up to my left, perfectly matching my stride.

"Yep," I replied.

"And your parents? The warrior and the witch? They are married? In my … understanding, it is unusual for a guardian to marry."

He stumbled over the word understanding. I was fairly certain he was going to say 'time,' but then didn't. I felt bad for him. Just for a second. Then I shook it off, reminding myself he was just doing his 'duty.' No less and no more.

"No," I said. "They … ah … the circumstances surrounding my birth were unprecedented."

"I imagine."

"They only just reconnected. About ten months ago."

"Do they plan on marrying?"

"Not that I know of. Why?"

Warner shrugged as he glanced around at the tiny village that had practically appeared out of nowhere on either side of the paved path. "It's good to know the customs of a strange land before walking there."

Right. It wasn't the first time I'd heard a dragon use the term "walking" when referring to visiting the human world. Haoxin had done so, in fact, speaking from the portal. But Warner seemed to be asking about

Adept customs — or, specifically, dragon customs — rather than human. Maybe he was wondering how to ask Haoxin out. Guardian dragons had to date, right? They couldn't all be nuns and monks. Otherwise, baby dragons like Drake couldn't go around breaking the necks of baby half-dragons like me.

The single-storey buildings and homes of Hope Town were all painted in bright colors, dominated by seashell pink. Kandy cut up between buildings toward the red-and-white-striped lighthouse that towered easily five storeys higher than any other building in the village. I spotted a few people dressed in bright colors, most of them shopping or hanging around a local coffee hut, but no one gave us a second glance. Kandy had outfitted us perfectly for what was obviously a tourist destination. The sparse population of three hundred — according to Kandy's brochures — appeared to be a mix of Caucasian and people of African ancestry, but the village didn't feel desolate. More like everyone was elsewhere — perhaps the cluster of taller buildings on the edge of town that the golf cart was zooming toward. A hotel, maybe.

My stomach grumbled, but I ignored it.

The lighthouse was before us. A pink rope hung across the entrance, which I took to mean it was normally open to the public. Just beyond and down a slight hill, the ocean lapped against a grassy shore. Tiny seaside houses on that shore had boats tied to individual wharves. The low buildings surrounding the lighthouse were painted pink with white-trimmed windows and balconies, which was an odd contrast to the thick red-and-white stripes of the lighthouse tower. We'd left the pine forest behind us. A few palm trees were mixed with the low buildings, but nothing as dense as where we'd come through.

I stopped and stared up at the lighthouse looming before us. Kandy tucked up to the back of my right shoulder, as she always did. Warner stood directly to my left, placed so he occupied too much of my peripheral vision.

"Do you taste that?" I asked. I took another step forward and held out my left arm to block Warner from following. He took my hint.

"Magic?" Kandy asked.

"Sorcerer, I think. Maybe witch."

Kandy stepped off to the right, her footsteps practically silent as she circled the buildings around the lighthouse. Over the six or so months since Pulou had first tasked us with collecting treasures for him, we'd fallen into a rhythm. Kandy would scout and secure the area while I dealt with the magic — whatever that entailed.

I closed my eyes and focused on the new flavor. It hovered just underneath the natural magic that had been dulling my senses since we'd come through the portal. I brushed my fingers over my invisible jade knife through the fabric of my skirt and then twined them through the wedding rings of my necklace. I'd been so unfocused — so distracted by wet jeans, hunky, unattainable dragons, and missions far beyond my comfort zone — that I'd been walking all over this new magic without noticing it.

But this was who I was ... fundamentally ... utterly. There was no use dancing around it. No use trying to be sunshine and light, trying to make up for all the darkness Sienna had left behind in my soul. My deep, deep core. The darkness was there ... and it was time to move through it. It was time to embrace the new, to relish the present.

I was a dowser ... an alchemist.

I was the warrior's daughter.

I had a job to do. A job I wanted to do.

"Sorcerer?" Warner prompted from just behind me.

I opened my eyes. The natural colors around me were a blur of green and blue, pink and white. I blinked and the colors settled into trees, lawn, and a dirt path. Kandy was crossing back toward us from around the other side of the lighthouse.

I turned my head toward Warner. He stepped closer. I leaned into him and whispered, "You taste just like black forest cake. I like black forest cake. A lot."

How was that for embracing the future?

Warner opened his mouth, apparently flustered by my confession.

I grinned, then laughed. A low, husky sound that I hadn't felt like making in a long time.

"Black forest cake," Warner said.

"It's an insanely delicious dessert made with layers of whipped cream, cherries, and chocolate cake."

"Cake?" Kandy asked as she jogged up to join us. "Who has cake?"

I laughed louder.

Kandy grinned. Then, playing the tourist guide, she swept her arm toward the lighthouse and said, "The Hope Town Lighthouse is one of only three manual lighthouses left in the entire world. It's operated by a spring mechanism that has to be hand cranked every few hours."

"Very informative," I said. Still grinning, I started toward the lighthouse.

Kandy slipped around to stand behind my right shoulder. Warner remained a step behind me.

"I can't smell any magic around the other side," Kandy said.

"It's strong here," I said, indicating over the pink rope hanging across the open doorway of the lighthouse. "Some kind of sorcery. Like a ward, but not."

"The lighthouse itself?"

"No. I think that's real ... built by humans, I mean."

"It's a doorway," Warner said. His tone was even, but I was aware he was repeating himself.

"Okay, sixteenth century," I said. "You're going to have to elaborate. I've never encountered a so-called 'doorway' of magic before."

"You encounter one every time you walk in or out of the nexus."

"Nexus?" I asked. "As opposed to a portal?"

"The nexus doesn't exist in the same pocket of time as this world does," Warner answered.

"Yeah, it's a magical construct," I said, still not completely following him. "That's why time is weird in the nexus. Like it's disrupted by the intense magic of the guardians. And the rooms are never in the same place. They can be bigger, or smaller, or missing altogether."

"I hadn't noticed that."

"Yeah, well, you're a dragon. I'm not."

"I still don't get it," Kandy said.

"The nexus is anchored at a physical location," Warner said. "A temple in Shanghai."

"I thought that was just the gateway to the far seer's territory," I said.

"It is, and more." Warner nodded toward the lighthouse entrance. "Something similar is situated before us."

Kandy looked at me. I glanced around to see that we were still unobserved by the locals, and nodded to the green-haired werewolf. She ducked under the pink rope and crossed into the lighthouse, cutting immediately right to disappear from sight. Though, I could still taste her berry-infused dark-chocolate magic.

"You let the wolf precede you?" Warner asked. Again, his tone was even, but I heard the rebuke nonetheless.

"We all have our talents. Kandy's is scouting ... and, you know, roughing people up. She's happier doing her thing, and so am I."

"I'm not questioning you, alchemist," he said. "I'm simply figuring you out."

I turned to look at him. The morning sun did wonderful things to his eyes ... or maybe it was the T-shirt Kandy had clothed him in. Either way, he was delectable.

"I'm an enigma."

"I don't think you are," Warner said. Then he grinned at me. "I would appreciate if you shared your thoughts about the magic you sense and what its presence means to you."

"I've been trying to perfect a black forest cupcake, but I can't quite nail it," I answered.

"I meant the sorcerer magic you're sensing here."

Ah, okay. I thought there'd been some flirting going on.

"Though I would be happy to taste any cupcakes you create, alchemist," he added.

"What the hell is with all the cupcake talk?" Kandy groused as she exited the lighthouse. "I'm starving."

"Me too," I admitted. "Warner would like us to share our process with him more."

"Yeah?" Kandy eyed Warner. "Thinking of sticking around?"

"It's my sworn duty," Warner said gruffly.

"That means nothing to us," Kandy said. "When the world falls on our heads, we make it through. Me, the dowser, and the vampire. You're just some dragon following us around and acting pissy about it."

"When the world falls in, I'll hold it up," Warner said, quietly and terribly deliberate.

"Don't tell me," Kandy said. "Jade is the one it always falls on first."

Warner looked at me. I caught his gaze and smiled. "Don't worry," I said. "I'll try not to get you killed."

Warner turned to look thoughtfully up at the lighthouse. "There is little in this world that can wound me, Jade Godfrey, warrior's daughter." He looked back at me, or rather at my necklace. "Except perhaps you and your creations."

Kandy laughed huskily. "He's no idiot."

"Nothing inside?" I asked her. I was fairly certain that what I was sensing wasn't something easily triggered by a tourist, or even a werewolf, wandering through the door of the lighthouse.

"Stairs," Kandy answered. "I popped the lock on the room at the very top. Nothing. You can walk right through here. There's a door directly on the other side."

"And what happens when the alchemist walks through?" Warner asked. I was already ahead of him, though.

I offered my right hand to Kandy and my left to Warner. "Let's find out." Then we stepped forward to awkwardly duck under the pink rope and squeeze through the door of the lighthouse.

Nothing happened. The round, white-painted room was empty except for a cloudy window, a set of open steel stairs that wound upward, and a doorway that matched the one we'd just crossed through, straight ahead. But I could feel the magic intensifying before us.

"Well, that was anticlimactic," I said. "Wrong door." Then I stepped forward to pass through the open door before us, which by all appearances simply led to the front lawn of the pink buildings that surrounded the lighthouse.

I could see a rainbow-colored beach ball abandoned off to one side of the lawn.

I took another step and the colors of the ball flared, intensifying, as did the lawn and the buildings. Then everything blurred before me.

Magic lapped against me. Sorcerer magic, to judge by its earthy base ... old, dry, untouched ... musty but not unpleasant.

"Ready?" I asked, already knowing the answer.

Kandy squeezed my hand. I stepped into the magic, stepped through it as if it were a fine spider web — and for a moment, the world was just a wash of colors ... a rainbow of gossamer light.

Warner grunted as if in pain.

I took another step and felt the magic of the web snap around Kandy and me, but not Warner. The ward was trying to deny him entry, even though I was pulling him through.

Warner's deep chocolate and cherry magic rose beside me. I could actually feel it shifting underneath my hand.

A third step left me standing on a grassy knoll and looking down at an austere temple sitting in the middle of a tropical jungle. The lighthouse, its surrounding pink buildings, and the village of Hope Town were nowhere to be seen. Oddly, the sun was directly overhead now, as if it was midday, not morning.

"Cool," Kandy said.

Warner grunted and dropped my hand. He brushed his arms and torso, then his legs, as if trying to remove the residual magical web. I felt nothing similar. Just the sorcerer magic of the entrance behind me. Though when I turned to look, all I could see was a slightly warped view of the beach and ocean beyond. No wharves or boats.

"Are you sure you should come with us?" I asked the sentinel. "I know your magic is different. Adaptive. And you told Pulou you'd stay with us, but ..."

"I will go as far as I can go by your side," he answered. "Then I will find another way."

He didn't mean it the way he said it. Not romantically at least. But damn if my stomach didn't flip at the inference.

"It looks more like a temple to me," I said, hoping to cover my reaction by keeping us on task. "Not a fortress."

"Yeah," Kandy said. "Isn't there supposed to be a moat?"

"That's castles."

"Blackwell's castle doesn't have a moat."

"There is no God here." Warner's tone was distant and darkly tinged, but not angry.

"Okay, then," Kandy said. "To the fortress we go?"

"Apparently," I answered.

The fortress — as Warner preferred to call it — wasn't terribly ornate, its builders obviously subscribing to the function-over-form method of design. It was built out of gray stone. Its curved roof and gargoyles appeared vaguely Asian influenced. A long sweep of stairs led to wide, blue-painted front doors. Though I couldn't see particularly well from this distance, I thought the door might be hanging open.

A dirt path led from the hidden entrance we'd just passed through to the wide stone stairs of the fortress. Dozens of two-by-two foot stone slabs — their color making them appear as though they were carved out of the same granite as the fortress — looked as if they'd been shifted or flipped to one side of the path.

I stepped onto the bare dirt and slowly walked toward the fortress. The flipped stones hummed with sorcerer magic as I passed.

"Don't touch the slabs," I said.

"Roger dodger." Kandy slipped by me to stride ahead.

"Someone lifted these," I said.

"Yes," Warner agreed.

"They look heavy ... and spelled."

"Yes," he agreed a second time. "More sorcerer magic."

I nodded and looked up at the fortress stairs as we neared. They were also constructed out of stone, but certain slabs appeared to be missing. "The magic in the slabs is in the stairs, too."

Kandy paused at the base of the fortress to look at the first empty slot. The stone that had previously capped it was flipped onto the neighboring stair. She sniffed the packed dirt that remained. Then she sniffed the air. "Magic all around," she said.

"The air is still. Almost stuffy," I said. "The natural magic isn't as strong here."

"Like it's been used up?" Warner asked. "It takes a lot of energy to create a pocket area this large and detailed."

"You think they stripped the naturally occurring magic to create the pocket and build the fortress?" I asked, attempting to follow his train of thought.

"And its defenses."

I gestured toward the stones that had been flipped. "Its disabled defenses. But sorcerers can't tap into and manipulate magic like that. It would have taken a lot of alchemists, wouldn't it?"

"Or one very powerful one," Warner answered without taking his eyes off the fortress above us.

Kandy, who was obviously tired of all the yammering about magic, stepped up on the first empty section of stair.

Nothing happened.

She pivoted and hopped to the next empty section, one stair up and to the left. The empty sections zigzagged up to the blue-painted doors of the fortress. Now that we were closer, I could see that they were indeed off their hinges, hanging to one side like they'd been half ripped off.

"Anyone else getting the feeling we aren't the first Adepts to come through here?" I asked.

"Yes," Warner answered. "That's obvious. But I assume they didn't get far."

"Why assume that?"

"Because I was called to you because you possessed the map, and not here to stop a theft." He stepped to follow Kandy up the stairs. His long stride closed the gaps between the empty treads effortlessly.

"If the guardians don't own this artifact we're looking for, how do you know it's theft?" I asked, just trying to play devil's advocate.

"What we seek shouldn't be in anyone's hands, Jade Godfrey. Not even the guardians. And I would hope that whoever it originally belonged to, whoever originally created it, is long dead. And that such deadly alchemy has died with its maker."

Ah, there it was. "I thought you didn't know what we're looking for."

"I know that I was tasked to protect the guardians from it."

"And now you're helping another alchemist to retrieve this deadly item."

Warner paused his ascent to look back at me. "I am." There was something in his tone, something dark and serious, but not toward me.

"Because I can perform deadly alchemy as well."

"I've held the knife you made, alchemist," he said. "I know of what you're capable."

"But you'll do your duty."

"To the end."

"And beyond."

"Always."

I nodded, then jumping from stair to stair, I climbed until I stood before him. He watched me as I approached.

"That makes two of us," I said.

"Yes. We are well matched."

"Really? Here I thought I was just a half-blood." Yeah, that still smarted.

"A powerful half-blood," Warner murmured. He was still looking at me, but I wasn't sure what he was looking for.

"You're killing my buzz, sixteenth century."

Warner raised an eyebrow questioningly.

"Yeah, sentinel," Kandy called from above us. "Don't block the dowser when she wants to dance."

"It was not I who brought up the world falling down on our heads."

Kandy laughed. "We aren't the dwelling type."

Well, not out loud anyway.

"Door's open," Kandy said. "Looks like we don't even need to knock. That's too bad. I like the knocking part."

I laughed. Warner and I climbed the last few steps to join Kandy on the landing. Two gargoyles — resembling some sort of demon I didn't recognize — were placed to either side of the landing. The double doors — one of which hung off its top hinge and one of which had fallen to the side — were carved along the edges with a series of runes, all of which had been scratched through.

"Does altering a rune, scoring through it like that, void the magic somehow?" I asked.

"If you're strong enough to affect it," Warner said. "Or die trying, when the displaced magic backlashes."

Kandy glanced around. "No dead bodies lying around."

"Other than the runes and the gargoyles, it's not very ornate," I said.

"Serviceable," Warner muttered. He turned to look back the way we'd come. I couldn't see the warp effect of the magical doorway from here. Just the crashing surf and the white sandy beach beyond.

"The nexus doesn't feel like this," I said. "It feels full and vibrant."

"It's not the same," Warner said. "This is just a pocket. The nexus is a universe. Nothing lives or grows here."

"Things die here, though," Kandy said. She'd stepped just inside the fortress doors. "I revise my previous no-dead-bodies-lying-around assessment."

Taking extra care to not accidentally brush against anything, Warner and I followed Kandy into the fortress.

Chapter Ten

Three more doors stood beyond the main fortress doors. These were closed, though. One was edged with an inlay of yellow runes, one with blue, and the third with red. Sand covered the smooth stone beneath our feet.

"Don't touch the doors," I cautioned as Warner cut left and Kandy circled right away from me. "More magic. Way more concentrated here." Actually, this sudden intensity of magic made me realize what I'd been tasting as we'd neared and entered the fortress. "Does the magic feel depleted to you? Like drained?" I asked Warner, not taking my eyes off the doors.

"Weak, yes," he answered. "But I have no sense as to whether it was ever stronger or not."

"Sorcerer magic," I said.

"From all the dead sorcerers?" Kandy asked.

I glanced over to her. She was leaning over what I'd assumed was a pile of sand blown up here from the beach in a storm or something. Except if Warner was right about this being a pocket of time, storms might not occur here. Kandy crossed to look at a second pile. There was also a third one against the wall she was standing by.

I turned to look at Warner. He was standing by two similar-looking piles. But farther into the entrance, propped in the corner next to the yellow-runed door, sat a partial skeleton. The sentinel hunched down to look at it. Then he reached into the rib section of the dry bones and picked up a silver metal rune that the corpse had worn on a leather tie, probably around his neck.

I couldn't feel any magic from the item Warner held, but he didn't lift his gaze from it until I spoke.

"This isn't sand." I was suddenly hyperaware of the grit I was walking on, but didn't want to appear squeamish about it in front of a dragon and a werewolf.

"No," Warner answered.

"We're walking on the disintegrated bones of ... Adepts?" Okay, I was getting a little squeamish. The leather tie of the metal rune had crumbled away when Warner touched it. He was now flipping the rune through his fingers one at a time. I wanted to make a snarky joke about magician's tricks and coins — you know, to cover my discomfort — but I didn't. See? I was all grown up now. "The rune emblem ... these were sorcerers?"

"Perhaps."

"What does the rune mean? Is it a word or just a letter? It looks like a decapitated, legless stick-person."

Kandy snorted at my description, but kept her attention glued to the puzzle of opening the doors. I was a little sketchy on how runes worked. It wasn't my kind of magic. Witches rarely used runes in their spellcasting, though Gran sometimes used specific ones to anchor her wards.

"Not all Adepts appreciate the protection of the guardian nine," Warner said.

"People generally don't like being told what to do."

"This symbol — the eternal life — represents one such sect of sorcerers. A sect I thought long gone."

"They are," I said, gesturing to the piles of disintegrated bones. "Someone stopped them from entering the fortress. Another sentinel perhaps? Or they died trying to get through the doors?"

Warner made a noncommittal noise, not ready to share his thoughts. At least he didn't just ignore me like some vampires I knew would have. Well, I only knew one vampire. And honestly, if the glimpse I'd had of Kett's maker in London was any way to judge, I was seriously happy to leave it that way. One vampire was enough.

Kandy started toward the blue-runed door.

"Wait," I said. "Wait. Wait. The doors are spelled. See the runes along the edges?"

"Yeah? So?" Kandy said. "We have the key." She pointed to an indentation in the center of the blue-runed door, which looked a lot like the artifact I'd pulled out of the map — including being set with thin stripes of red, yellow, orange, blue, and violet.

"Fine," I said, as I dug into my ruined satchel to retrieve the artifact. "But you don't know we're supposed to go through the blue door."

"Blue and yellow make green."

"There's a yellow door right there." I gestured toward the door on the far left. "Why pick blue?"

"I like blue."

Warner laughed, calling my attention back to him. He was digging through the other disintegrated remains and retrieving more identical silver runes. It seemed he found Kandy's methodology amusing.

Tucking the runes into his pocket, Warner straightened from his crouch and turned to look at the three doors. "The magic on the doors appears untouched?"

"The magic that I guess once coated the walls, stairs, and front doors is diminished. As if it was drained or transferred somehow. But these three doors don't taste weak like that. I don't recognize the spells, but each door is spelled differently by the same group of Adepts."

"No one stopped these guys," Kandy said. "Look at how they were sitting."

I wasn't sure that piles of disintegrating bone could be described as "sitting," and the one that was partially preserved looked more like it was slumped. "They could have been thrown there. Their necks broken, maybe? I mean, I'm not the only one that happens to, right?"

Warner furrowed his brow at me, and Kandy didn't look much happier. Okay, so joking about broken necks wasn't funny. Got it.

"If a sentinel like him ..." — Kandy nodded to Warner — "...came through here, the sorcerers would have been ripped apart."

"More likely decapitated if they fought," Warner said. "Most likely apprehended and imprisoned."

"Sorry?" I asked, snagging on to that last nugget of information. "There's a dragon prison?"

"I thought you were the treasure keeper's apprentice?"

"I work for him, but I'm not his apprentice. Not like Drake is Chi Wen's successor, if that's what you mean. But what does that have to do with a dragon prison?"

"The treasure keeper keeps more than just treasure. But these interlopers would have simply been turned over to the sorcerers' League for punishment."

Note to self — don't do anything so crazy that the dragons decide to punish me. I'd take the Convocation over Suanmi any day.

"I didn't mean to imply you were in line for ascension," Warner continued. "Very few dragons are capable of surviving the ceremony and accepting the mantle of a guardian. This Drake you speak of must be very powerful."

"And prone to prison breaks," Kandy added. "Key, please? Or are we going to order tea and crumpets?"

"I have no idea what crumpets have to do with it," I muttered. I handed the artifact I'd retrieved from the map to Kandy.

She slowly turned the circle in her hand, then peered at the indentation on the blue door. She held the key up to the door but didn't insert it. Then she turned it in her hand again, as if attempting to line it up with the door's indentations.

"Chi Wen is the eldest now?" Warner asked as Kandy worked.

"Yes," I answered. "Drake is Suanmi's ward, but the far seer's apprentice."

"Suanmi," Warner repeated, with just enough edge that I suddenly liked him a whole lot more. "I have slept for half of Chi Wen's ascension."

"No one's feeling sorry for you, buddy," Kandy growled as she stalked over to the yellow door.

"Kandy," I admonished, though I knew she was probably just bitchy about figuring out she'd chosen the wrong door. "I guess the colors didn't line up?"

"I'm just saying we all go through shit. He's lucky he slept through most of his."

"Except, of course, his very existence is tied to shit going down."

"Except this," Warner muttered. "Why wasn't I called to this?"

"Because they didn't have the map?" I asked as Kandy slotted the key in the indentation of the yellow-runed door. She'd turned it upside down, if I remembered correctly, opposite to how the key had worked on the map.

"I'm tasked to protect the locations of the instruments of assassination. An incursion here should have woken me."

"Always?"

"Yes," Warner replied tersely.

Figuring I'd press him until he stopped answering, I said, "Maybe someone out there knows how to get around triggering you."

Warner frowned and — as expected — let the conversation drop. Instead, he crossed to examine the corpses on the other side of the entranceway — the ones Kandy had been hovering over earlier.

Kandy turned the key.

"Wait," I cried, but was too late to stop her.

Somewhere beside or behind the door, large gears creaked as if they were turning for the first time in what sounded like over a century, if not longer. Though, given the supposedly timeless nature of the pocket that concealed the fortress from the human world, that was just an impression, not the reality.

Nothing else happened.

Kandy smirked, then wagged her eyebrows at me.

"Sorry," I said. "With the map, I had to be the one to hold the key."

"That was a map conceived by the former treasure keeper and tattooed by an alchemist," Warner said. "Here, the key would have to be usable by sorcerers." He retrieved a rune from the piles of bones he'd been digging through. He now had five of the silver 'eternal life' pendants.

Magic rolled through the runes at the edges of the yellow door. Each one glowed briefly with a wash of blue sorcerer magic before that magic moved up to the next. Then the door opened about a foot wide.

Shadows, Maps, and Other Ancient Magic

Kandy slipped through without another word. Warner straightened from gathering his clues and tucked a sixth metal rune into his pocket. I knew I should have been more interested, but frankly, bone dust freaked me out, and I wasn't here to figure out some incursion that happened centuries ago. I was here to retrieve an artifact for the treasure keeper. Also, I had a hard time wrapping my head around time like that. I didn't like to frustrate myself by thinking of things I really couldn't comprehend for too long. It gave me headaches, and my chocolate stash was a world away.

I followed Kandy into the next chamber. "The magic is still active," I said. I had to push the door open a bit wider to get through.

Kandy was standing, staring at three more doors. They were edged with orange, green, and violet runes. More skeletons lined the walls here, but the bones were better preserved.

"Well, that's a game changer," I said.

Kandy growled something and tossed the key up in the air with her right hand, then caught it again. Like pitchers did before they threw.

"If you break the key, we won't get much farther."

Kandy sighed and wandered over to peer at the indentations on the orange door. Then she looked closely at the key, comparing the two. "Is the magic the same here?" she asked.

"Yep," I answered, reaching out with my dowser senses to confirm. "Same spells on all the doors. Well, different spells on each, but the same magic."

Warner entered through the door behind me and immediately crossed to the three corpses slumped to the right side of the small chamber. Dust hung suspended in the late-afternoon light that filtered in through windows cut into the stone along the top edge of the wall above him.

I tried to block out the idea that the dust was from the disintegrating corpses, and that I was currently breathing it into my lungs.

"No clothing to help identify the time period," the sentinel said. "More of these." He held up the silver 'eternal life' runes for me to see.

"Yeah," I said. "I was kind of hoping the ones in the entrance died from the utter boredom of not being able to get through the doors."

"Only three corpses in here," Kandy said as she crossed to the green door. "Six in the last room."

"I guess they were getting better at getting through the spells," I said. "Question is, what killed them? And is it coming for us?"

Neither Kandy nor Warner answered. I couldn't feel anything malignant in the magic the doors held, but the diminished magic all around worried me because I couldn't get a specific read on it. I couldn't really taste it, except for its sorcerer roots.

"So, did these eternal life sorcerers hate dragons?" I asked Warner.

"Immortality seekers," he answered.

"And dragons don't like to share?"

"Dragons aren't immortal. And guardians don't believe in immortality. Such power usually has terrible side effects."

"Evil side effects."

"No one should live forever."

"That's why you hate vampires?"

"Vampires take life to live."

"They don't have to."

"Any one of them who tells you that is lying."

"They have rules."

"About not getting caught, and not drawing attention."

A loud click drew my attention back to Kandy. She'd inserted the key into the green-runed door.

For a nanosecond, nothing happened. No gears turned. The door didn't open.

Kandy turned to look at me. Her eyes glowed green to match her hair. "Sorry, Jade," she whispered. "Wrong door."

Sorcerer magic boiled up at her feet, just as her own shapeshifter magic rolled over her torso, arms, and legs. I lunged for her, but my outstretched fingers only brushed the fabric of her tank top as the ground beneath her feet dropped away. She plummeted down, even as she transformed into her six-foot-tall half-beast form.

She didn't even scream.

I tried to fling myself after her, only to have Warner wrap his arm around my waist and lift me off the ground.

"Hey!" I shouted, twisting and turning in his iron grip. "Asshole! That's my friend."

Far beneath us, a series of somethings snapped and cracked. I panicked, thinking I was hearing Kandy's bones shattering. I slammed my head back into Warner's mouth and nose in my effort to get away from him. He grunted in pain but didn't loosen his hold. Starbursts exploded before my eyes as I felt what I assumed were his teeth denting my skull.

"I'm okay," Kandy called up the dark shaft beneath my dangling feet. Her voice echoed, and her words sounded mangled by her three-inch incisors. "But yuck. I'm not the first one down here."

The creaky gears of the open door behind us started to turn. The door slammed shut.

Warner set me on my feet, a step away from the trapdoor that had swallowed Kandy. I weighed nothing to him. And while the idea of being petite to anyone was utterly intoxicating, I was seriously pissed. Pissed enough to completely ignore him as I knelt on the stone at the edge of the opening, peering down into the darkness.

The sides of the stone shaft that had just swallowed my best friend appeared to be coated in blue sorcerer magic.

"I can't climb back up," Kandy called.

"Sorcerer magic on the walls," I yelled down at her.

"Yeah," she said. Her voice sounded like she'd reversed her transformation and was once again in her human form. "Plus, you know, nothing to hold on to."

"We'll find you a rope."

Warner snorted. I continued to ignore him.

Something crashed and splintered below. "Kandy!?"

"Never mind the rope," she yelled. "I made a door. I can see a corridor. I'll come to you. Plus, you know, I kind of have the key."

I glanced up at the green-runed door before me. The indentation in the center was empty.

Warner laughed quietly as he continued to search the three skeletons against the wall. There was nothing snarky about the laugh, but I wasn't amused by his amusement. I glared at his back as I strained to hear the sounds of Kandy breaking through something else, God-knows-how-far below me.

"Stairs," Kandy yelled, her voice faint and echoing now. "It's slimy and wet. No more spiked corpses, though."

I closed my eyes and tried to imagine her progress back ... a hall, some stairs ... obviously, the sorcerers who'd built the fortress wanted multiple ways to move behind and through their magical traps. If we knew where we were going, we could probably just use Kandy's cuffs to demolish the magic-depleted walls and avoid the doors altogether.

I pulled the map out of my satchel. Maybe I could trigger it to reveal more detail, getting it to zoom in again until I could see the passages and actual rooms. Then I remembered that Kandy had the key. And this wasn't a video game.

"You're mad at me," Warner said without looking at me.

"No shit, Sherlock."

"You wish I'd let you fling yourself to certain death."

"Uncertain death, but yes."

Warner tugged the pendant off the skeleton he was crouched in front of. The bones shifted to the side, but they didn't crumble into dust as they had in the entrance. "I understand you care for the wolf," he said. "But you can aid her alive far more than you can dead."

"That's your opinion."

"That's fact, warrior's daughter. Your petulance aside." Warner straightened from his crouch. I mimicked his movement. The trapdoor slid shut behind me. Its magic settled until I couldn't distinguish it from the runes surrounding the doors. I briefly wondered if my presence had held it open, but I was too busy being pissy with Warner to think about it too long.

"You're such a sweet talker, sentinel."

"Is that what 'Sherlock' means?"

"No."

He shrugged his shoulders and turned to look at the final corpse. Apparently, dead sorcerers interested him more than I did.

"How many of the silver runes do you need to collect to confirm your suspicions, sixteenth century?" I was attempting to be sarcastic — my default comfort blanket — but I wasn't pulling it off. The fact that Warner seemed impervious to it didn't help.

"None," he answered. "What do you think happened here, alchemist?"

"Well, obviously they didn't have a key. Unless there are two."

"Doubtful."

"So they used magic to get through the doors." Yeah, so I was being drawn into his ancient mystery against my will. I guess I wasn't exactly known for my outstanding willpower.

"Sacrificial magic."

Blood magic. I couldn't pick up any residual. Though that was odd. Terrible spells normally came with a terrible taste, which usually made me puke my guts out. Maybe magic faded over time, just like the bones of mortal sorcerers. The idea of the skeletons being connected to blood magic should have probably already occurred to me. Except I actively ignored such possibilities. Just as I actively ignored the ability to perform such dark magic myself. Ever since the events of London and then Tofino, I could feel that darkness dwelling contentedly within me. Hell, it more than dwelled. It manifested the second I was under extreme stress. I had the sacrificial knife as evidence, tucked into my ruined satchel right now.

"It appears so," I said, aware that enough time had passed that Warner would know I was uncomfortable. But then, he already knew that, didn't he? He'd offered to relieve me of the burden of the sacrificial knife. "But the magic on the doors either regenerated or reset. The other magic — the path, the stairs — not so much."

"The builders of the fortress put more energy into the doors."

"Makes sense."

"Six corpses in the first room. Three here."

"You think they sacrificed themselves willingly. And were more efficient with the casting the second time."

"Yes."

"Who does that? I thought they were immortality seekers?"

Warner shook his head, but didn't answer. He straightened to gaze at the three doors blocking our forward progress.

"Don't step between me and a friend again," I told Warner's broad shoulders.

He turned to look at me. "I'll step between you and whatever I perceive as dangerous, any and every time."

"Because I'm a weak half-blood."

"Because you're valuable. Unique."

He held out the nine silver runes he'd collected. I offered my open palm to him and he dropped them into my hand. I instantly tasted their residual magic.

"Sorcerer," I said. "Different than whoever built the fortress, though."

"Yes? That makes sense."

"No key."

Warner nodded his agreement. "I couldn't feel any magic on the runes."

"Residual." I tucked the pendants into my satchel. My fingers brushed the bundle of my wet T-shirt, which I'd wrapped around the sacrificial knife. Yes, over the tea towel I'd already wrapped it with, so maybe I was a little OCD about it. The touch of its magic made me instantly uneasy. Of course, standing around hoping

Kandy showed up soon might have contributed to the feeling.

"I haven't done anything particularly unique in your presence," I said, bringing the conversation back around to my being pissed at him. Or, rather, my attempt to be pissed at him.

"You walk the earth, warrior's daughter."

I wasn't sure how to take that. I wasn't sure I wanted to know how to take that.

Jesus, I was afraid.

I was practically running scared, yet desperately trying to keep from moving. I was scared Kandy wasn't going to make it back. I was afraid I had no idea what was going on ... or where life was taking me ... or who I was becoming.

Yeah, I was lumping everything together and mixing everything up. I'm a baker and an alchemist, I do that. A lot. Normally, when things got this amped up in my head, I'd dig into my satchel for a bar of 70 percent single-origin cocoa from Madagascar to distract myself, but I didn't have any.

I did, however, have black forest cake.

Yeah, Warner suddenly looked ... delectable. He'd stepped forward into a pool of sunlight still filtering into the chamber through the high, narrow windows, and the warmth of it colored him with a welcoming sort of light. Especially his green eyes. Though, again, that might have had more to do with him wearing the perfect color of T-shirt rather than the light. Kandy obviously had a previously unknown flair for color combinations.

"I've got this thing for kissing inappropriate men in inappropriate situations ... and places. You game?"

"I don't like games of chance. I like to know I'll be keeping the spoils."

"I can't figure out if that's a yes or a no."

Warner reached for me, wrapping one arm around my back and pressing between my shoulder blades to pull me forward to meet his lips. Nothing the least bit gentle in his touch, though his lips were soft as they closed over mine.

I swayed into him, burying myself in the kiss but not touching him further. I luxuriated in the moment. I gave myself the tiny gift of the warmth of his skin, of the strength of his limbs. He brought his hand up against the back of my neck, as if he was worried I would pull away. But I already wasn't close enough, and I wasn't even ten seconds into the lip lock.

And his magic ... the taste of his magic. Oh, God. He was all deep, smoky cocoa and sweet, sweet cherries delivered with a creamy smooth finish. I parted my lips underneath his, just ever so slightly to taste him better. And I swear I actually breathed in his magic. It went straight to my head, making me instantly, delightfully tipsy.

It had been a long time since I'd gotten drunk on magic. It had been a long time since I'd felt safe enough to do so.

Warner brushed his fingers through the curls at the side of my head, teasing the tip of his tongue against mine. The touch of his magic lingered across my cheek, ear, and neck even longer than the warmth of his hand.

It had been a long time since I'd felt I deserved to feel this way ... wanted, maybe even adored.

Yeah, Warner packed a lot into a simple kiss.

Behind us, the gears of the yellow-runed door clicked and then turned. Warner didn't break the kiss, so neither did I.

"Christ," Kandy said. "I almost get my ass skewered and the two of you are standing around macking on each other."

"Macking?" Warner mumbled the word against my lips in a way that sounded as if maybe he hadn't heard Kandy return at all.

I laughed and stepped back from the embrace. Warner's arms stretched between us, his fingers brushing against my shoulders before they fell to his sides. He wasn't smiling, and he hadn't taken his eyes off me yet. I couldn't help but grin at him, pleased that he was obviously into me as much as I was into him.

"Took you long enough," Kandy muttered as she attempted to brush by me. Attempted, because she had to suffer a one-armed hug around her neck before I'd let her pass. "I've been deliberately leaving you two alone since he showed up."

"Don't even try to pretend you deliberately went through the wrong door, taking the key with you."

Kandy offered me her patented nonsmile as an answer. Then she tossed the key up into the air, caught it, and sauntered toward the violet door. She inserted the key into the indentation there without any other preamble.

"Wait!" I cried. The warm cocoon I'd found while in Warner's arms stripped away instantly. I really couldn't bear to watch Kandy fall a second time. "How do you know it's the purple door?"

"Violet," Kandy corrected. "It's how the colors line up. Red and blue make violet."

"But you just thought yellow and blue made green."

"They do," Kandy smirked. "I assumed green, because that was what worked the first two times, with the map and the first door. But the second key, the second almost-a-rainbow on the tattoo, wasn't the same. It was missing violet, remember? I just didn't get the connection between the second door and the second tattoo. Both sets have to line up. Tricky."

Warner grunted like maybe he thought it wasn't so tricky. I was pretty much lost, though I couldn't dispute Kandy's logic. There was a second key on the tattooed map that we hadn't utilized in any way yet. Questions of how Pulou-who-was knew to tattoo any of this on his back arose in my mind, but I tamped them down. Now wasn't the time to try to untangle that mystery, if I could even hope to understand the ways of a guardian at all.

Kandy turned the key, then quickly stepped to the side. Just in case she was wrong a second time and the floor was about to drop out from underneath her. The gears in the door creaked and the door opened, all the way this time. A long hallway appeared beyond it.

"No lights," I murmured.

"No problem," Kandy said. With her shapeshifter magic glowing in her eyes, she stepped through into the stone-walled corridor — which was suddenly uncomfortably reminiscent of a tunnel.

"Maybe I should lead?" I asked. "Last time we were in a tunnel, you got swallowed by the wall."

"The wall swallowed you?" Warner asked as we both followed Kandy through the violet-runed door.

"Yeah," Kandy answered. "Asshole sorcerer."

"Different lifetime," I murmured.

"I don't know, Jade," Kandy said. "Blackwell's got it pretty bad for you. According to Audrey, he pays thousands to get his hands on any or all of Rochelle's charcoals."

"Audrey?" Warner repeated. "Rochelle? Charcoals?"

"Audrey is the beta werewolf of Kandy's pack," I said, attempting to quickly fill in the blanks for Warner. "Rochelle is an oracle, under the far seer's mentorship, who presents her visions in charcoal on paper. She has some peace treaty with the sorcerer Blackwell, who's a pain in our collective asses. But who's also deemed by the treasure keeper as not worth our time."

"He is undoubtedly correct."

"Yeah," Kandy snarled. "He still dislocated my shoulder with that tunnel trap and directly contributed to the death of a pack mate."

I ran into Kandy in the dark because I hadn't realized she'd stopped. I whacked my chin on her head and bit my tongue.

"Ow!" she cried.

"Jesus, your skull is like a freaking brick!"

She chortled a laugh, but then said, "I can't actually see any farther. A light spell or a flashlight would help."

"I'm not that kind of witch ... or Girl Scout," I muttered. "Though I excelled at selling cookies." I reached sideways until I could touch the stone wall to my right. When no magic instantly leaped out and attempted to eat my arm, I pressed my palm fully to the wall and tried to dowse for any magic nearby.

"This would be perfect timing for one of those shadow demons to attack," Kandy said. Her tone was far too gleeful.

"It's odd that they have left us alone," Warner said.

"It isn't after sunset here yet." Yeah, I could add two plus two. It was only when the numbers went into double digits that I got into trouble. "The magic feels stripped all along here."

"Not just weak or muted?" Warner asked.

"Yeah, I'm not really sure how I can tell the difference, but it's diminished somehow."

"Someone's been here before us, like in the other rooms," Kandy said.

"And left no magic behind? If they didn't have the key and used some powerful magic to get through the doors, that should have left a trace."

"We should've brought the reconstructionist," Warner said. His voice was warm comfort at my back, but my arm felt exposed and vulnerable pressed against the wall.

"She doesn't like us much," Kandy said.

"Me. She doesn't like me," I said.

"She's afraid of you, warrior's daughter," Warner interjected. "That's not the same thing."

I reached out to the magic I'd been searching for in the stone wall. Then, ever so carefully, I added a little bit of my power to it. Pale blue lights glimmered along the edge of the ceiling, and then all along the tunnel in front of us — glowing brighter the closer they were to me. Then they dimmed and we were plunged into darkness again. I pushed another pulse of magic into the wall, following its path in my mind to the light I'd seen nearest to me. I twined my magic into the glimmer of the magic I'd found that triggered the lights.

The light over my head glowed pale blue again. Then a few more glowed farther along the windowless hall.

"See? You are that kind of witch." Kandy started walking again along the corridor.

Something clanked in the wall ahead of us. Next thing I saw was Warner holding a steel arrow about an inch away from Kandy's heart. He'd gotten in front of the werewolf and me in the blink of an eye. As I stared, the sentinel snapped the arrow in half and dropped the pieces to the ground.

"Apparently, you woke up more than just the lights," he said. "Shall I go first?"

"With reflexes like that, hell yeah," Kandy answered.

Warner stepped ahead of us. My legs felt numb, shaky, but they seemed to still function as I followed. I really wasn't sure that a werewolf could survive getting skewered through the heart.

"It's just like Indiana Jones," Kandy said, grinning back over her shoulder at me.

"Sure. Great," I answered.

No more arrows attempted to pierce our hearts as we continued forward until the corridor dead-ended at a stone door. Some complicated-looking runes were etched into the stone tiles that encircled the door. A few of those tiles appeared to be depressed, as if they'd been pushed farther into the wall.

"The magic, alchemist?" Warner prompted.

I shook my rekindled fear for Kandy out of my head and peered at the door. And the runes. "Diminished as before."

"We could trigger it, just to see what it does," Kandy mused.

"No," Warner and I said in unison.

"Spoilsports," the green-haired werewolf said gleefully. At least one of us was having a ball. "It's broken anyway." She pressed her fingers to the stone door, which opened farther but bumped against something. I hadn't seen that it was open at all. Despite my half-dragon DNA, my eyes still weren't as sharp as a werewolf's. I assumed that made me prey, in the dark at least.

Through the door, stone stairs dropped off sharply to the left.

Kandy stepped through the door and down the first couple of steps, then turned to look behind it. "Another body," she said.

The light from the corridor barely penetrated the stairs, even with the door wide open, but I was fairly certain the corpse blocking the door was wearing the same rune pendant. The skeleton was better preserved, with bits of hair and patches of clothing hanging off it. Probably because there weren't any doors or windows around. Though if this was a pocket of time, should the sacrificed sorcerers even be decaying at all? Maybe time just moved super slow here.

"How many is that now?" I asked. The preservation of this corpse made it much more difficult to ignore the mounting death toll.

"Ten that haven't succumbed to the elements," Warner answered. "Could've been more."

"This one is sitting like the others. As if accepting his fate."

"Yes. Without flesh, it's difficult to know what killed him, but they do appear to have sacrificed themselves."

"To counter the magical traps of the fortress," I said. "That's a lot of people willing to die for their cause."

Warner made a noncommittal noise. "I'm concerned we might come up empty-handed. But how anyone could gain access to the instruments of assassination without my sensing it, I don't know."

"Magic has its limits," I said. "Even Guardian magic."

Warner nodded, and then took the lead down the stairs. Kandy and I followed.

Chapter Eleven

We went down and down in a slow, wide spiral. Down and down until I wasn't sure how long we'd been walking. Lights flickered on intermittently as we passed, but most of the magic that I presumed once coated these walls and steps was diminished. The walls became damp and slimy, and though I attempted not to rub against them, I wasn't completely successful.

We stepped over three more corpses — Warner pulling a pendant from each — as we descended. Again, these skeletons were better preserved ... almost mummified. This state of preservation made me fret about the oxygen levels, though I wasn't silly enough to say so out loud. The utterly fearless werewolf and dragon would sneer at me for sure. The air didn't taste stale. But it was oxygen that caused things to decay, right?

Each corpse was placed before what I assumed had been some sort of magic trap along the way.

"Thirteen now," Kandy said from up ahead as we passed another skeleton. She didn't sound so gleeful anymore.

Warner grumbled something under his breath. I took it that he wasn't a fan of the number thirteen, but I'd grown up with witches who didn't believe in such superstition. In fact, many witches promoted such superstitions to create a powerful aura among the Adepts, which had subsequently leaked out into the human world through centuries of practicing witchcraft.

The perfect number for a coven was thirteen, actually, though given the low birth rate of most Adepts, that wasn't always possible. The Convocation was traditionally made up of thirteen witches from all over the world. One of those spots had formerly stood empty for years, however, waiting for a witch powerful enough to fill it. Scarlett was the witch who eventually stepped up … a sacrifice of her freedom that my mother had made to protect me.

Most dragons were too impervious to magic to be bothered by it, just as Warner had asserted in my bakery kitchen only a day ago. But ideas penetrated where magic couldn't. And thirteen corpses spread throughout a fortress that contained something called the 'instruments of assassination' created a pretty pervasive impression.

Someone scary powerful had walked these steps before us. Someone who had followers willing to sacrifice themselves to thwart the magic protecting whatever we were currently hunting.

My toes were getting wet. I hated having damp feet. I loved walking in rainstorms, but only when I was wearing proper shoes. I know I was just wearing flip-flops, but it was weird to be surrounded by so much stone and still get wet, wasn't it? Yeah, I'd gotten my neck broken two days ago and hadn't given it a second thought, but wet feet bothered me.

"What's with the damp?" I asked, then flinched as my too loud voice echoed back and around me. I modulated my tone to a whisper. "Where is the water coming from?"

"It was slimy like this in the spike-filled, corpse-riddled hole," Kandy said.

Warner grunted, but didn't offer his opinion.

A terrible idea occurred to me. "How far do you think we've walked? Far enough to get to the other side of the island? Near the ocean?" The beach we'd swum up on had tapered for hundreds of feet out into the sea, maybe more. And now I was wondering why.

"Could be," Kandy answered.

"And deep enough to be in an underwater cavern?"

"Jesus, I hope not," Kandy said. The green of her shapeshifter magic shone so brightly in her eyes it practically obscured her face. "But I guess it would make sense to fortify a powerful artifact that way. And digging through stone with magic would be an insane feat, wouldn't it?"

"It would," Warner said. He turned back to look at us. He'd reached some sort of landing at the base of the stone stairs. He lifted his foot and deliberately placed it down again. Water sloshed.

Possible underwater cavern? Check.

I hated being right about all the terrible shit.

A wooden door stood open before the sentinel, half off its hinges as the entrance door had been. The runes that had once decorated its edges were scratched and marred. No corpses were slumped against the walls, though. Whoever had led the siege hadn't needed to sacrifice a follower to get through this door. Or the main entrance, now that I thought about it. Though maybe any corpses outside the protection of the fortress would have succumbed to the elements.

Golden dragon magic rolled across Warner's eyes. I'd never seen dragon magic do that, except with Chi Wen. After meeting Rochelle last January, I'd assumed the magic I'd seen in the far seer's eyes was a manifestation of his oracle power. I guessed all dragons held their magic differently. I didn't know Jiaotu either; maybe Warner took after his mother.

"Shadow scouts ahead," Warner said.

"Waiting for sunset?" I asked as I joined him on the landing. The water was ankle deep here. I was going to have to work through my wet feet issues whether I wanted to or not.

Kandy bent down to touch the water; then she licked her fingers and spat. "Salty."

I sighed.

The green-haired werewolf began prowling the perimeter, which was rather tight, so she brushed by Warner and me each time she passed. Her eyes were full-on glowing green. She kept clicking wolf claws in and out of her fingertips. I wondered if it hurt her to do so.

"Alchemist?" Warner asked. "Are we continuing?"

"Why wouldn't we?" I said, attempting to shake off the sense of doom that seemed to be pressing down between my shoulder blades.

"He thinks old dead things should scare us," Kandy said as she circled us again.

"He also probably thinks you're pacing."

"I'm not pacing," Kandy snapped at Warner. "I'm securing the area while you stop for tea and crumpets."

Warner raised an eyebrow at the green-haired werewolf. I wondered where he'd picked up that affectation. Pulou maybe.

"That crumpets line really isn't working," I said.

"I know, okay? This place stinks of death. Dry, dusty death."

I reached out to touch Kandy but managed only to brush my fingers across her hand and bracelet as she passed. She stopped pacing and looked down at me touching the cuff.

The alchemist magic tingled underneath my fingers. I dropped my hand.

"I didn't think we'd get to the end so quickly," Kandy murmured. She lifted her wrist to look at the cuff and then locked her gaze to me.

"Chi Wen ... the far seer isn't usually literal," I said. "Are you worried about what lies ahead through those doors?"

Kandy snorted. "Not for me."

"I don't understand."

"I'm not wearing these for me, am I? The far seer's gaze isn't fixed to me."

"The far seer isn't known for his understanding of time," Warner said. I was relieved at his interjection. "You could wear the cuffs for the next fifty years before you know why you were given them."

Kandy shifted her green gaze from me to Warner. "Yeah?" Her tone was deep and deadly. "You think that's happening here?"

Warner turned to look at me. He shook his head. "No."

The green-haired werewolf returned her gaze to me as well.

With their expectant eyes locked on me, I turned to look at the dark doorway looming in front of us. I pulled my knife and twirled my wrist to needlessly loosen it.

"Shall we dance?" I asked Kandy.

Kandy laughed, low and husky.

I stepped through into what appeared to be the main chamber of the fortress without waiting for an answer. Fretful or not, the werewolf was always up for dancing.

Magical sconces flared as I entered the circular room. The vaulted ceiling was supported by impossibly tall pillars ... nine plain stone pillars. The similarities to the dragon nexus stopped there, though. There was nothing gilded about this round room, and no immediately apparent doors leading from it. The decor was entirely gray on gray. Slab tiles carved out of stone spread out before us in concentric circles. Those circles radiated inward to a set of stairs that rose, also in a circular pattern, to create a simple stone dais. A statue stood before an altar on top of the dais. But as far as I could see, there were no other statues in the room.

"No magic," I whispered.

"None?" Warner asked. "See the path?"

Certain stones had been removed from the concentric circles, as they had been outside and on the stairs leading up to the entrance.

"None except for up there." I pointed to the statue at the altar. "It's as if it's been stripped, even more so here than in the halls. Not a drop of residual magic."

I started to cross the concentric circles, carefully stepping within the edges of the missing stone slabs. I wasn't terribly concerned about making a misstep, seeing as I couldn't feel any magic in this area of the chamber. But it was never stupid to be wary. I approached the bottom of the stairs, noting that there were nine steps, not counting the top of the dais. I could feel Warner and Kandy mimicking my movements behind me. I was happy to taste Kandy and her dark-chocolate berry-infused magic behind me. Not that I knew for sure that placed her out of harm's way, but it felt better to lead right now.

I paused and reached out with my dowser senses to taste the power at the top of the dais again. "I can't place the magic ... sorcerer maybe. Alchemist for sure."

According to Pulou, I was the only alchemist currently practicing anywhere in the world. Whatever was on the altar was at least older than me. But I was betting it was way, way older than that.

I shifted my focus, reaching out to the farthest edges of the round chamber, but I still couldn't taste any other magic around us. "I thought you sensed shadow demons here?" I asked Warner.

"They're here. I can feel them," he answered. "Waiting."

"Waiting for what?" Kandy said. "I thought they wanted the map?"

"Perhaps they just wanted to give us a push," Warner answered.

I jogged up the nine stairs and stepped in behind the statue, skirting around it to see that it depicted a woman. The detail of the carving was intricate, and in complete contrast with the utilitarian fortress. The woman was wearing a wide skirt, so long that only the tips of her shoes showed at the hem. Her bodice was laced at the back and cut square along her collarbone. Her neck and hands were bare of jewelry, but what appeared to be a circlet rested on her forehead. Her eyes were wide open and staring at her outstretched hand, which hovered a couple of inches away from a rough-hewn wooden box that sat in the very center of the stone altar.

"Hello, *Game of Thrones*," I muttered. "Someone wants their costume back." Then I called out to Kandy and Warner, who were still ascending behind me. "It's weird, isn't it? That the statue doesn't match anything else around here? Look at the detail … her hair falling over her shoulder, the way her feet are placed, as if in midstep. Then look at the altar, the dais, and the box. All of which are just basic. Serviceable."

"Maybe something used to sit there instead of the box?" Kandy offered. "And whoever came before us took it and left the box?"

"What does the magic tell you, alchemist?" Warner asked. "The runes along the edges of the altar are inert, yes?"

A thick layer of dust practically obscured the carved runes Warner was referencing, but I was way more interested in the wooden box. "The box holds ... something ... but I taste nothing from the statue or the altar." I skirted the altar until I was standing opposite the statue. From there, I could see her eyes were fixed on the wooden box. "Does she look surprised to you?"

Something was really bugging me, but I just couldn't figure out what. I looked up to meet Warner's gaze. He was staring at me — not the statue or the box. Figuring me out, not the puzzle standing right in front of him. I could feel myself start to blush — yes, like a silly teenager — just as something occurred to me. My stomach bottomed out at the thought.

"What did you just realize?" Warner asked, his tone low and intimate.

"She's not ... I mean, you've been concerned about the fortress being broken into and why you weren't ... woken."

"She's not."

"Not what?" Kandy asked.

"A sentinel," Warner answered.

I looked back at the statue, my stomach rolling uncomfortably at the idea of Warner 'sleeping' encased in stone like this. He had screamed when he appeared in front of Kandy and me in the alley. I'd assumed that the magic of whatever transportation spell had sent him there had just overwhelmed him ... but ... what if ...

I looked back at Warner, who offered me a curl of his lips. Not really a smile, but an attempt at one. Then, failing that, he shook his head emphatically.

"She could be a warden of some other kind," Kandy said. "You know, like a gargoyle or a nondragon guardian. But neutralized or petrified. Another trap that's already been triggered?"

This pulled my attention back to the present. I couldn't figure out Warner's potentially terrible past right now. I wasn't sure I actually wanted to know the details of what his sentinel duties meant for him when he was 'sleeping.'

"Not that I can taste," I answered Kandy.

I reached over to the box and lifted the lid.

Warner hissed harshly, like he was really pissed off all of a sudden. Yeah, I had just touched an unknown magical object without laying down protection spells or anything. I got that reaction a lot, but I wasn't a protection-spell-laying kind of witch.

Nothing happened.

"Well, that was oddly easy," I said.

"Oh, fuck," Kandy snarled. "You had to say that out loud."

We glanced around the fortress to see what karma was going to rise up to kick our asses.

Nothing happened.

I leaned forward, placing the lid to one side of the altar as I peered inside the eight-by-six-inch wooden box. Three braids of what appeared to be silk thread were coiled inside.

"Hmmm," I muttered. "Usually these sorts of things come with velvet cushions and diamonds. Or at least some kind of precious metal. I wasn't expecting hair ribbons."

Warner didn't step any closer, but Kandy lifted up on her toes to look. "Ribbons?"

I reached out with my dowser senses, trying to get a taste of the alchemist magic that coated the braids. Each tiny rope, or ribbon, or whatever they were, was braided with five individually colored silk threads. At least, I assumed the braids were magical in nature. It might just have been the wooden box I was tasting. "Red, orange, yellow, blue, and violet," I said to Warner and Kandy, both of whom had smartly stayed a step away from the altar.

"Like the key and the doors," Kandy said.

"I don't understand," I said. "We're here to pick up rainbow-colored braids?"

"Almost a rainbow," Kandy corrected.

I glanced at Warner, who did not look like a happy camper. His teeth were clenched so tightly I could see the strain across his jaw and cheeks. "Is this what we're here for?" I asked. "Or is it some weird message from whoever got here before us?"

"You can't feel the magic?" he asked. His voice was strained.

"Not as much as you seem to."

He met my gaze intently and then nodded his head.

Okay, weird. But whatever. I picked up the lid, intending to replace it before I took the box off the altar.

"Destroy it," Warner said.

"What?"

"I think you should destroy it."

"That's not what we're here to do," I said. "Pulou …"

"We tell the treasure keeper we couldn't find it."

I stared at Warner. Even Kandy stopped her pacing to look at him. Then she started laughing.

"What about duty?" she asked him. "Loyalty? And how do you know the fucking thing won't backlash and kill Jade if she tries to do what you ask? For someone who said he'd hold up the world if it came crashing down, you have a pretty loose understanding of the concept of protection ... and friendship."

I wasn't sure I'd ever heard Kandy so quietly angry, so utterly affronted.

I placed the lid back on the box.

Warner shook his head as if clearing it. Then he grimaced. "I'm sorry," he said. "If you could feel it, you would understand. It's like millions of lightning bugs crawling underneath my skin, digging into my brain, heart, and lungs. I've never felt the like."

"I still wouldn't have asked Jade to do something so stupid. She does stupid things just fine on her own."

"Thanks," I said dryly.

"You know what I mean," the green-haired werewolf continued. "You already take too many risks too easily."

Warner focused on me. "I apologize, alchemist," he said, his words carefully deliberate. "I spoke before I thought. I will bring the matter up with the treasure keeper. Perhaps he will feel the same way as I do. It was an instant reaction."

"Let's keep moving," Kandy said. "The statue is starting to creep me out."

I totally got what Kandy was talking about, as I nodded to acknowledge Warner's apology. Then I reached to touch the sides of the wooden box with my fingertips. Runes glowed underneath a layer of dust on the altar that I hadn't paid much attention to when investigating. I supposed dust just wasn't pretty enough to draw my attention. I wasn't going to make any excuses for being a magical magpie — not even to myself. Such things were in my DNA, after all.

I swiped my left hand across the runes nearest to me.

"What is it?" Kandy asked.

"Um," I answered. "I can't move my feet."

"What?"

"Step back," I said.

Warner and Kandy took a step away from the altar to stand on the second stair of the dais. I stared at the incomprehensible runes, glowing blue before me now. "It's sorcerer magic, but I can't read it."

"Even an expert would need hours to discern the runes, alchemist," Warner said. "Many are interchangeable. The intent of the use is usually key to the spell."

Wasn't that sweet? The sentinel was trying to make me feel better about my ignorance. Yeah, I kind of missed Kett right now. Who knew I'd prefer tough-love mentorship. But then, Warner wasn't my mentor — he was an equal. Or at least I should be seeing him that way.

I cleared more dust to reveal more runes. The magic that was binding my feet to the dais crept up my calves.

Kandy moaned. "Is that stone?"

I looked down, assuming that the magic would appear the same way it tasted. But my feet now appeared to be encased in stone.

I glanced back up at the statue that stood with her hand outstretched across the altar from me. "Same stone," I said. "She tried to touch the box?"

"Trying to move it seems to be the trigger," Warner said. "It obviously encased whoever she was, but more quickly. From the rate it's attaching to you, I assume you can break free?"

The stone spell spread up and over my knees. It didn't hurt, but it was exceedingly distracting. I ran my fingertips along the runes, finding a spot that appeared to be a circle with five grooves.

"Alchemist?" Warner asked again. "You can break the hold of the spell, can't you?"

"Haven't tried yet," I muttered. "Kandy, toss me the key."

The stone made it up to my waist as I caught the key that Kandy threw.

"To delay seems moot," Warner said. He sounded like he was attempting to modulate the harshness of his tone.

"Gotcha, sentinel," I said. "But I'd like to figure it out properly, you know?"

"No," he growled as the stone climbed up underneath my breasts. "I don't 'you know.'"

Ignoring him, I pressed the key into the indentation. The dais absorbed it. Something shifted in the magic of the runes, but the stone continued to roll up over my shoulders and started to spread down my arms.

"Well, that didn't work," I muttered.

"You disabled the spell from triggering again, Jade. Not from its current manifestation."

If Warner's use of my first name wasn't an indication of how angry he was, his tone certainly conveyed his ire. I couldn't see his face, because as the stone spell crawled its way up my neck, I was having a difficult time moving my head. As it hit the edge of my jaw, I felt the first pulse of panic.

I closed my eyes to focus, reaching out to the magic of my necklace and knife. Though they were encased in the stone, they still responded to me. I drew what shielding power they offered. Then — painfully, slowly — the upward creeping of the spell stopped, just as it encased my chin.

"Jade?" Kandy asked. She sounded concerned. Scared, even. I didn't like scaring her.

I stretched my dowser senses out to taste the magic of the stone spell. For the first time since I'd ruined it in Tofino, I wished that I still had the sword my father had commissioned as a vessel for my alchemist powers. But the katana was hidden away now in a treasure trove from which I'd plucked the key to the map and the fortress — filled with and twisted around Sienna's dark magic.

That was a mystery for another day. Unless I didn't manage to break out of the stone spell.

So, yeah, it would certainly have been handy to have the sword now.

I focused on the flavors filling my mouth in an attempt to sort through the magic. If I could understand it, I could try to manipulate it.

I tasted rich, fertile earth. "Mushrooms. Moss. And something almost sweet ... honeysuckle or ..."

"What?" Warner asked.

"The magic," Kandy answered. "She's tasting the magic."

Now that I'd identified the root of the spell, I attempted to channel its magic into my necklace. The stone crept farther around the back of my head, even as it covered my mouth.

"Jade!" Kandy shouted, but her cry was muffled as the stone poured into my ears.

I'm not going to panic. I'm not going to panic. No panicking. Come on, Jade! You're a freaking alchemist! And a half-dragon. What would a dragon do now?

I visualized the stone everywhere it touched my skin. I visualized my magic coating me like a protective layer. Then, just as the stone flooded over the top of my head, I visualized thousands of spikes of magic shooting out of me.

The stone exploded in a burst of energy that struck Warner to my left. He stumbled down another step, shaking his head as bits of stone rained down around and behind him.

The blast hit Kandy to my right, throwing her clear of the dais altogether.

The blast hit the statue across from me, cracking it in a series of radiating hairline fractures. As I watched, those cracks began to spread, widen, and crumble.

"Kandy?" I called.

"I'm okay."

I reached for the closed wooden box as the statue crumbled before me, revealing a young girl who looked to be about four years old. Same clothing and everything, but with a younger person inside them.

"What the hell?" I murmured, even as I felt Warner step up on the dais behind me.

The child opened her eyes, and for a moment, I could have sworn they glowed with the golden magic of the portals. But then they cleared to light brown orbs that were way too large for her gaunt face.

No child should be that close to starved. The circlet that the woman-sized statue had worn fell down around the girl's neck. Her long, light brown hair looked as if it had never been cut.

There was nothing childlike about the intensity of her sooty, sweet magic, though.

Not even remotely hampered by the bodice and skirt that were now far too large for her, she lunged across the altar for the box. "Mine!" she declared. Her accent was so heavily English and posh, it was disconcerting to hear it coming out of a child's mouth.

I lifted the box that contained the five-strand braids, holding it out of her reach. With the box clear of the altar, I could feel the intense magic thrumming within it. It momentarily scrambled my brain, which wasn't completely clear of the stone spell yet — discombobulating me just long enough for the child to scramble up and across the altar and try to wrestle the wooden box from my grasp.

Warner swore something German-sounding under his breath as he stepped forward, but then paused as if unsure if he should interfere.

"Jesus," Kandy whispered as she stepped up to my right.

The girl was oddly strong for a four-year-old. But then, by the sooty taste of her magic and the gold that had rolled over her eyes, I could tell she was a fledgling dragon.

"Hey!" I said, unsure of what else to say to the half-starved dragon toddler before me. I'd always been terrible with kids. I usually just ended up feeding them too many cookies, but cookies were something I obviously had no current ability to make.

The girl, who was half-hanging off the altar and half-hanging off the box, chomped down on my wrist. And drew blood.

I shrieked and snapped my wrist to shake her off. The girl tumbled back onto the altar, then sat on her haunches and licked her lips.

"Enough," Warner said. The dust on the altar rippled from the power of his rebuke, but the girl simply grinned at him.

"Jesus," Kandy repeated. "What the hell?"

Yeah, the supposedly powerful adults just stood there staring like idiots at the four-year-old on the stone altar. The bite on my wrist had already healed, but it continued to sting as if it was infected.

"She's dressed like, what?" I whispered. "Eighteen hundreds?"

"Sixteen hundreds," Warner said. He sounded terribly grim.

"Jesus," Kandy repeated.

"What's a four-year-old from your century doing here?" I asked Warner.

The kid started messing with her clothes, yanking the bodice and skirt off, tearing through the fabric until she was free of it. She then tied one side of her chemise in a knot. Her feet were bare. If I looked on the other side of the altar, I'd probably find her too-big shoes abandoned there.

And yes, we were still just standing there staring at her.

"Look closer at her magic," Warner said.

The child smiled at me. The expression stretched her thin face further, and a pang of pain went through my heart. She was just a little girl —

"Hail, sister," she said. "I like your blood. Spicy sweet."

"Dragons don't consume each other's blood," Warner said, instantly going all big brother on the kid.

The child cackled. All the hair on the back of my neck stood up. I finally saw what Warner had picked up before me.

"Her magic is diminished," he said. "Locked away."

"Contained."

"In the form of a toddler."

"Preschooler," Kandy corrected. Like that made a difference.

"Hail, sister," the kid tried again.

"Yeah, I wouldn't play the sister card," I said. "I don't have a great track record with siblings." I couldn't figure out if I felt sorry for her or if she scared the crap out of me.

I cracked open my ruined satchel — willfully ignoring the bits of its vegan 'leather' that were now crumbling off it — and started to try to wedge the box into it. Frustratingly, it didn't seem to fit.

Warner thrust his hand past mine to yank out the sacrificial knife, which was still bundled in my wet T-shirt and the tea towel. He ripped the T-shirt and towel off the knife, then shoved them back in the satchel. I stumbled against him as the force of him doing so pulled down on my right shoulder.

I would have sworn the knife started purring contentedly in his hand the second he unwrapped it. You know, if I believed that magical objects could have moods.

"Hey!" I cried.

Shadow demons rose out of the ground all around the top stair of the dais.

The child clapped her hands, which shifted her firmly into the scared-the-crap-out-of-me category. God, I hated that clapping-while-diabolically-pleased thing. Sienna used to do that all the time.

In a blur of motion, Warner spun around and slashed the shadow demon nearest to us in half. No ripping necessary. The sacrificial knife, which was deadly enough to kill an ancient vampire, sliced through the creature like butter.

"What is it?" Kandy screamed. She couldn't see or scent the enemy right in front of her.

"Shadows have come to play, wolf," the child answered.

"Stay right beside me," I said to Kandy as Warner slashed through a second shadow. Then he pressed his back to mine. The remainder of the shadow demons stayed back from us, as if waiting for some signal.

"Come," I said to the kid, who was still perched on the altar like a malevolent vulture. "We'll get you out of here, get you to the guardians. They'll figure out what's wrong with your magic." I held my hand out to her.

She glowered at me. "I don't need the help of a half-blood."

"Well, there goes the sister bond I was so hoping for."

"Give me the garrote vil."

"What?"

"The instrument of assassination. Now!"

"This?" I held up the box. "It's braided threads. They aren't murdering anyone."

The kid snarled at me.

"Rabid," Kandy said.

"Being stripped of magic would make anyone crazy," I said. "Who's your mother?"

"Mother?" the child echoed.

"I'm laying money on Suanmi. You've got that instant-hate-for-me thing in common."

"Who's my mother?" the kid repeated, obviously confused.

I sighed. "Come on. Warner, can you cut us a path?"

"If we move quickly."

I held my hand out to the kid again. "Don't bite me," I said. Then I wiggled my fingers at her like she was a pretty kitty.

She grabbed my hand, yanked me forward, and kicked me in the side of the head.

Yeah, a four-year-old kicked me in the head. I stumbled sideways and knocked Kandy off the dais for the second time.

The shadow demons swarmed the green-haired werewolf. Kandy might not have been able to see them, but by her terrified screams she could feel them.

I shook off the kick to the head — freaking dragon kids — then cradled the box in my left hand as I willed my knife into my right. I spun, stepping out of the kid's path as she leaped for me from the altar. Then I made a beeline for Kandy.

Warner got to the werewolf before I did. Even as they swarmed and attached themselves to him, he slashed the shadows away from Kandy. I could actually see them sucking the shapeshifter magic out of my friend, like leeches.

Warner freed Kandy and shoved her behind him. Her arms, neck, and face were covered with red hickey-like marks as she pivoted, spotted something behind me, and lunged forward.

I felt the child make a second attempt to jump on my back. Kandy threw a punch over my shoulder and knocked her off.

"Fuck!" Kandy screamed, shaking her fist. "The kid has a hard head."

I spun to see the kid fly back and tumble down the stairs of the dais. The crazy child was cackling with some sort of evil glee. I lost sight of her in the midst of the shadow leech swarm.

"Jesus, Kandy," I said. "She's a preschooler."

"She kicked you in the head first."

"Go now!" Warner yelled. The shadows were pressing him as he continued to slash them away. His arm and the sacrificial knife were a blur of motion, the magic of the knife flashing and humming as it cut through the leeches. Cutting through magic was what the knife seemed to be made for, but it was insane that I felt like this made it happy. That was way too far down the crazy road, even for me.

"Behind me," I said to Kandy as I pressed the wooden box with the five-stranded braids into her hands. She couldn't see the shadows, so she couldn't hope to fight them. And I needed my hands free.

I sprinted for the entrance, but got only three stairs down before the shadow leeches pressed against us. Warner shifted along the edge of their mass and moved to block them from me. I thrust my knife into what looked like the head of the nearest leech and felt its magic grab hold of the magic in my blade.

"Not for you," I muttered as I sent a pulse of my power through the knife. The shadow leech exploded.

The others nearby backed off.

"What the hell are they?" Kandy asked. I could feel her frantically looking around behind me.

"Magical leeches of some kind," I answered as I flew down three more steps. "Sentient, though. They're scared of my knife."

"Yeah," Kandy snarked. "I think it's the warrior's daughter who really freaks them out."

From out of the shadows, the kid appeared before me and kicked out the side of my right knee in the same instant. Bone crunched, fiery pain exploded in my knee, and I stumbled. Then the kid leaped by me and tackled Kandy.

The shadow leeches swarmed over all of us, sucking at any hint of magic they could find. Kandy shrieked, but in frustration rather than fear. She couldn't get the kid and the leeches off her at the same time, but the kid couldn't get the box away from the werewolf either.

As I stumbled around, still half upright but with a useless right leg, the leeches tried to attach themselves to me. I pulled magic from my necklace and knife to create a personal shield between them and me. It didn't stop them from constantly trying to suck on me though, which was seriously creepy.

Warner stepped between Kandy and me. He was attempting to wrestle the kid off the werewolf, even as he kept fighting the leeches. I managed to grab the kid's legs and half-yank her off Kandy.

The green-haired werewolf tore the box from the kid's loosened grasp. Then she proceeded to smash it into the tiny, crazy dragon's face. The wooden box splintered into pieces.

The kid cackled gleefully again. Though I still had her legs pinned, she grabbed for the braided threads as they fell free from the box. She snagged two, but then immediately shrieked when she touched them. I got my arm around her waist, clumsily yanked her off Kandy, and threw her down the remainder of the stairs for the second time. The shadows swarmed her, swallowing her so completely that I couldn't taste her magic anymore.

My right leg was still a fiery column of pain as I stood to scoop up the three five-stranded braids off Kandy's chest. They didn't burn or hurt me in whatever way they'd hurt the kid. But I'd already put two and two together before I touched them. Though they felt benign to me, they — along with the magic of the fortress — were obviously dragon-kryptonite somehow.

Warner stepped almost rhythmically around us, slicing through leeches, though I wasn't sure he was actually vanquishing any. He might have been weakening them, but he wasn't reducing their numbers.

Kandy scrambled to her feet, gave me her shoulder, and started half-dragging me down the stairs toward the entrance. She was limping herself, and her other arm — her bad one — didn't seem to be fully functioning.

"The kid!" I cried.

"Screw the kid," Kandy snarled.

My right leg was definitely not happy about the quick pace. As we moved, I twisted the three braids together, then knotted them around my left wrist. Their sorcerer-alchemist magic prickled against my skin, but didn't seem to affect me adversely in any other way.

We stepped off the stairs and the earthquake hit.

The ground suddenly cracked open before Kandy and me. We dove in opposite directions to avoid falling into the fissure that appeared in front of us.

Warner, slightly behind us, tumbled out of my sight. Despite the rolling ground, I could see Kandy gaining her feet to my left. She was close to the exit.

I tried to stand. The ground underneath me continued to roll and crack. The leeches had all disappeared.

"Remember Indiana Jones?" Kandy shouted from the relatively safe entrance archway, which had held against the earthquake so far. She was still having way too much fun.

I laughed. Even with my leg hurting and Warner currently missing in action, I couldn't help it. "I'll race you out," I called.

Kandy lost the smile. "Jade!" she screamed as she pointed up over my head.

I looked up, even as I saw Kandy dive through the stone-framed entranceway.

I had a split second to hope she made it out of the fortress safely. Then the high-vaulted ceiling crashed down over my head.

I ducked, hunkering down next to a portion of the ground that had swelled upward from the earthquake.

I wasn't sure that would offer any protection, but I also wasn't sure what else I could do at the moment.

I was, however, sure that half-dragon/half-witches didn't survive being crushed by thousands of pounds of stone.

Chapter Twelve

Someone was calling my name. Screaming it, actually. But I couldn't open my eyes … or my mouth, for that matter. All the bones in my face felt like I'd run into a concrete wall nose first. Yeah, unfortunately, I knew what that felt like.

"Jade!"

Kandy … Kandy was screaming for me. She sounded terrified, and that just wasn't right. My vibrant, brash best friend should never sound that way, especially not when calling my name.

I opened my eyes. I still couldn't see anything. It felt like some sort of liquid was screening my sight.

Blood. My eyes were flooded with blood.

I lifted my arm to wipe my face. I could feel the bones knitting together as I moved. It hurt. Enough to wake me up a bit more.

My hand came away bloody, but at least I could see again.

" … not much longer," Kandy screamed.

I lifted my head. I was lying on my side, so I rolled over onto my back. Kandy was standing over me. She appeared to be carrying a boulder large enough to obliterate the sky above her.

Sky … that didn't make sense. Rock … the fortress ceiling had collapsed on me. Though the earthquake had apparently abated.

"Move your ass, dowser!" Kandy shrieked. She was shaking with the effort of holding the boulder off me.

My survival instincts kicked in. I rolled. The rock slammed down exactly where I'd been lying.

I sat up to see Kandy collapse. She fell, first to her knees, then all the way over onto her side and a craggy pile of massive chunks of granite.

"Sorry," she whispered. "I couldn't hold it."

Then she stopped talking.

I crawled to her. My hands and arms were the only part of me that seemed to be working, so it was slow going. I left bloody handprints in my wake. I got halfway to her before the bones in my left leg had knit together enough that I thought they might be able to help. My right leg was still useless, though. The one the dragon kid kicked.

"Kandy?" I whispered. I could taste the werewolf's magic, but it was as dim as it had ever been. Beyond that, I could taste only the magic of the braids that were still tied around my left wrist, and the magic of the cuffs that Kandy wore. No kid and no Warner, though I had the distinct impression that my magic was concentrating on healing bones and mending lacerations, not on dowsing. So they could both have been nearby.

I reached Kandy. I could see the slow, steady rise of her chest, so she wasn't dead. Her arms were sprawled out to the side. I don't think she'd even tried to stop her fall. Her palms looked like hunks of bloody, shredded meat.

I lifted her into my arms, somehow finding my feet despite the fact that my legs didn't feel whole yet. She was too light. I'd carried her like this in London and she'd been epically heavy for someone so tiny. But then, a lot had happened since London, and my magic was different now. I'd been so badly hurt in Sienna's final circle — had used so much of myself to contain her magic in my sword — that when my magic came back, it was as if it filled up all the empty spaces and burrowed even deeper into my flesh and bones.

"Why are you carrying me like a baby?" Kandy murmured.

"I didn't like you lying on the ground," I answered.

"That's no excuse."

"You dug me out."

"What did you think the cuffs were for?" Kandy sneered, which was an impressive feat when she hadn't actually opened her eyes yet. "Yoga?"

I coughed out a laugh, along with a mouthful of blood.

"Eww," Kandy said, opening her blazing green eyes. "Did you just spit blood up on me? Put me down."

I tried to prop Kandy up on her legs, but she was having some trouble taking any weight on them. "Umm," she said. "Just put me over there for second. I don't think I can stand up yet." I set her down, half propped up on one of the large jutting slabs of the floor … or maybe it was a piece of ceiling. I couldn't tell. The place was a dangerous freaking mess.

"Just because you can lift heavy things with the cuffs doesn't mean your legs can take the weight," I snarled, suddenly irrationally angry that Kandy was even in this situation.

"What are you, my mother?"

"You're hurt, and —"

"And you feel bad, like usual. I thought I was a member of this team?"

"You are, but —"

"Get your shit together, dowser. Find the sentinel and get us out of here."

I clenched my jaw and then my fists. Happily, they both seemed to be working just fine now. Counting to ten in my head, I looked around at the caved-in disaster area that was the fortress.

Yeah, look at me being all grown up again.

The dais and the altar were gone. I couldn't even see where they'd once been.

"Did you see where he fell?" I asked Kandy.

She shook her head but seemed more interested in breathing than in talking. Her berry-infused dark-chocolate magic intensified. I took that as a sign that she was going to be okay.

I hoisted myself up on the next section of jutted floor, careful to avoid falling into the chasm that looked as though it dropped into nowhere on the other side. Apparently the entire ceiling hadn't collapsed — just the center section. I could see darkness above, but it didn't feel like sky — no stars and no fresh air. I couldn't see the entrance, if it even still existed.

No kid. No shadows.

And my freaking right leg still wasn't functioning properly.

"Sentinel!" I yelled. Then I waited, but there was no answer. Not even an echo of my call. "Something's coming," I muttered. I didn't like the stillness of the air, or the lack of magic. Though that wasn't new, since it had felt stripped away since we stepped through the lighthouse doorway.

"You've ruined that pretty skirt." Kandy shifted into a seated position behind me and then slowly rose to her feet.

I glanced down at my skirt. It was covered in blood — Kandy's and mine, I guessed — and shredded in numerous places. I was also missing my flip-flops. Thankfully, I still seemed to have my satchel.

"At least the blood matches," I said.

Kandy snorted. Then, painfully slowly, she climbed up onto the boulder opposite me to look toward where the entrance had been.

"Warner!" I shouted again.

A pile of rocks on the other side of where the altar had stood shifted. I clambered down the side of my perch, then leaped over a fissure between me and the shifting rocks. As soon as my feet touched down on the granite on the other side, I could taste Warner's black-forest-cake magic. Further evidence that the entire fortress somehow absorbed magic, or dulled it, or something.

I could feel Kandy following, but she was still unsteady on her feet and moving slowly. I crushed the spike of fear I felt when glancing back at her. We'd get out of here and she'd heal. I'd take her to Qiuniu if necessary, though owing too many favors to the Brazilian guardian probably wasn't a fantastic idea. I was fairly certain it wasn't cupcakes he wanted in trade.

I reached Warner where he'd half-dug himself out of the rubble of the floor and ceiling. Though he was covered in rock dust, he didn't appear to have a scratch on him. Of course.

I grabbed his arm and hauled him the rest of the way out. He groaned in pain but did most of the work on his own. I wasn't sure I could have moved him any other way. He tried to stand, swayed, and then fell against the nearest pile of rubble.

"Legs broken," he said. "Long fall ... the climb up wasn't short either." Then he lifted his head as if hearing something.

I glanced around but I couldn't hear anything. However, Kandy was perched on the far side of the fissure from us and was looking around as well. Beyond her, I could see where the entrance had once stood. It was blocked by a cave-in now.

"What's that?" she called.

"Water," Warner muttered. He straightened and, oddly, twined his fingers through those of my right hand.

"I might need that hand," I joked.

"Is that ... water?" Kandy called. She was looking back toward the blocked entrance.

I still couldn't hear anything.

"We need an exit, wolf. Now," Warner said. "Fresh air would be the best indication of one."

Kandy lifted her head as green rolled over her eyes. Then she pointed toward a half-collapsed wall behind us, where I could see only rock piled on more rock. Kandy began climbing down the boulder she'd been perched on. The large fissure was still between her and us.

Then I heard the water. A rushing sound like a thundering tide.

"Not a tide ..." I said, voicing my fear out loud. "A river."

Rock and debris blew open the former entrance behind Kandy. Water flooded into the chamber.

"Kandy!" I screamed as I lunged forward. She was poised to leap the chasm before her, but I could tell she wasn't going to make the jump. Warner held me back, so firmly that my right shoulder actually dislocated with a pop and a flash of pain.

The torrential flood — boiling with all the rock and debris it had gathered in its path — crashed into Kandy in midair.

Still fighting Warner, I lost sight of my friend. The water hit us at waist height, with more continuing to flood into the chamber.

I was still screaming and fighting when the sentinel picked me up, then threw me toward the back wall like I was a freaking football. I flew toward the opening that Kandy had scented, just as the water burst through three more sections of the ruined fortress and crashed into Warner.

I hit rock, cracked my head, and was swallowed by the flood.

I was dreaming. A floating, peaceful dream. I felt free, weightless, and warm. I was enveloped and held lovingly by a warm blanket of ... water.

Water.

I was surrounded by water.

I opened my eyes.

I was surrounded by endless blue. Blue ... blue ... salty water.

Peacefully slipping away in the deep, deep water.

And I couldn't breathe.

I shouldn't breathe.

I was drowning.

I was dying, actually.

I screamed, involuntarily thrashed my arms and legs, and instantly knew that was the wrong thing to do. I snapped my mouth closed in an attempt to preserve whatever oxygen still filled my lungs. Pain lanced through my chest as my body demanded more air.

I kicked out with my legs. I didn't know where to go, what to do, but this couldn't be it. This couldn't be the end.

Then I remembered.

Just before the synapses of my brain fizzed out from oxygen deprivation, I remembered Chi Wen brushing by me in the nexus. I remembered the glimpse of the vision he'd shared with me. I remembered the instance of drowning.

I remembered breaking through into the sunshine.

I kicked again. I lifted my arms up and over my head and pulled myself through the water, having no idea if I was going in the correct direction.

I had to believe.

I had to trust.

If I was going to carry the yoke of destiny like a freaking albatross — if I was going to run scared from fate, even as I blindly stepped forward onto its path — then I was going to believe, going to trust the far seer. I was going to trust in magic. Trust in the spirit that flowed through us all, as Gran would say after too many chocolate chip cookies.

My fingers broke through into unresisting air, slapping down against the surface of the water as my head followed through into sunlight.

I breathed, gasping for air. Coughing and choking on the water I inhaled in my haste.

A hand grasped my left wrist. A shock of smoky dragon magic flashed through my senses.

Not dragon. Guardian.

"Pulou," I gasped, looking up through the mop of wet curls that obscured my vision. The treasure keeper was hunched down, holding me from a portal that hovered about three feet above the water.

He was peering down at my wrist, but didn't seem to be all that surprised to be holding me half out of the water in the middle of the Bahamas. "Are you wearing one of the three ways to kill a guardian — an ancient relic of grave importance — as a bracelet? A now soaking-wet bracelet?"

His proper English accent made his casually posed question seem like a scathing condemnation.

"Umm," I said. "You didn't actually mention the guardian killing part."

Warner broke through the surface of the water beside me. Kandy was in his arms.

I wasn't sure she was breathing.

Without even thinking about it, I wrenched my arm from Pulou's grasp and threw my head back to scream into the golden magic of the portal.

"Qiuniu!"

Warner lifted Kandy up out of the water and Pulou knelt down to take her from him.

"Qiuniu!" I screamed again.

The treasure keeper stepped back into the golden magic of the portal as Warner somehow grabbed the edge of the portal like it was a physical object and hoisted himself out of the water. Kneeling, he spun to reach back for me. I grasped his hand and heaved myself up. My heart thumped wildly in my chest. I hadn't quite caught my breath from drowning, and now I wasn't sure I was ever going to be able to breathe naturally again.

Warner and I tumbled back into the dragon nexus in a tangle of limbs and slid across the floor.

"Kandy ... Kandy ... Kandy ..." I realized I was repeating my friend's name over and over in time with my heartbeat, so I clamped my mouth shut.

Qiuniu was already standing over Kandy, who was supine on the floor at the exact center of the nine nexus doors. Pulou stood to one side with his hands on his head as though he didn't know what else to do.

I scrambled forward, not bothering to stand. Qiuniu lifted his beautiful brown eyes to me.

"She's too far gone," he said.

The words warped around in my head as I refused to actually hear them.

As if to confirm Qiuniu's terminal diagnosis, the cuffs fell off Kandy's wrists with two terribly audible clicks.

"No!" I shouted. "No!"

I shoved past the healer, gaining my feet as I did so. He fell to the side with a surprised grunt. I gathered the green-haired werewolf in my arms. "No! No! No!" I repeated the word over and over, forcing my denial of the possibility of Kandy's demise into the ears of all the magical witnesses in the vicinity.

Kandy was a child of the magic that ran through us all. And that magic wasn't ready to let this vessel go.

"Warrior's daughter —" I could hear the attempt at reason in the healer's voice.

"I can still taste her magic!" I snapped at him, not even remotely caring that one didn't shove past guardians and then shriek demands in their faces.

Qiuniu shook his head sadly.

But not sadly enough for me.

"Portland," I said. I stood, still unsteady on my feet but buoyed by my anger. Epically angry and determined.

"Where?" Pulou asked, his question gentle.

"Desmond ... the Alpha's home."

"I don't know where that is ..." Pulou said.

Ignoring him, I turned toward the native-carved door.

"Jade," Qiuniu said behind me.

"She needs the magic of the pack! Portland!"

Pulou stepped up behind me and wrapped his hand around my upper left arm. The door to North America blew open before me. "Show me," the treasure keeper said as we stepped together into the golden magic of the portal.

I could feel Qiuniu and Warner following us. And I momentarily panicked. I was dragging all of us into magic I couldn't actually control. What happened if we got lost in here?

Pulou squeezed my arm. It hurt. "Focus, Jade Godfrey." I heard him in my head rather than with my ears. "Take us to the pack."

I visualized Desmond's living room. The massive stone fireplace, the large trestle dining room table, the perfect chef's kitchen ... I wondered if he'd fixed the granite island that he'd broken when I'd come to read Rochelle's oracle magic last January ...

Pulou grunted, satisfied.

And we tumbled out of the golden magic into Desmond Charles Llewelyn's living room.

I knew we were going to scare the shit out of any member of the West Coast North American Pack in the house at the time. But Kandy's life was worth potentially getting torn limb from limb by the teeth and claws of her pack mates.

Even with Pulou's hand at my back, I landed on Desmond's square glass coffee table on my knees, shattering it. You'd think Desmond would have replaced it with something sturdier after it had gotten smashed in January, during Kandy and Audrey's dominance fight.

Pulou dragged me to my feet by the back of my still-soaking-wet tank top. It hurt like hell, mostly because my right leg was still acting like it was shattered beyond repair. I kept hold of Kandy and tried desperately to ignore the fact that she wasn't breathing.

Pulou drew a nasty-looking blade with a gigantic emerald embedded in the center of its guard — the magic of which momentarily warped my eyesight. He slid one leg through the shattered glass in front of me as a seven-foot-tall monster with double fangs burst into the room from the west wing of the house.

McGrowly had arrived.

He chucked the couch out of his way as he barreled toward us. It crashed through two of the huge living room windows.

A just-as-tall werewolf in half-beast form appeared behind him. Her pelt was dark gray, her eyes blazing green. Her canines were almost as long as McGrowly's, and just as sharp.

Hello, Audrey.

McGrowly — stupidly — attacked Pulou, who backhanded him almost nonchalantly across the face. He flew past where the couch had been and slammed into the wooden trestle table in the open dining room. As massive as the table was, it cracked in half underneath McGrowly's weight.

Audrey snarled fiercely, but stopped a few feet back to assess the situation. She always was a quick learner.

Warner and Qiuniu stepped out of the portal behind us and it snapped shut.

Only seconds had passed.

A snarl from McGrowly rippled through the room as he pulled himself off the ruins of his dining room table.

Heedless of his aggression, I stepped forward with Kandy in my arms. Audrey moved to intercept me.

"Open your eyes, wolf," I snapped.

She backed off. McGrowly stepped forward, his magic rolling up and around him as he transformed into his human visage. His T-shirt was seriously stretched to hell, but nothing mattered now except Kandy.

"Please," I said. I begged. "Please." Faced with the fierce scowl etched across Desmond's granite-like features, I couldn't manage to articulate anything else.

He took Kandy from me without a word, turning to lay her on the granite kitchen island in a fluid motion. Without her weight to hold me — to give me purpose — I fell to my knees.

Audrey stepped around me, transforming into her human self as she joined Desmond.

"Call the pack," he barked at her. He ran his hand over Kandy's forehead, down the sides of her face, and to her shoulders. He rested his hand against her chest above her heart … her agonizingly still heart.

Audrey threw her head back and howled inhumanly. The undulating noise entered my ears and rattled my brain.

The front door burst open, and two people I didn't recognize barreled through. Three more joined the group in the kitchen from deeper inside the house, including Lara of the bee-stung lips. I assumed the shifters were already in position, waiting in reserve against the attack Desmond and Audrey thought they'd been facing. I barely saw or felt them, though. I could only see

Kandy's profile. Her wet green hair was slicked to her forehead. Her eyes were closed, perhaps forever.

Qiuniu stepped up behind me and brushed his fingers through my curls. His healing magic — accompanied by the sweet music that always followed him — flooded through me.

My anger returned in a savage rush to shock me out of my premature mourning. "Not me," I snapped as I slapped the healer's hand away.

Warner moaned as if I might have just signed my own death warrant. And maybe I had. But for Kandy, I'd walk through hell with no way back. She'd done the same for me, more than once.

I swallowed my anger, nearly choking on it, as I felt the pack magic that Desmond commanded rise in a swirl around Kandy. I spun, still partially kneeling in the shattered glass of Desmond's coffee table, and took Qiuniu's hand — the one I'd just slapped.

"Healer." I pressed my lips to the back of that hand. "Anything. Anything you can do to aid the pack. Please."

"Life is a gift," he said. "And I'm no god."

"She is strong, so strong," I whispered into his warm skin. "She was injured in service to the guardian nine."

"A service of utmost consequence," Pulou said behind me. His tone was even, as if he was simply verifying information and not trying to influence the outcome.

"She … I can still taste her magic," I continued. "She's still here. Please. I would do anything. I would trade my life for hers if I could. Please."

"Thankfully that isn't an option, Jade Godfrey." Qiuniu sounded angry, but he shook off my hold and stepped around me to approach the gathering of shapeshifters at the kitchen island.

Soft melodic music rose to dance among the pack magic whirling around Kandy. Qiuniu's toasted-coffee-and-Brazilian-chocolate magic joined the healing magic I'd seen Desmond call from the pack to heal Lara more than a year ago.

Warner stepped up beside me. I hadn't risen from my knees, though Qiuniu had healed my leg with his brief touch. "You make deals with guardians that you can only hope to uphold," he said. He didn't sound accusatory. Just matter-of-fact.

"Thankfully, all we ask in return is her very best," Pulou said.

I didn't take my eyes off Kandy on the kitchen island. More shapeshifters had arrived, filtering one at a time in through the front door without a single glance at the strangers in the living room. They'd linked hands and formed a circle around the island, encircling Kandy between Desmond and Qiuniu. The healer stood with his eyes closed and one of his hands on the crown of Kandy's head. He'd placed his second hand over Desmond's, both of them touching Kandy's chest over her heart.

"How long …" I murmured. "How long can the brain be oxygen deprived?"

Magic undulated around Kandy in a whirl of gold and green. It settled down over her like a gossamer blanket.

She opened her eyes and screamed, "Jade!"

Then she began to convulse.

Desmond snarled and rolled her over onto her side.

I started crying, not realizing that I hadn't been before. Loud, ragged sobs tore through me and out of my throat.

Qiuniu lifted his gaze to meet mine. He still looked angry, but then he smiled tightly. With a nod, he stepped away from the shapeshifters. The circle closed behind him.

Desmond was crooning to Kandy, whispering, "Come, little wolf. Change for me. Come, wolf."

Kandy continued to convulse.

I rose. Brushing shoulders with Qiuniu as I passed, I stepped up to the island and reached through the swaying shapeshifters to place my hand on Kandy's back. She was still in the midst of some sort of seizure. Her muscles were taut with what felt like unbearable tension.

"Kandy," I said. My voice cracked, and I was suddenly afraid I wouldn't get the words out through the sobs that still lurked in my throat. Words that I needed to say. "Kandy," I repeated. "You saved me. Me and Warner. Mission accomplished. We got the treasure. Come back, my friend. Come back to me."

Kandy stilled. Then her blazing green, berry-infused dark-chocolate shapeshifter magic rolled over her. She transformed into a gray wolf.

I backed away.

Her metamorphosis looked painful. Even Desmond lifted his hands away from her as she transformed.

Desmond looked at me, then. The first time he'd acknowledged my presence at all. Green flecks of his magic still whirled in his topaz-brown eyes. "Go now, Jade," he whispered. "I can't look at you."

Then he gathered Kandy into his arms and walked out of the kitchen, surrounded by his pack.

"Stay," Audrey murmured as she passed by me to follow him. "Kandy will want to see you. She'll need to see you in order to concentrate on her own healing. Desmond will sleep soon enough."

She walked away without another glance. Behind her, Lara wrapped her arms around me in a crushing hug before jogging off to join the rest of her pack.

Then I was alone in Desmond's thoroughly trashed living room with the dragons.

"Was it worth it, then?" Qiuniu asked quietly, but he wasn't speaking to me. He sounded weary. I'm not sure I'd ever heard a guardian sound even slightly diminished before.

Pulou nodded. "The warrior's daughter has completed her first task."

"First?" I asked. "What the hell were all the other retrievals?" I felt lightheaded — epically empty. So much so that my voice sounded disembodied to my own ears.

"First of three. If the myths hold true," Pulou answered. He looked at Warner. The sentinel shook his head wearily, as if he didn't know anything anymore. "The other retrievals were training."

"I'm not sure anything qualifies as training for what we just did. Without Kandy, I'd be trapped underneath thousands of pounds of rock. Then I would have drowned. Without Warner, Kandy would be dead."

Pulou inclined his head without answering. Then he held a golden diamond-encrusted box toward me. Its lid was hinged open and ready.

I stepped forward, loosening the knot of the ribbons I'd tied around my wrist as I did so. I lifted the five-colored silk braids before me, the three of them still twisted together into one. With them held aloft, I could taste their sorcerer-alchemist magic much more intensely. That magic thrummed contentedly with its joyful, deadly power, despite almost being lost at sea.

Qiuniu hissed and recoiled. "I didn't feel that before."

Pulou and Warner gritted their teeth.

"The alchemist's magic acts like a shield. A buffer," Pulou said, as if this talent was common knowledge and not something I'd just figured out with the map and the shadow demons myself.

I dropped the tangled braids into the golden box and Pulou snapped its lid shut with a shudder.

"Then the warrior's daughter is the only one who could wield such a weapon without our knowledge," Qiuniu said.

"If that were so, then the guardians would be at no risk," Pulou responded.

Qiuniu nodded. He hadn't stopped staring at me since I'd turned to face them in the living room. Though I couldn't read his exact expression, it held no hint of his usual flirty admiration.

"Thank you, healer," I said. "I'm indebted to you."

"It is the wolf who holds that burden now," he said mildly.

I lifted my chin defiantly. "Then I accept the debt, twofold." Some kind of dragon-scented magic shifted between us as if held at the ready, but it didn't settle.

Warner sighed.

Pulou laughed. "The warrior's daughter is not an easy protection duty, sentinel. Are you still on task?"

"Always," Warner answered.

Portal magic bloomed and grew behind Pulou. Qiuniu turned without another word and walked into its golden wash. The magic that had risen between us stretched as he did so, thinning to almost nothing as the portal magic swallowed the healer. He hadn't accepted the debt I'd claimed, but I wondered if he could call upon it at whim now.

Pulou reached into his pockets and pulled out Kandy's cuffs. "These belong to the wolf. She's more than earned them today."

"She's done her duty."

"These were a gift from the far seer," Pulou said. "And not for you to return."

I took the cuffs from him.

Pulou turned and walked into the golden magic of the portal. "Let that be the wolf's choice, Jade." His voice once again sounded in my head, not my ears. The magic of the portal obviously facilitated a level of telepathy among the dragons … and me, I guessed.

The portal swallowed the treasure keeper from my sight.

"I'll let you see to your friend," Warner said. His tone was formal, as was his slight bow.

"Yeah," I answered. "Okay."

He touched my cheek so lightly that I probably wouldn't have felt it, except for the taste of black forest cake that came with it. The tense knot in my chest eased a bit. I looked up to meet his green eyes and he smiled at me. "Kandy is blessed to have you as a friend."

"This isn't the first time I've almost gotten her killed."

"And she chooses to remain by your side. She wouldn't do so unless she wanted to be there. Dangerous beauty, tasty magic, and all. As the wolf would say."

Then he turned and walked into the portal.

The magic snapped closed behind him. I felt bereft without its warm glow to comfort me.

I felt alone.

And, no matter how childish it probably was, I felt like I deserved to be alone.

Chapter Thirteen

I straightened the couch and swept up the broken glass of the coffee table as best I could. I didn't cut myself. But then, I didn't expect to. I was tougher, harder than that now, as if I was coated in my inherited dragon magic. But that didn't explain why my heart still felt so mangled. Magic only healed wounds, not souls.

I didn't bake, though I seriously wanted to soothe my aching heart. It wasn't my kitchen. It was never going to be my kitchen, and I was okay with that. I had my own home.

Plus, some part of me knew I really didn't deserve to be soothed. I had dragged Kandy treasure hunting numerous times in the last ten months, and we had come out relatively unscathed. She relished the hunt almost as much as I did. Almost.

I should have known this one would be different. The first freaking clue was tattooed on the skin of a former guardian, after all.

I went out and sat on the front stoop. I had no idea what time it was in Portland. The sun had been in the west when Pulou pulled us out of the ocean, so even though time hadn't seemed to exist in the magic pocket of the fortress it, had continued in the actual world.

That would make it midafternoon here, I thought. Portland was still warm in September, with a lovely, light breeze playing across the laurel hedges that blocked the views of the house from the street.

I was exhausted.

I could taste the individual magic of all the shapeshifters in the house behind me. Including Kandy's, which was stronger than before but still so much weaker than I'd ever tasted.

"Diluted," I murmured. "The leeches." We'd thought the shadow demons had been after the map. Then we'd thought they'd been after the braids, except … except they hadn't tried to take the artifact from me. Not that I could remember, anyway.

'Scouts,' Warner had called them. I'd jumped to the conclusion that demon shadow scouts would be scouting for some other demon looking to break through into our dimension. But there had to be some connection between the way they'd leeched magic from us and the diluted magic of the fortress.

The door opened behind me. I'd already felt Audrey approaching, and knew that she'd hesitated before stepping outside. Maybe steeling herself before dealing with me. The beta werewolf's magic was a cool white-chocolate mint. Like the iced tea I'd made from the plant I'd grown on my balcony this year. She settled down beside me and lifted her face to the sun, her eyes closed, her brunette waves cascading elegantly down her back.

"Those were the most powerful beings I've ever scented." She meant Warner, Pulou, and Qiuniu.

"You've met Qiuniu. He brought you part of the way back on the beach in Tofino. After you sacrificed yourself to save Kandy's life."

Audrey laughed softly. "You have a romanticized view of the world, alchemist. I fought because my pack needed me. It's my duty and my privilege."

"And now you're beta, with even more responsibility and personal peril."

"Again, you think you hold some responsibility for that. You think that none of us would have been on that beach without you. Your ego is massive."

"I made the knife that Sienna used —"

Audrey snorted. "Spare me. I was there. I chose to be there. Just like Kandy chose to be with you wherever you just came from."

"Shoving that opinion down my throat seems to be the theme of the day."

Audrey turned toward me as she opened her eyes. "Then chew it, swallow, and move on." She regarded me through slits of gleaming green, and for the first time since we'd met, I was the one to break my gaze from hers.

Audrey lifted her face back up to the sun. "I don't remember," she murmured. "I don't remember Desmond making me beta." She sounded sad, and I was seriously surprised she hadn't bothered to rub in the fact that I'd just backed down from a fight. "I remember you falling to the black witch. And the four of us trying to break through her circle to you. Desmond, Kandy, me, and the vampire. But without the protection of the witches, the sea demons were overrunning the shapeshifters on the beach and I had to turn back. I don't remember much after that. Except waking up to find the pack tied through me to Desmond."

I waited for her to continue, but she didn't. This was the longest civilized conversation we'd ever had, and I wondered if it was Audrey or me who'd changed and made that possible.

"You will always be a friend of the pack," she said, abruptly changing the subject.

"Are you breaking up with me, Audrey?"

She laughed, a low, husky sound. I didn't think I'd ever heard anything resembling pure amusement without an edge from her before. "Kandy will need to stay," she said.

"I know."

"She won't heal properly any other way. Six months, maybe more."

"I know."

"You'll have to convince her. And ... after today, I wouldn't advise you to visit. Not right away. Christmas maybe, if Desmond goes to his parents'."

"She's my friend."

"We take our friendships very seriously in the pack, alchemist. We understand loyalty. But Desmond ..."

"Is angry."

"For now. But you returned Kandy to us, so balance will eventually be restored."

"If I stay away."

"For now."

Silence fell between us. Normally, that would have bothered me. Normally, I would bristle against anything that came out of Audrey's mouth. But I knew she was right.

"Thank you, beta," I said, acknowledging the vital role that Audrey seemed to be settling into well.

"Till next time, alchemist," Audrey said, baring her teeth at me in an arrogant display of aggression. "And maybe you could be more careful of the furniture?"

I laughed. That was the Audrey I'd expected.

"I'd like to see Kandy before I go."

"Then Lara will drive you to the portal."

Audrey stood in one fluid movement that I could never hope to emulate, dragon training or no dragon training. So I didn't even try as I followed her into the house. She turned right toward the guest wing. I noticed she was barefoot, and just barely managed to stop myself from remarking on the opal polish that prettified her toes and stood out against the dark walnut flooring of the hall. I was ninety-five percent sure it was OPI's *I'm a Princess, You're Not*, which was a go-to favorite of mine. But Audrey wasn't a friend, and I didn't want to risk getting my eyes gouged out over nail polish.

An hour ago, Audrey had been a seven-foot, toothy, terrifying monster, but I couldn't see a hint of it on her now. Whereas my hair had dried in fuzzy clumps of curls. My skirt and tank top were water stained and ripped. I had no idea where my shoes were. And I still wasn't ready to acknowledge my ruined satchel.

But even as those thoughts popped into my head to distract me, I knew none of that mattered. That was just silly busywork for my mind, so I didn't have to anticipate the next moment more than my wrenched gut already did.

Audrey led me to one of the guest bedrooms halfway down the hall at the front of the house, but she didn't enter after she opened the door.

"Desmond's sleeping," she whispered. "But you shouldn't linger."

"The warrior's daughter doesn't take orders from you, beta," Kandy snapped from inside the bedroom.

A massive grin spread across my face as I dashed into the room. Audrey chuckled behind me and closed the door.

Kandy was lying in the center of a king-sized bed. She had the emerald-green duvet tucked up to her chin and underneath her bare arms. Her hair was mousy brown. She looked like she'd lost ten pounds that she couldn't afford to lose.

"You look terrible," she said. Then she offered me one of her nonsmiles.

I started to sit in the green brocade chair beside the bed, then changed my mind. I tossed my ruined satchel to the chair instead, crawling onto the bed beside her.

"Good girl," she murmured, her words suddenly heavy with sleep.

Careful to not actually touch her, I curled up close, nestling my head on the second pillow. I closed my eyes to listen to the deep, full sound of her breath.

I drifted.

I woke. Maybe ten minutes had passed ... the filtered afternoon light in the room hadn't changed. Yeah, I noticed things like that now.

Kandy was sleeping. I eased off the bed, pulled the strap of my satchel over my head and shoulder, and carefully placed the cuffs from Chi Wen on the side table.

"I'm going to be out of commission for a while," Kandy murmured, though she didn't open her eyes.

"We'll Skype."

She laughed quietly. "I mean the cuffs. You should take them. Keep them safe."

"They're yours."

"One doesn't accept gifts from dragons lightly."

"No."

"I didn't, Jade." Kandy opened her eyes to lock her gaze to me. She looked as exhausted as I'd felt before the nap. Weak and utterly determined.

"I know."

Kandy nodded and closed her eyes again. Her breathing fell into that deep rhythm almost instantly.

"Sleep well, my friend," I whispered. Then I turned to the door.

"Give him a chance," Kandy said behind me. "The sentinel. He's no Hudson, but he'll do."

"That's high praise from you."

"Yep." She laughed.

I waited until the sound faded away before I closed the door behind me.

Desmond was waiting for me in the entranceway. I could taste his magic from Kandy's room. His citrus-finished dark chocolate was easily at half strength. Moreover, the taste didn't comfort me as it once had, when for an ever-so-brief moment I'd thought I might find a haven in his arms.

A haven from the terror that my sister had wrought in my life.

The realization that I didn't need that from him — from anyone but myself — hit me as his gaunt face came into view. The magic he'd expended to heal Kandy had hardened his visage further. Maybe even eaten away at him.

His eyes glittered with shifter magic and animosity, but I didn't feel like smirking at all the cracks that had suddenly appeared in his armor. He was usually so political, so careful to protect his alliances, his investments. But now he was eager to kick my ass. Warrior's daughter or no warrior's daughter.

"I absolve you," he said.

That stopped me in my tracks. "Excuse me?"

"You heard me."

"What, are you a priest now?"

He glowered at me, clenching and unclenching his hands.

"Imagining strangling me isn't going to help with whatever lame diplomacy you're going for, Desmond."

He growled. A low rumble that spread through the entranceway. I swear I could feel the granite tiles vibrating underneath my bare feet.

"You invaded my home —"

"You thought I invaded your home."

"Who was that dragon?" He didn't mean Pulou or Qiuniu. He'd already met or seen both of them in Tofino ten months ago.

He couldn't figure out if he wanted to strangle me for almost getting Kandy killed, or whether he wanted to own me. He was still jealous. Jesus, shapeshifters and their freaking territory issues.

"You mean Warner," I answered. "The guy who saved Kandy's life."

"The life you put in jeopardy."

"No."

Desmond looked as surprised as I felt at my denial.

"No?"

"No." The second time I said it, I felt the truth of it. We all made choices. We all did our best. Warner, Audrey, and Kandy were right. It was utterly egotistical of me to take the blame for everything bad that ever happened around me. I wasn't a god. I wasn't the devil or some minion of evil. I was simply Jade Godfrey, half-witch, half-dragon, baker of cupcakes, treasure hunter, and warrior's daughter. That was more than enough mantles for one person.

Desmond and I stared at each other until Audrey appeared in the hall behind her alpha, looking anxious.

And not just for the furniture. All three of us knew that Desmond couldn't take me in a fair fight — and that I wouldn't submit to his authority, with or without one.

"So ... Lara is cool to drive me to the portal?" I asked.

Desmond nodded and stepped away from the front door. I resisted the urge to punch him in the gut. You know, just to prove I didn't need his permission to exit.

"Thank you for bringing our pack mate back to us," Audrey said. Her tone was cool and formal as she closed the gap between her and Desmond. "We will meet again."

"Far too soon," Desmond snapped. Then he turned his back on me and walked away.

Well, that was that.

I could hear an SUV idling in the driveway. I locked my gaze to Audrey's. She smiled. Yeah, there was no love lost between us, but she was even more political than Desmond. I'd just tumbled into the living room with an impossible amount of power and prestige at my back. Audrey knew gold when she smelled it.

I had a bunch of nasty things I wanted to say, childish denials of guilt and whatever. Instead, I nodded. "I thank the pack for its hospitality, and for taking care of my friend."

Audrey nodded back, though she lost the smile.

I thought my formality disappointed her somehow. Perhaps I didn't conform to the box she'd shoved me into and labeled in her mind.

I left.

I didn't look back. But I did text Kandy a chocolate bar emoticon on the drive to the portal from Lara's phone, tagging it with the letter J. Sure, Kandy's cell was probably completely fried from the portal magic and the double near-drownings — like mine was — but I already missed her. She'd get the message the first time she booted up her new phone.

Anyway, I left my best friend to heal her wounds, surrounded by the magic and care of her pack family. I was going to miss her terribly, but I tried to not be sad about it. Kandy would kick my ass if she found me moping.

Chapter Fourteen

A dragon was cooking pancakes in my apartment kitchen. Badly. I could see — even before I'd fully entered the living room — that half of his first attempts were burnt and tossed to the side. He was currently undercooking the second batch.

He'd gotten past my wards somehow. Though as they folded around me, I could feel that they were intact. So he hadn't damaged them to get into the apartment.

I stopped. Just stopped right there at the top of the stairs that led down to the bakery. The door, the exit, was still open behind me. The living room and the kitchen island were between me and Warner at the stove.

I could turn around. I could walk away. I wasn't sure that thought had ever occurred to me before. I could leave the map and the responsibility of it to Warner. It was his job — his sworn duty — after all. I wasn't even a full-blooded dragon. No one would question me taking a step back. No one would question that I hadn't realized the burden I'd accepted when I'd taken the map from Pulou.

A map that led to artifacts that could be used to kill guardian dragons.

My ruined satchel was suddenly epically heavy. I pulled it off over my head, then dropped it to the worn hardwood floor beside me. I thought about taking two steps and face-planting onto my leather couch, but I didn't feel like moving any farther.

Warner lifted his attention from the raw dough in the frying pan and turned his head to catch my gaze. "The wolf?" he asked.

"She'll live. Thank you."

He raised an eyebrow. "You don't thank me, alchemist. We all do our parts. It's been a long time since I've worked as part of a team. I'll do better next time."

I didn't respond. Though the words 'next time' were literally rattling around in my empty head.

He flipped the pancake. It broke, oozing raw dough everywhere. He grumbled as he scraped the frying pan clean in the kitchen sink.

The sentinel had placed the sacrificial knife he'd 'borrowed' in the fortress on the granite counter of my kitchen island. Returning it to me, unasked. Returning the responsibility of my own creation.

I should move. I should shower. I should strip off my ruined clothing. I should find some shoes. I should fix the safe and get the map and knife locked away. If I was going to continue forward, I should be asking questions, demanding answers.

I did none of those things.

I watched Warner adjust the heat of the element and spoon more batter into the frying pan. He had one of my old cookbooks open on the kitchen counter between the stove and the fridge. The one I always went to first, so much so that its binding was broken and its pages of recipes were really just a pile of loose printed paper.

I wondered why he'd chosen that cookbook over all the fancy hardcovers I had shoved away in the cupboard above the overhead fan. Yeah, people bought me cookbooks, which I guess made sense. But I always preferred fine chocolate as a go-to gift.

"Your mother and grandmother are at a coven meeting," Warner said without looking up from his cooking.

"Did Scarlett let you in?" I thought I'd adjusted the wards enough that I was the only one who could invite — or uninvite — Adepts into the apartment.

Warner looked up at that, surprised. "No," he said. "You did." Then he laid a blazing, sexy-as-hell grin on me. Like he could smile like that every day ... at me. Warmth curled in my belly.

"The kiss," I murmured as I clicked together the pieces of the puzzle that his chameleon magic presented. He borrowed. He adapted, like the ability to change his accent or clothing. That was a bit of alchemy in itself — though he transformed himself, not magical objects as I did.

Here, he'd obviously absorbed the bit of my magic that he'd gotten while kissing me, and had used it to pass through my wards. I certainly had invited him.

Warner's grin widened, turning intimate and smoldering before he laughed and returned his attention to the pancakes.

For some reason, I felt like moving again. I sauntered over to the kitchen island and climbed up on a stool to prop my chin on my hands.

This third batch of pancakes looked perfectly edible. His ability to absorb new situations, learn languages, and adapt in general was impressive. He was my complete opposite. I had to be beaten over the head before I absorbed any important information.

Warner deemed these pancakes acceptable and put them in the oven to keep them warm. Someone had obviously read more of the cookbook than just the pancake recipe.

"The shadow demons," I said, even though I would have sworn I wasn't remotely interested in talking about anything of substance. "I think they stripped the magic from the fortress. Like magical leeches. Maybe even weakening it so much that the pocket that hid the fortress collapsed when we tried to remove the instrument."

"Or the earthquake was the final trap laid by the sorcerers who built the fortress."

"It could have been. Except then, how would we have wound up in the ocean without walking back through the doorway or deliberately cutting another exit through the barrier?"

Warner nodded thoughtfully while flipping another round of pancakes.

"But the leeches couldn't touch the braids," I said, continuing to voice my thoughts out loud. "Or wouldn't."

"I think you're right."

"So they weren't trying to take the map."

"Just attracted to its magic."

"Or to the key it held?"

"Yes."

"For who? You said they were demon scouts. In the service of what sorcerer? If they're a form of demon, then they've been called to this dimension, but by who?"

Warner frowned. "Dimension?"

"That's how my father explained demons to me. Not of this world."

Warner nodded. "The corpses," he said.

I didn't immediately follow what seemed like a change of subject. Then I remembered London, and

Sienna calling demons forth through the sorcerers. While they were still alive.

"The skeletons of the sorcerers in the fortress," I said thoughtfully. "Willingly sacrificed before each magical trap. Did you show Pulou the runes?"

"Not yet."

"Because I still have them." I'd tucked them in my satchel for safekeeping after Warner had given them to me in the fortress. I laughed at myself, then smiled. Kett would have frozen me out for making such a blunder. For opening my mouth to question what I should already know.

Warner simply answered the question. "Yes."

"You think someone used the sorcerers to gain entry to the fortress. Performed some sort of black magic, blood magic, to call the leech demons through them."

"To bind them to her."

"But she had to try to take the braids herself, because the leeches are only capable of draining magic. Maybe even sustained by it."

"Eternal life, as they wished," Warner said grimly.

I shuddered. I couldn't imagine that was the existence — the shadow leech form — that the sorcerers would have devoted their lives to achieving. "The child dragon," I said.

"She wears the form of a child now."

"Now? You think she survived the earthquake? The flood?"

"Dragons are difficult to kill."

"Do dragons always revert to a younger form like that when their magic has been drained or compromised?"

Warner shook his head. "I've never seen or heard of the like."

"Maybe it's a lingering effect of the stone spell," I said, shuddering at the memory of slowly being encased myself.

Warner nodded, but didn't answer. I could tell he was still peeved I hadn't countered the spell on the altar more quickly. But the fact he didn't bring it up pleased me. He might be pissed, but he wasn't going to fight about it. Like maybe he trusted my judgement.

"How many leeches did you kill?" I asked, changing the subject slightly. "They disappeared at the same time as the kid."

"If I was truly vanquishing them. If they don't just regenerate. Not enough."

I nodded. I was too exhausted to think about it anymore. I felt — utterly selfishly — bereft without Kandy.

Warner stepped over to the fridge and pulled out two plastic containers and an aerosol can of whipped cream. He placed these before me on the island, then grabbed two plates out of the cupboard and two sets of forks and knives.

I watched him as he moved around the kitchen with utter confidence, like he'd lived and cooked here for months. I'd been invaded, and I didn't seem to mind one bit.

I blamed the exhaustion.

Warner pulled the pancakes out of the oven and set two onto plates. He opened one of the containers — which appeared to hold some sort of stewed sweet cherry — and spooned the fruit onto the center of the pancake. The second container held chocolate shavings.

My heart started to beat erratically as I watched him spray whipped cream from the can on top of the cherries, then sprinkle chocolate over his concoction.

He put the plate before me.

Oh, God. He'd made me black forest pancakes. I looked up to watch him as he put together a second plate.

"You cooked for me."

"I was going to try cupcakes, but didn't think I had the time to figure them out. Or your magic to pull them off. Gran thought pancakes would do."

Gran. He was calling my grandmother by the nickname I used.

He was in cahoots with Gran. She'd probably found the cherries, then dragged my mother away for an impromptu coven meeting. And here I thought she had plans for Qiuniu and me, but Warner was clearly an acceptable alternative for one of the guardian nine.

That said a lot, actually, about what Gran thought of the sentinel.

Warner caught my eye. His smile was softer, more tentative now. "That's what you do, Jade Godfrey. To express your feelings. You bake for the people you care about."

"You're learning my language."

"So I can communicate effectively."

"Communicate your feelings."

His grin widened, smoldering on the edges again. "Yes, but I gather that's obvious."

"I usually need things spelled out for me."

"I'll remember that."

I answered his smile. Then I laughed. I threw back my head and laughed.

I picked up the can of whipped cream and sprayed it directly in my mouth. It tasted like chemical-infused milk. Yeah, absolutely terrible.

Warner laughed at me. The apartment wards rippled at the power that rolled off him. I breathed in his black-forest-cake magic, savoring the deep-cocoa-and-sweet-cherry taste of it.

Then I ate my pancakes.

I was really in trouble now.

Acknowledgments

<u>With thanks to:</u>

<u>My story & line editor</u>
Scott Fitzgerald Gray

<u>My Proofreader</u>
Pauline Nolet
Indie Solutions by Murphy Rae

<u>My beta readers</u>
Leiah Cooper, Terry Daigle, Angela Flannery, Gael Fleming,
Desi Hartzel, Heather Lewis, Mandy Reed, and Karen Turkal.

<u>For their continual encouragement, feedback,
& general advice</u>
Luch Balao – for the Martial Arts training
The Retreat

<u>For her Art</u>
Elizabeth Mackey

Meghan Ciana Doidge is an award-winning writer based out of Salt Spring Island, British Columbia, Canada. She has a penchant for bloody love stories, superheroes, and the supernatural. She also has a thing for chocolate, potatoes, and sock yarn.

Novels

After The Virus
Spirit Binder
Time Walker
Cupcakes, Trinkets, and Other Deadly Magic (Dowser 1)
Trinkets, Treasures, and Other Bloody Magic (Dowser 2)
Treasures, Demons, and Other Black Magic (Dowser 3)
I See Me (Oracle 1)
Shadows, Maps, and Other Ancient Magic (Dowser 4)
Maps, Artifacts, and Other Arcane Magic (Dowser 5)
I See You (Oracle 2)

Novellas/Shorts

Love Lies Bleeding
The Graveyard Kiss

For giveaways, news, and glimpses of upcoming stories, please connect with Meghan on her:

Personal blog, www.madebymeghan.ca
Twitter, @mcdoidge
And/or Facebook, Meghan Ciana Doidge

Please also consider leaving an honest review at your point of sale outlet

Catch a glimpse of
the dowser universe
through Rochelle's eyes...

The day I turned nineteen, I expected to gain what little freedom I could within the restrictions of my bank account and the hallucinations that had haunted me for the last six years. I expected to drive away from a life that had been dictated by the tragedy of others and shaped by the care of strangers. I expected to be alone.

Actually, I relished the idea of being alone.

Instead, I found fear I thought I'd overcome. Uncertainty I thought I'd painstakingly planned away. And terror that was more real than anything I'd ever hallucinated before.

I'd seen terrible, fantastical, and utterly impossible things ... but not love. Not until I saw him.